Karen -
thank you for reading.

Red Fabric Chairs

Bruce Cashbaugh

This is a work of fiction. All names, characters, places and incidents are products of the author's imagination or are used fictitiously. Any resemblance to any events or locales, or to any actual persons, living or dead, is entirely coincidental.

ISBN: 9798408156689

1 Words in a doorframe

"Arvin, before you leave tonight, can I have a quick word with you?"

I look up from my keyboard to see Bill Hanlow leaning into my office, left hand on the door frame, shirt sleeves rolled up nearly to the elbows, two pens in the left breast pocket of his light blue button-down dress shirt.

"Sure, Bill, no problem. The girls have practice tonight, so I'll be leaving at five on the dot," I say.

I wrap up the last few entries for Smeltzer Clothiers and shut down the computer. Since my evening will consist of a quick, light dinner, then practice with the girl's combined fifth and sixth grade spring rec league basketball team, I don't bother to pack anything into my briefcase. Other nights, I'd take it home with some mild work in it, but rarely does the case get opened, much less any work get done. I feel that the simple act of carrying work home makes me look more professional.

I walk into Bill's office and see he's busy, with papers strewn all over his desk, credenza, and a portion of the floor and a spreadsheet active on his screen. That's not uncommon in an accounting firm – we're paid to do all but the most mundane tasks. Sometimes, for some accounts, we do the mundane tasks too. As the owner of the firm, Bill's office is the largest in the building, if you want to call a 12' x

15' office large. Bill doesn't believe in spending any money that doesn't have to be spent. The firm, which consists of four CPAs, three assistants and an office manager, has offices in an old house on the outskirts of downtown Stillwell, Iowa. The house was built in the early 1960s, ranch style, fake limestone and wide aluminum siding that was originally white. Original steel casement windows that leak air. The garage is now the storage area, the three bedrooms each converted into offices, with Bill claiming the dining room. The entrance to it, off what used to be the kitchen, has been closed off so there is only the one entrance to his office.

Bill takes off his glasses and places them on top of one of the piles of paper on his desk. Usually, he has neat piles of paper, those posted, those waiting to be posted, client A and client B. Not today.

"Arvin," he begins, "I know this is going to be a surprise, but I have to let you go. With the loss of the Mercury Glass business we have to reduce expenses, and most of our expenses are salary. I'm sorry."

He pauses, then goes on.

"This is uncomfortable, but I'm sure you understand. I have to ask you to clean out your desk, now, while I watch."

So there. My thoughts of basketball practice turn instantly to thoughts of, of nothing. I'm stunned into non-thinking-ness. Numbed. Do I ask the dozen or thirty questions half-congealing in my brain? Do I slug the son of a bitch in the face?

I say nothing. Walk out his door and go to my, what used to be, my desk in an office that at one time was a bedroom. I share this, used to share this office, with Carson, a relatively new CPA hire. She's conveniently left early today.

I open my pencil drawer and wonder which of the jumble of pens and pencils are actually mine and which belong to the SOB standing in the doorway, leaning on the frame. Will Bill know? My pocket calculator, old but familiar, I know is mine, along with the Cross pen and pencil set Laura and the girls gave me for Christmas a couple of years ago. Last season's Cyclones basketball pocket schedule. I glance around the office.

A couple of school textbooks in the bookcase, those are mine. I haven't looked at them in years, but I know they have my name and my outlines and my yellow highlighter marks and my blue-pen scribbled notes, just in case Bill will ask for proof of ownership. The photos, Laura at the picnic table, Jan and Jess the day we brought Jess home from the hospital.

Bill leaves the doorway for a moment, comes back with a banker's box and places it on my desk. I put the books in, then the calculator, the pictures, then toss whatever is left that looks like mine into the box. It comes complete with lid, which I use.

Then I walk out the door and get in my car. I make the six-minute drive home last as long as I can. I stretch it out to eight minutes

This time of year, we don't try to cram the car into the unconnected garage at the side of the house. It's filled with the mower, five bicycles for the four of us, a fertilizer spreader, unused fencing, garden edging and more stuff that just seems to grow by the month. The bankers' box with my briefcase on top of it stays in the back seat.

“I have news,” I say as I walk in the back door of the house. It opens into the kitchen; I sit down and look at Laura.

Laura is the love of my life. Two years younger than me, we’d met through a mutual acquaintance my first year back in Stillwell after four years at Iowa State. If you want an example of love at first sight, ours is it. I look at her standing by the range, mixing something in a frying pan, and for an instant my mind goes back to that moment when we learned each other’s names, and I offered her a handshake and she laughed and shook her dark brown hair off her shoulders onto that deep yellow top she used to wear.

But then my reverie is broken by her voice.

“Don’t you have practice tonight . . . “she started.

“I just got fired.”

“What?”

“Don’t make me say it again. I just got fired. I was wrapping up, Bill came in, and said I didn’t have a job anymore.”

Laura takes this smoother than I. She stops stirring whatever is going to be dinner and sits down gracefully at our small kitchen table.

“Did he say why?”

“We lost Mercury Glass.”

“Do you work on Mercury Glass?” Laura questions.

“No, not one hour. Bill kept Carson. Not me. Carson

worked on Mercury. She'll have to . . ." It's hard to continue. I choke a bit. It's impossible to continue. I stand.

"I had no notice, no warning, just another day. That son-of-a-bitch kept Carson and fired me."

Laura keeps her head.

"Arv, it'll be OK." She gets up, walks around our little table, puts her arms around my shoulders and hugs me. It feels like a stranger's hug.

"What did he say?" Laura asks.

"We lost the business, he needs to reduce costs, and I'm the cost he reduced. I get an entire 30 days severance pay. Five-and-a-half years, I get 30 days. And he stood by while I packed up my desk. Like a third grader being sent back to second grade for bad spelling."

I walk over to the top right cabinet nearest the door, grab the bottle of Jack, decide against drinking straight from the bottle with Laura watching, pick a glass from the same cabinet, pour too much into it and drink. It doesn't burn, doesn't warm, doesn't do a damn thing.

"Arvin, let me call Jake and tell him you'll miss practice tonight. I can pick up the girls later."

She walks into the front room and picks up her phone. I heard her tell Jake, my coaching partner, that I won't be able to be there tonight, but that Jan, along with Jess at two years younger the unofficial team manager, will be. I wonder vaguely what I will be missing, who will time the drills and work on free throws. But I don't wonder long. My mind suddenly snaps back to how unfairly I have been treated. I pour another glass of whiskey and drink it. Still no help.

Laura comes back into the kitchen and puts her hands on my shoulders, rubs them gently, concentrating on whatever those ropy muscles at the top are and then the smaller vertical muscles in my neck. It's not my shoulders that hurt. It's my pride. But I don't verbalize that.

"I'm really sorry, dear. I know it's not your fault. Things happen. We'll be fine. We'll adjust. We'll be fine."

I'm too numb to listen. She may be cheerleading; she may be speaking the truth. I can't tell, but neither can I keep a single thought in my head for more than three seconds. What matters is that she's there, and is projecting calm. I'm anything but calm, my mind racing over the practice I'm about to miss, the box of my office effects still sitting on the car seat, the quarter-inch of my second glass of whiskey staring at me, daring me, Bill's face as he asked me to "have a word," and the pit of my stomach, hollow, empty, void, scared, searing.

"I'm going to take Jan and Jess to practice," Laura says. "You try to relax. Put some music on. I love you." A soft kiss on my forehead.

"I love you," I whisper back. I feel like crying. I'm drained, empty. I can't remember the last time I cried. I don't want Laura to leave, yet I don't want her near me as I choke back my whimper, my voice soft enough to fold. I hear the door close, her car start. The hell with it. Just the hell with it. Don't need ice, just pour it in the glass. No music, no input, no noise, no, no, no, nothing. Maximum sensory deprivation. I don't taste the Jack going down my throat.

I wake up next morning while Laura is in the shower. I sit up, think "I need to be in there first," swing around and put my feet on the floor. Then I remember. I have nothing to do. After I take the girls to school today, I have nothing to do. Nothing. I sink back into my depression in the bed and listen to the vague sound of the shower running, stopping, the shower curtain being pulled back. I never heard the alarm clock; how did Laura know to wake up on time? Yes, I check the time, it's 6:11, the time I'm usually in the shower. I think back to last night and sit up again. No headache, I must not have had that much whiskey. It was a bad idea to drink however much I drank.

I stand up, wobble a tad, grab my robe and tap on the bathroom door.

"Good morning."

"Good morning, dear," I hear back. The door to the bathroom opens. God, she's beautiful with wet hair wearing only a towel wrapped around her torso.

"How are you doing?"

"I'll go make coffee," I mutter. I didn't want to answer any questions. I flip on the radio to catch the local news at the bottom of the hour.

I make coffee almost every day. Today, Thursday, is the first time in years I have to think mechanically through every step. Measure out the coffee. No, get the filter first. No, damn, water first. Then the filter, then the coffee, then turn the switch. Think, force yourself. Each. Movement.

I think it's a demonstration of cliched suburban inanity to go outside wearing a bathrobe. The neighborhood of the small town we live in is hardly a suburb, but I walk out to the mailbox for the newspaper without bothering to pull on jeans. I've never been outdoors in my bathrobe before, but don't give it a second thought this morning.

I look for a headline "local accountant fired." No. Is there another, this stating "local accountant found dead in home, apparent suicide?" No. Just the usual local police activity and national politics. I shove the paper aside, waiting for the coffee to finish, and catch the chatter between the two morning hosts on the local radio station. Why do we even subscribe to the paper, I wonder?

2 Home Alone

Laura's off to her classes and I take the girls to school. Then back home.

I've never been home alone during a weekday. Never took a sick day off in 5-1/2 years. So I spend much of this morning on our family computer updating, then composing a new resume. I never thought I'd have to do that again, after getting the job at Hanlow Accounting. Thought I was set for life. I never expected to own the business, but I sure never expected to get fired, either.

Fired. That word is taking me a while to wrap my brain around. Had Bill said "laid off"? I can't remember his exact words after "now, while I watch," but the precise words don't matter. Precision is for numbers. With words, you can change the order around, swap one for another yet the impact is the same. Was I incompetent? No. Unproductive, a poor employee? No. Why did I get fired and Carson didn't?

Carson. Four years younger. Female. Married, but I haven't met her husband. Nice looking, conservative dresser, quiet, modest. Never saw any connection between Carson and Bill, in fact, I always thought Bill went out of his way to treat Carson and I equally. Except she still has a job and I don't. Except she worked on the Mercury Glass account and I didn't. And I got fired and she didn't.

While shaving, I look at the mirror and see a 36-year-old

guy, whose once-coal-black hair is beginning to lighten. My green eyes are still green, my face still clean shaven, sideburns about a half-inch longer than the current fashion. My skin is showing some of the wear that comes with being a kid and a young adult before lotions were in everyone's pocket. Nothing here to brag about. Nothing here to take a photo of for inclusion on a resume.

I allow myself the rest of this week plus all of the next week to get my head together, do the online job hunt, and print up a resume and business cards. In between resume drafts, I create a pro forma for our household expenses. I mow the grass. Two days later, I mow it again, right after filing for unemployment.

Unemployment income, I find out, will pay about a third of my old salary, and that for only a few months. Thirty days severance only goes so far and delays my unemployment claim. The house payment, the two car payments, Laura's gasoline and school expenses, Laura's tuition two or three times a year, the girl's clothes, insurance, cable, city utilities, all those bills are still due. Thirty days severance. Thirty days seems so unfair after 5-1/2 years.

Tomorrow morning, I go job hunting in person. The newspaper and online job boards don't offer much. I suppose we're lucky to still have a newspaper here in a town of this size, and don't have to depend on Des Moines for that, too. Still, there's no listing I've found in the newspaper or on the on-line boards for an accountant in this area. The four other accounting firms are one-person shops, and I've already posted my resume on all the major job boards. Checking those each day at 7:50 shows how little time it takes to find nothing.

I plan to go up and down Main Street to offer my services. I have the right experience. I have a decent suit, tie and shirt to wear. I'm not the most outgoing person, but I don't stutter or smell bad. I've printed 35 copies of my resume, and my new business card that lists my home address and my cell number.

I have to do this. I have to think positive and I have to act like I enjoy meeting the business owners and asking them about their accounting services. I've prepared a list of questions to ask, have practiced and am as ready as I can be. Tomorrow is going to be a good day.

Tomorrow.

Miserable. Beyond difficult. Am I an idiot? I have a college education, albeit just a 4-year degree, yet from a respected state university. I've worked in my field since a week after I graduated. I've been loyal and productive. My clients have always liked my work. I can help, I know it, I know it.

3 Tomorrow is now today

I walk the girls to school, just because I can and it won't look so much like killing time. It's the last week of school before summer vacation, and their excitement is evident. They pull out more colorful tops and get to wear jeans this week. They chat about everything and everyone along the way. I shuffle behind them, hands in my jean pockets, considering what I have to do when I get back home. It's a pretty day for late May, and I notice the trees have greened up, a few lawns need mowing, and I can't keep my mind focused on anything but stepping up my courage to go look for employment.

I look up out of a trance and find that I'm on my way back home. Did I say good-bye to Jan and Jess or did I just turn around when they melded into the crowd at the front of the school? It's a 15-minute walk home. I shave, shower, get into my whitest white shirt, knot up my newest bland tie, pick up my portfolio and resumes and walk downtown.

Stillwell is one of those typical Midwestern towns that grew up around a courthouse. The courthouse square is still the center of the town's retail. I figure the small, locally owned stores and businesses downtown are my best prospects. I've done accounting for a few of them over the years, helping out at tax time or when an owner dies and the business goes with her. But I'm not taking the easy way today, not starting with the three places I'm familiar with. Today, now, I'm starting on the northwest corner opposite the courthouse and going door-to-door, one at a time. I've timed this well. It's 9:18 am, just after most stores are open but before many customers are likely to come in.

The dress shop on the corner is first. I take a deep, long, cleansing breath that I learned from Lamaze class with Laura and walk in. I see a stylishly dressed, middle-aged woman behind the jewelry and watch counter and walk over.

"Hi, I'm wondering if the owner is in?"

"Yes, that's me," she says. "What may I help you with?"

"My name is Arvin Miller, and I'm an accountant." I notice suddenly that I've forgotten to ask her name and forgotten to extend my hand for a hand shake. Too late now. I stumble ahead with my lightly practiced sales pitch. She cuts me off before I get far.

"My brother-in-law does our books every month, and does our taxes too," she informs me politely, firmly, yet with a hint of warmth in her tonality.

I realize I haven't practiced a line for this situation. I haven't thought of what to say when I get a firm "no" answer. I'm searching for a cohesive thought to communicate. I'll settle for a word or two. But my mind and voice are in separate counties. I can feel my mouth opening and staying open.

She leans forward ever-so-slightly and ever-so-graciously. "Thank you for coming in," she says as our eyes lock, ever-so-briefly.

I'm able to reply, because I identify this as my chance to get out of the dress shop. "Thank you," comes out of my mouth, and I turn and get to the door as quickly as I can walk without actually running.

Once outside, I turn left and go to Marvin's Trains and Toys. I have no idea who the owner is so I go inside and ask.

"I am," says an older gentleman, wearing dark chinos and a light, mint-green shirt open at the neck. I go into my spiel.

"Whoa, whoa, whoa," he interrupts. "This is my store. I decide what merchandise to stock. I decide my opening and closing hours. If I get in early in the morning, I'm open early. If I decide to take off at 4:42 pm, I'm closed early. I do my own bookkeeping, my own accounting, my own taxes, and I sweep the floor and make my own lunches back in the stock room."

"Ohhh, I see," happy that a word came out of my mouth. "Well, thank you," I say and turn to leave.

"Those new Brio trucks just came in, you might take a look at those," I hear as I'm two steps from the door. I give him a short wave, grab the door knob and walk out.

A left turn, a walk past the display window of the insurance store, a glance at the faded photos of smiling people in front of shiny new cars, obviously reproduced from 1950s magazine ads, and I walk into the Shultz Insurance Agency.

"Do it myself."

Meyer's Ace Hardware. "Been using Julie Kemp for years. She works outta her home."

Blint's Blintzes. "My dad does it."

Weber & Weber Opticians. "I do it. Every Monday, first thing on my to-do list."

San Miguel Tacos, the last store on the block. "No. My wife. But I'll take your card and give it to her." I count that as a victory. My first.

In Stillwell, a pedestrian waits at stop lights even when no traffic is coming. I do a quick analysis of my first of four blocks. Seven doors, seven attempts on Center Street. I handed out one business card, no resumes and I haven't taken a single note. Haven't even written down a single name of a single person in case I want to come back later. That was something I had planned on doing. I wonder how I forgot, but then the light changes, the orange hand is replaced by the white walking symbol and I do as electronically instructed.

I turn right at the corner and I wait at the light. The White Horse Inn Bar & Grille on Main Street doesn't open until 4 pm. I peek through the door, and don't see a light or a sign of life. I skip it. Tempted to write that down for later, but I'm on a roll of no note-taking so I go with the flow.

Terry's Men's Wear is next, and I know Terry died about three years ago. His wife kept the business for a short time, but I think someone new took over. I get his name, Karl Thomas, and I get the same answer. "I have that covered."

The pet and garden supply store. John's Ace hardware store. Doug's Barber Shop. Turn left, walk across Maple Street then right across Main. The Hair and Nails Emporium. Carmen's Deli. The Brass Rail. El Maguey. Past two empty storefronts, cross the street, turn right, cross the street. Bill's Bail Bonds. Meridian Therapy. L&M Auto Parts. Vic's Ice Cream. Samantha's Shoes. Jason's Jewelry. Classic Jewels. The Coffee Beanery. Salon Perfumeria. Jurn's Family Dentistry. That's on the corner across the street from the dress shop where I started. I've completed my trip around the courthouse square.

I decide to take a break. Halfway down the block is the library, where I pull out a chair from a small table. I do a quick inventory of my sales materials. 32 resumes left, so I've handed out three. I started with 15 business cards, and I have 12 left, so I've managed to hand out three cards as well. My watch says 10:37. An hour and 19 minutes, three resumes, three business cards and not a single opportunity. Not one. I'm as hollow as I was twelve days ago, when Bill fired me.

Suddenly, I snap awake, as if I had been sleeping. I have no idea how long I've sat there at the library desk. I glance at my watch, 10:53 and then look at my calculation on my notepad, which say I've been in the library for all of 16 minutes. I'm numb, seeing no difference between staying at the library staring into the unfocused space between my eyes and the reference stacks, going home and staring into the unfocused space between my eyes and the family photos on the sideboard and going out trying to find work to do. But my cards and my resumes are there, my notepad is handy, so I gather things up, walk out the door and turn left.

I walk down to Jefferson Street, where I know there are a few other small businesses. Although I've driven down this street many times, I've never actually walked down this section of Jefferson before, but there's a sidewalk and I'm OK with walking. I spot a sign for Dr. Joseph, Pediatrician, and walk in.

It's a converted older home, not unlike the one I spent over five years working in at Hanlow Accounting. The woman behind the small desk looks familiar, but I can't place her.

"Hi, can you tell me who does the accounting for you, please?" I ask.

"Hi, Arvin, nice to see you," she says.

I pause. I'm not good with names and faces and conversations. I'm not good at many things.

"I'm JoAnn, Ann Lopes' mom. You coached her basketball team last year."

"Oh, yes, I'm so sorry I didn't recognize you," I reply. I do, in fact, remember Ann and maybe I remember JoAnn dropping her off or picking her up from practices. I struggle not to stare too hard at her while deciding if I truly remember her or not.

"We used to use Kay Johnson, but she got sick a few weeks ago and hasn't been in. I hear you aren't with Bill Hanlow anymore."

"No, I'm, not, I'm on my own now." The words form and I can hear myself speak but my brain isn't processing anything.

"I think Doctor Joseph might be interested in talking with you. He has an opening at 1:20 today, if you'd like to come back, I can book you in."

"Sure! Yes!" Maybe I shouldn't look so excited. But I am.

I go back to the library and read magazines I didn't know existed until 1:05 pm. A 5-minute walk back to the good doctor's office makes me early. I say hello to JoAnn, grab a seat and a magazine.

Dr. Joseph's personal office is tiny, cramped, his desk is stacked with files and brochures and papers 4" deep. He has a large monitor and keyboard on a side desk, an old-fashioned wood desk chair that I've only seen on old TV shows, and a hard-plastic orange side chair that might be as old as I am.

"JoAnn tells me you're an accountant," he jumps right in.

"Yes." A long pause I finally fill. "I've my BS degree from Iowa State and have worked professionally in the field for 14 years. Here's my resume." I can't believe these words are coming out of my mouth. Do I sound as good, as positive and as firm, as I think?

Dr. Joseph adds my resume to one of the larger piles on his desk. It's unread, unglanced-upon. "I've used Kay Johnson for years, but she's having some health issues and won't be able to work for some months. She comes in here on Mondays, picks up the invoices and the checks from JoAnn, and comes back in on Thursdays with everything done, checks written for me to sign. Can you do that?"

"Yes."

"I pay her — I paid her $85 a week. I'll pay you the same until Kay is back. I'll have JoAnn call Kay and arrange an appointment for you to pick up what you need from her."

The Doctor stands up, and does not extend his hand to be shaken. "I need to move along."

I stand up and turn sideways so he can walk past me into the hallway where he disappears into a doorway. JoAnn is waiting for me in the lobby, where she hands me a slip of paper.

"That's Kay's address. I'll set up an appointment at her home for you tomorrow at 9 am, if that's OK. Give me your card. I'll call you if that time doesn't work for her." She smiles at me while she says this, as if she is handing me the keys to a kingdom of vast wealth.

"Yes, sure," I reply. "Tomorrow at 9 am. Thanks, JoAnn, nice to see you. Thanks again."

I'm through the door and onto the sidewalk before I'm aware I've moved. I think I have my first client! I've worked with physicians in the past, not at Hanlow, but at my first accounting job, Randall C. Meyer Accountants. In fact, a doctor was one of the first clients that I handled myself. I walk down the street and turn right at the first street with a sidewalk.

I feel accomplished. I sold somebody something. Never, never did I think I could sell anything to anybody. I feel elated. I cross the street and turn around to head home. Cannot wait until Laura gets home and I tell her.

I hear her car pull into the driveway as I sit and watch TV. She comes in through the garage, glides through the kitchen and into the living room then pauses when she sees me holding two glasses of whiskey. Two ice cubes in hers, mine is neat.

"You must have had a good day!" she smiles as she takes her glass. We clink and drink. "What's your news?"

"I'm pretty sure I have a client. I'm meeting with the ex-accountant for Dr. Joseph tomorrow morning and she's turning over all the files to me."

"Oh, honey, that's wonderful! Dr. Joseph over on Dubuque Street?"

"The very one. JoAnn Lopes is his receptionist, I coached her daughter last year. She put me right into his appointment book. We chatted for less than five minutes and I have the assignment."

"I'm not surprised. You look very presentable with that

new haircut. What kind of work does the good Doctor expect you to do?"

"Everything," I reply with an expansive gesture across the room. "I pick up the weeks' worth of work on Mondays and take it back to him on Thursdays. I'll write his checks, monitor cash flow, balance his books, just like a real accountant."

Laura sets her half-empty glass on the table by my chair. Comes over and gives me a small, shy hug.

"And just what does this mean for our family finances?"

"Well, we will be improving."

"Can you be just slightly more specific?" Her eyebrows go up and she does that little head tilt to the left and down that I've seen and loved since we met.

It takes some doing, and a good quick effort at another cleansing breath, but I get it out. "$85 a week."

The pause in her breathing matches the pallor that instantly appears on her face. "Is there the opportunity for advancement?"

"Doubtful the Doctor's practice is going to grow a lot in the short term."

"Mmmm, I can see that. Who is the meeting with tomorrow?"

"Kay somebody. Has been doing his books for years, I guess. She's having some health issues and can't work for the next couple of months."

"So, Arv, is this a temporary assignment or a full-time, first-client for your new accounting firm?"

"At this time, it's temporary." I don't need to exhale that last breath, as all the wind goes out of me. My high achievement looks more like a C+ on a seventh-grade spelling test.

Laura turns around toward the kitchen, turns back, picks up her glass, takes a healthy swill, heads into the kitchen, glass in hand.

"I'll start dinner. The girls should be back from school and practice in a few minutes."

"Hon, I'm sorry. I went first thing to the dress shop and could hardly speak a word. The owner, I don't know her name, I forgot to ask. I went to the toy shop, the insurance agent, I went to every single business around the square, and got nothing. I handed out three - three — resumes and three cards. I happen to walk by Dr. Joseph's office, I go in and bingo. I'm no salesperson, you know that."

A deep breath, and I go on. "So I found work, I have no idea how much work there is, I'll find that out tomorrow. $85 a week. Laura, that was my hourly billing rate at Hanlow, I figured I'd start at $60 an hour, that's substantially lower so I can save companies some money. But it's more than Bill was paying me so I can work a bit fewer hours and make a few dollars more. That's what I thought. Now what? $85 a week, I don't care how many hours it takes to do the work. We can't survive on that. And I have way too much time on my hands."

The front door opens and Jan and Jess come trotting in. "Hi, Mom, Hi, Dad! What's for dinner? Tomorrow is orange day; we're supposed to wear as much orange as we can! Can I wear my new swimsuit top if I wear a sweater over it? Can we stay up late tonight because we're not doing anything in school tomorrow?"

The girls' questions and excitement overcome and truncate my explanation the way Laura's coolness trumped my own enthusiasm. The day recedes into evening.

4 Dr. Joseph's assignment

Kay's house at 9 am looks much less interesting than I had imagined it would. Although it's a 5-minute drive, I drive because I think it's more professional than walking. I ring the bell and an older woman I presume to be Kay answers the door.

"You must be Arvin, I'm Kay," she says as she reaches out her right hand and gives me a firm handshake. "I have things here for you, come step this way." She takes charge and I follow her over the threshold, through the front sitting room and into what I take is a small dining room. The exterior wall is loaded with family pictures, and the small desk has a keyboard and an ancient monitor.

I'm guessing Kay is at least 70, a small, slim woman who looks like she could be swept away like Dorothy during a middling Iowa summer rain storm. About five feet, two inches, she has short, curly grey hair, and is wearing a faded dress that I think is listed in the dictionary as "house dress."

We pull out chairs. "I've been doing Albert's books for decades," she says. "I used to be his receptionist too, but retired seven years ago. I do his books to support my needlepoint habit."

She points to the wall opposite me, where the evidence of her habit is hung in a myriad of frame styles and sizes. I gaze around and see that almost every inch of wall space on all the walls of the dining room are covered with needlepoints.

"Since my husband died, this is my comfort. I get satisfaction from making progress one stitch at a time and soon enough, I can see how my work turns into a flower, or a garden or a building. I think it's like accounting, don't you?"

Fifteen minutes later I'm back in my car. My head whirls with this assignment, because now, today, I can get back into accounting, what I do best. I have invoices, receipts, checks, records and a flash drive containing every monthly statement dating back over three years. At home, I tap the computer into life and dive in.

I wrap up before I get hungry. I'm so used to keeping track of my time that I record the hours worked. I'm surprised when I look up that it's after 3 pm. But I feel good, satisfied, and pleased that I am productive.

A few minutes spent tidying things up, papers, envelopes. I email JoAnn asking if Thursday at 9 am is a good time for me to bring my work in. I relax with a cup of Earl Grey and check out last night's NBA scores on my tablet. The strong tea warms me as I pause and relax on the couch. It's my night to make dinner and get the girls ready for bed while Laura goes to class. She has two semesters left to earn her BS nursing degree.

My famous breakfast for dinner menu takes 20 minutes to prepare. Scrambled eggs (with my signature hint of mustard), white toast and sausage patties. Keeps the kids happy and nourished. We josh about homework over dinner and I insist they spend time reading books while I do dishes and clean up the kitchen. Laura puts in a full day as an LPN at the hospital, then has class until 8:30. It's a long day for her.

Next day at nine I walk into Dr. Joseph's office. JoAnn and I chat while we wait for him to finish with a patient. Then the three of us sit down and I walk them through the weeks' worth of materials. It's not difficult work, there is nothing complex, the volume is small and we get through quickly. Neither one of them has any questions, I have no questions so we take our leave until next Monday.

The hardest part of the day is going back to an empty home. I toss my keys into the desk drawer next to my resumes and business cards and dread what I know I have to do tomorrow.

5 I have to do this

Resumes, cards, notebook, pen and backup pen. I practiced all Sunday night after the girls went to bed while Laura was studying. Walk in, greeting, pitch, typical questions, ask. My route of prospects is clearly in front of me, this time the small manufacturing plants on the north and east sides of the city. I spent two days reviewing sales techniques online and at the library. I'm ready. I've even done a drive-by on the highway, divided it into sections based on the speed limit as it goes from 25 to 30 to 40 and then 55 as it heads south to Medina.

I start with the smaller stores in the 25 portion. These are similar to those downtown. My plan is to hone my presentation on them, then polish it on the 30 section. The used car dealer. The next used car dealer. The auto alignment place. The used building materials store. The Hispanic grocery store. This group gets my business card.

Turn the corner and into the industrial park. There, I enter into another world. Long streets full of factories on each side, large hulking buildings with large, proud signs and small places with no apparent office, just a door inserted into the side of a sheet-metal building. Some with no signs. Parking lots full, or not full, of older model cars along with a small handful of new, upscale models, these consistently clean and pristine.

I stop at 11 factories, get past seven front doors and talk to four actual accountants. I leave a resume at every place; in two I leave it sitting on a table in what used to be a reception room. The actual live human beings I talk to get my best presentation, ending with an intelligent question. The best I get back; "Yeah, can't use you."

The results alter my noon lunch arrangements. I had promised to treat myself to a fish and chips at the Appleby's near the east end of the industrial park. That option looks too positive, too encouraging after this day, so I do a one-eighty and head back towards downtown. I hit a red light and sit there looking off to my left, I'm kitty-corner from the Fourway Bar and on a whim, turn in.

The hand-lettered sign on the whiteboard inside the door says "Seat Yourself Margarita Special $4." I find a seat and a Margarita while I check out the menu. One hour and forty minutes, two mediocre street tacos and three Margaritas later, I head back home.

"What in the hell were you thinking today?" Laura doesn't swear much, so I know I'm in deep trouble. "The girls said you came home at 1:45, and you were wobbling on your feet. I could smell the alcohol on your breath when I got home for dinner. Did you drink all day and then again tonight when I was at school?"

"I did my best today, Laura, I really did. You know how I practiced and practiced on Sunday. I made more sales calls on a few stores to practice and get over my nerves, then I went on to that industrial section off the Parkway. I went into 11 factories and had to rouse people out of their offices. I left resumes at every place. Laura, I'm not a sales person. I did the best I can possibly do. I can't do that again. The rejection is killing me."

Her features soften a tad. "Did you talk to the owner or the accounting staff? Did you get a reaction?"

"I had one guy at . . . ah, heck, I don't remember what the name of the place was. He listened to me. He said, and I quote, 'yeah, we can't use you."

"So what made you decide to drink?"

"I had promised to reward myself after a successful day with lunch at Appleby's. I caught a red light on the way, saw a bar and went in. They had a special on margaritas."

"Margaritas?"

"Yes, I know. It could have been Mad Dog 4040 and I'd have ordered it. I just wanted — needed — to have something go well, something go easy, some reason not to think, not to have to climb outside my comfort zone. I picked the special because it was easy, street tacos were the daily feature so I picked those. I heard 'no' all day, 'no' from here, 'no' from there, 'no' from the three women and the one guy I talked to, 'no' from the people I spoke to when I just walked right into their offices, 'no' like I heard it 26 times on my trip around the courthouse square. When the waitress came by and asked if I wanted another margarita, I said 'yes' just to hear the sound of the word."

"I'm so sorry, Arv. I know this is hard for you."

"I'm just an accountant. I'm not the smartest person in the room. I've focused on one thing, one narrow skill, and I'm good at it. I don't want to work for myself, to have to go find new clients. I want to sit in an office, do my work and come home at five o'clock."

"You're a very good accountant . . ." she starts to say, but suddenly I'm in a talking mood.

"I don't have big dreams; we don't have expensive tastes. We have a nice home here, it's not fancy but we're all comfortable. The girls each have a room of their own. We have two cars, one of which is almost paid off. We always pay our bills on time. I have to produce my share of the income to support that. I have to produce my share of the income to feel like I deserve to live here with you."

I collapse onto the bed, exhausted from talking, thinking, the tequila and the couple, ok several, shots of Jack I had after dinner. Laura sits down next to me and wraps her arm around my shoulder.

"I can see the toll this is taking on you Arv. I can feel it, too. You want to work. You're good at what you do, you're very good at it. You'll find something."

Her hug is warming, and I feel my back muscles loosening. The touch of her fingers on my shoulder is like cool lotion on a fresh sunburn.

But her words fall from me like water off a raincoat.

"Laura, are you comfortable here in Stillwell? I know you like your job at the hospital, I know you have just, what four classes, over two semesters of work left on your degree?"

She nods.

"And I know that the hospital has all but guaranteed you a new position when you graduate. You have a firm, planned track ahead of you. You have a successful career in front of you. I don't know if I can make it here in Stillwell. There aren't opportunities here for me. But we've lived all our lives together here, you have a fine and wonderful future here. Your Mom is here. It doesn't seem that there's a place for me."

"Oh, no," she says as the cool touch on my shoulders is

replaced by cold hard rain of words. These stick into my skin like needles. "We agreed years ago when Jess was born and I started nursing school that we are here long term. Don't get liquored up one night and decide to pull up stakes on me, the girls, and my Mom. My Mom is the only grandparent our girls have, now that your Dad has passed on."

"Arvin," she turns and puts a searing stare into my eyes, "you need to get out of this funk and find something to do with yourself. So we can live here. In Stillwell."

Next day, I wake up before anyone else and go out to the front room to fire up the computer. The map shows Stillwell to be a reasonable facsimile of a circle, so I decide to do quadrants. I've hit the north and the east a bit but I zoom in to each and looks for stores, service companies and manufacturing plants.

Screw it. I'll just drive out.

I've always been comfortable with numbers, less so with words and much, much less so with people. Laura told me this morning that my analytical abilities should help me in organizing my job search and in reviewing sales techniques and using the ones that work better than others. She's right, but what analysis doesn't help is that feeling in the pit of my stomach or the sense that I'm trying to swim in jello.

So I sort every business establishment I drive by into one of two groups, using my sales material as a base; the free-lance business card group or the resume group. The fitness center, the other fitness center, another Hispanic grocery, the two-person auto repair shop, the small factory with eight cars in the parking lot but a locked entry door, the recently built factory that's been turned into a church, each gets the appropriate knock on the door, quick question, polite or curt rejection and, when something seems not to be an immediate 'no,' the appropriate piece of paper.

I do the northeast quadrant in the morning and the northwest in the afternoon. I start to hand out resumes and cards almost every place I stop, knowing that for $20 The Depot will reprint them while I wait.

It's an expense I don't make. It's taken me two days since Laura and I argued to visit what to my judgement is the vast majority of businesses in the city and close environs. I have a short list of three people to call back and set up appointments, all for freelance work.

Since it's Thursday, Laura will go straight from work to school and won't be home until almost 10 pm. Dinner is up to me, and I stop at the local Hy-Vee for a large frozen pizza, some deli sharp cheddar, a few slices of ham and a green and a red pepper. Laura taught me how to dress up a frozen pizza years ago before Jan was born, and it's one of my "Dinner by Dad" favorites that the girls love. There will be a slice for Laura when she gets home tonight too. On my way to the checkout I happen to walk down the liquor aisle and pick up a plastic bottle of vodka.

Jan and Jess and I have a ball making the pizza, timing it in the oven, and arguing over who gets the green and who the red peppers. It's the best time I've had with the girls since I've been home. We laugh a lot, do the dishes together and when everything is clean and sparkling, the girls jump into their pajamas, I switch out my jeans and collared shirt for sweats and a Cyclones t-shirt, and Jess picks the night's movie. It's summer vacation and I make a new rule that on Mom's Late Thursday Nights, they can stay up till she gets home. Twenty minutes into the movie, I make myself the evening's first vodka martini.

The movie isn't very good but there's enough comedy to keep one of us laughing every once in a while, and that's enough sound to keep the other two of us awake. My eyes go to the backs of two beautiful young girls as one lays on the floor while the other slouches over the side of a chair. What do they think of me being unemployed? Are they worried about our financial situation? What has Laura told them? What should I be telling them? Full of questions, I try to watch the movie and see it from their eyes. I have no answers, and the vodka isn't contributing.

The movie ends a few minutes before Laura is due home and for the first time since we've been married, I'm not enthusiastic about her coming home. I have no progress to relate, no discovery, no success. The best thing I've done since our argument was to make tonight's pizza.

Which Laura enjoys. Jess is the microwave expert and she nukes up one of the two remaining slices of pizza while Laura doffs her work clothes for her own pajamas. We all laugh and joke about ham pizza and which color of pepper is better. I wish the pizza would last for longer than it does, because when it's gone, the girls are off to bed and Laura turns to me.

She surprises me with her first comment. "You look happy tonight."

I pause before answering. She's right, I suppose. Although I don't know how I look, I feel if not happy, then less unhappy. This was a good family night. I've never minded Laura's hard work at school and the hours away it meant, because it gave the girls and me time together. And after the last two days, that time baking, joking, eating, watching and snoozing was food for my soul.

I try to synopsize that into a coherent sentence and fail.

"Tonight with the girls and when you got home was wonderful. Today was only a tiny fraction better than yesterday. I don't think there's any real work here for me. I have travelled all over the city, have discovered places and businesses I never knew existed. Laura, I have done 100% of what I can do and have done it as well as I can do it. I don't see a way through."

She surprised me again. "What are you drinking?"

"Oh, it's a vodka martini with a splash of that white wine you like instead of vermouth. Would you like one?"

Tonight is a night for surprises, as she says "sure." So I make two.

"I know you've worked, I truly do," she says as I shake up the drinks. "It would be hard for someone who sells for a living to do what you've done over the past couple of weeks. I'm proud of you for trying as hard as you have. And I can see that you've really put your heart and mind into it."

I hand her the martini. We don't have the classic tapered glass with a long thin stem, but we do have some nicely shaped stemmed wine glasses that suffice. She sips carefully, again, then takes a good drink.

"Actually, this is pretty good. I'm not much on vodka, what did you do?"

"It's that white wine you like, the fairly dry one." This is starting to feel good, more like home, more like us, but then she changes course.

"So what are you doing next?"

I have no answer.

6 Medina

Two days later, I take the girls to Laura's Mom's for the day and drive to Medina. Laura has made this trip two or three or four times a week for almost four years and will be doing it at least through the end of this year. I've replenished my supply of business cards and resumes and am as ready as I will ever be for more disappointment.

I start out downtown, on the main street, Fourth Street. These are all business-card drops. I warm to the task or become oblivious to the rejections I receive. I begin to drive out to the industrial area when I drive right past an accounting firm. I pull a U-turn, park and go in.

"We sure could have used you during tax season, but right now, I have nothing to offer you." That's what I hear from Kate Spivey, owner of Medina Accounting. Her office is covered with photos of her two girls, one of them also named Jessica, and their artwork. She has four employees and no admin, as I discovered when I walked in the place and simply knocked on the door of the first office I saw.

I'm struck by the similarity and sameness of the businesses I visit. My "resume bucket" companies, the factories and so on that occupy large tracts of suburban land, are all ugly. They all appear to have been built for another time, when businesses were visited by customers and vendors, when a first impression mattered. On the front of the buildings there is an architectural nod to design, maybe some limestone highlights or a few bricks. Glass around the entryway. There's the leftover of a lobby, maybe a counter or a sliding plastic window that now looks over an empty desk. A few photos or plaques on the walls where chairs or couches used to be. Sometimes a phone with a list next to it so you can call the person you are there to see. The lists are always names and numbers, never titles, so I stand and call until someone, anyone, answers and I ask for the accounting department. It is, I suppose, efficient yet cold, impersonal, unimpressive, as if the purpose is to demonstrate frugality. The back portions of the buildings, the parts I rarely get a glimpse of, are often two story or larger, with metal siding. The image of an airplane hangar at a small local airport comes to mind.

I trudge on, following one street after another, from one parking lot to the next, one aluminum and glass entryway into the following one. I'm soulless, my interest in the few people I do see is less than minimal, a negative number if possible, caring only if they can give me a name or tell me who to talk to. I barely need to open my mouth, knowing in advance what I'm going to hear from them in reply before I begin to speak.

Still, I continue, having learned the blind squirrel and acorn parable is sometimes, unaccountably, randomly true. I'm becoming comfortable with my perpetual boredom. My non-thinking groove of movement and meaningless activity is better than cleaning and reorganizing the garage, which I've already done three times. It gives me a reason to shower, shave and get dressed each morning, to head out to the car and drive somewhere, anywhere, to replicate a small semblance of what used to be normal.

"Hi, Dad!" A small voice breaks me from my reverie. It's Jess speaking, and I'm home. Home looks familiar but feels just a bit off, as if the garbage from last night's dinner wasn't taken out to the trash can.

"Jess, I sure could use a hug." I get a big, long one. Just what the doctor ordered.

As I glance at the clock, I realize Laura will be home soon. Wednesday this semester means no classes and typically she makes dinner.

"Let's surprise Mom and you and I make dinner tonight, what do you say, Jess?"

"Yes! She will be surprised unless it's one of your breakfast-for-dinner specials."

"Are you saying you don't like the very best thing I make? You know, there are people in Kokomo who think my breakfast-for-dinner is the best thing they ever ate!"

She gives me that nine-year-old, no-school-summer-vacation, smarty-pants look. "Where is KoKoKo? Isn't that a gorilla?"

"Nope." I head for the refrigerator to see what we may have that doesn't include eggs and sausage. "I'll have you know Kokomo — KokoMO, with an M — is a very exotic place. One of my college roommates was from Kokomo and when it was my turn to cook, he'd hardly ever let me make anything except breakfast-for-dinner. That was fifteen years ago, and he still hasn't figured out my secret ingredient."

Jess smiles at me and steps beside me so she can peer into the fridge along with me. "There's your secret ingredient right there" she whispers and points to a bulbous yellow plastic bottle with a red top.

"Well, don't you let the bag out of the cat," I joke back.

She looks at me as if I had said something forbidden.

"Dad, I think you meant cat out of the bag."

"Nope. And do you know who Mrs. Malaprop is?"

"Is she from KokoMO too?"

"We'll all be in Kokomo if you and I don't start dinner soon. We want it well along by the time Mom gets here. I'm thinking vegetarian tonight, what do you think?"

"Mom likes that better than Jan and I do. Any other ideas?"

"Yes, I think we have just what we need in the cupboard." I walk to the cupboard wall, Jess trailing, and find a jar of some red tomatoey sauce and a box of rotini pasta. Perfect.

I hold them up, one in each hand, like an actor who has just won his second Academy Award of the night. Jess agrees on this plan, and we spend the next five minutes discussing the various skills involved in boiling water without burning it.

When Laura walks in the door, the table is set with our "fancy" napkins, utensils are laid out and matching drink glasses are ready for the water, all courtesy of Jan. Jess and I have the water almost to a boil, the sauce simmering and can of green beans open and ready to go in the pot with a dollop of butter waiting.

"Oh, this is a wonderful surprise," she smiles and turns to me. "You must have had a good day."

"Not as good as this dinner is going to be. Let's enjoy this fabulous repast prepared by chef Jess and chef Jan and sous chef Dad. We'll talk about today later."

We speak in hushed tones after the girls go to bed and while Laura is removing her makeup. The discussion goes about as well as it can. I plan to go back tomorrow one more time, stopping at the Medina library first to see if they still have a telephone book. The online Yellow Pages didn't list Medina Accounting and I want to be absolutely positive I've covered every accounting firm I can drive to.

I take the girls to Laura's Mom's house the next day to give them something different to do beside hang around our house alone all day. I hit the Medina library, two more industrial areas and a couple handfuls of other stores and service businesses. The highlight was thumbing through the Medina Yellow Pages, looking at the ads.

It's a bit out of my way home, but when I've covered Medina as well as it can be covered, I make the short side trip and stop off at the Fourway Bar.

It's mid-afternoon. I ate a cheese sandwich I made at home while sitting in the car in a small Medina city park. So I choose to sit at the bar in Fourway, which I've never done before. The drink special is martinis today, and I ask the bartender if that includes vodka martinis or just gin.

"Martini is a martini. Four bucks, any well booze you like. You can have a bourbon martini if you like."

"I've not heard of that, and it sounds interesting, but let's go with vodka. Keep it on the dry side if you would, please."

He smiles, nods, and in about eleven seconds I'm sipping. The first one goes down quickly so I order a second. I glance around and notice that I'm one of three people in the place, and the only one at the bar.

My solitude lasts for just a couple of healthy hits of my drink, and another customer sits down a seat away from me.

"What's on special today, Melvin," he asks?

"Martinis," replies the bartender. I like this, now, because I feel like an insider, the warm glow of the ice-cold vodka letting a smile come to my face. Melvin, I believe, is the first bartender whose name I ever knew.

The newbie gets his drink, takes a healthy dose, and turns his head right and left. "Afternoon," he says to me, "here's to us."

We lift glasses and drink.

He's somewhat older than I, maybe mid to late 40s with thinning and greying light brown hair. We stare straight ahead at the collection of bottles on the shelves behind the six beer taps. I take the last sip and turn to go. The greying man points to my empty glass.

"I'll stand you another one if you'd like. You look like you could use it."

I pause for a moment. I'm not used to people talking to me in a polite manner and in complete sentences. And offering me something. It's an oddly warm feeling after all the rejection and empty faces with cold voices I've encountered all day.

"No, but thanks." I try to put a smile on the comment like the TV newscasters.

"Maybe next time."

I make the short drive back to Lorna's house to pick up the girls. The man's 'next time' banging from place to place in my brain. He's a complete stranger. Why would he buy me a drink? Is he trying to pick me up? How bad do I look? I check out my face in the rear-view mirror while waiting for a light to change. I think I look the same as ever. Might need a haircut soon. That hair is still black, unlike Mr. Graying Hair.

Three days and one more garage cleaning and lawn mower tune up later I review my notes from my sales efforts. I realize I never kept track of the places I called on and wonder why. Now is not the time to re-create my activities. I check my receipts from The Depot and see I've printed 200 resumes and business cards. I have 37 and 10 left respectively. I record the places where I can specifically remember I didn't get an immediate 'no' and map out two routes, one in Stillwell and one in Medina. After dinner, I put everything together for one last try, one last effort, one last long, drawn-out day of petrified boredom. I know in my gut what the outcome will be.

The next day doesn't fail to disappoint. I toss my portfolio on the back seat of the car and hang my suit jacket on the hook and climb behind the wheel. A morning in Stillwell and the afternoon in Medina has only resulted in moving pieces of paper from my portfolio into a few hands, onto a few desks and countertops, destined no doubt for the trash. On the positive side, it's all recyclable.

It's just after 4pm when I pull into the small parking lot next to the Fourway. The sign still says martinis, Melvin is still behind the bar, and I'm still the only customer. As Melvin places the drink on the bar in front of me, a voice comes from just beyond me.

"That one's on me."

I watch the martini glass settle on the bar top and turn around. It's Mr. Greying Hair.

"What's this for?" I ask.

"I promised you a drink a few days ago, and I keep my promises."

"And I'll drink it." I do exactly that. "Thank you."

He pulls onto the barstool next to me.

"So why are you buying a complete stranger a drink?"

"You look like you could use one. You looked like that a few days ago and you look more like that now."

"I do?

"Yes, you do."

I reach for my glass to find it empty.

"Melvin, another one for the gentleman here. May as well make it a double. And one for me."

The deep cleanliness and wonderful cold washes over and through my mouth.

"So what is it that brings you to see Melvin and the Fourway today?"

"Lost my job. Can't find a new one. Got bills to pay."

"What kind of work do you do?"

The bottles on the backbar are an attractive display of shapes, colors, graphics, tastes, hopes, fears, celebrations and tears. My glance goes from the good stuff at the top left, down past the beer taps to the just-a-drink-level in the well on the right. My current level.

"I'm an accountant. Was. Was an accountant."

"Pretty tough out there?"

"Impossible."

"Mmm. Money getting tight?"

"I'm used to paying my bills on time."

I see him look past my upraised right arm to my left hand where it holds the bar steady. Looking at my wedding ring or my fingers or gauging the size of my hand?

"Might you need some extra cash?"

"Cash is good. Cash is real good."

"Are you available for employment?"

"Depends on the nature of the work. And the pay."

"Intermittent. Strictly cash. Few hours at a time."

"Yeah. Yeah, I'd be up to give it a try."

"Good. Meet me here next Wednesday, about the same time. I'm interested in a piece of real estate and you can find me some information."

7 Just a key

"No last names. I don't care if that isn't your real first name. Actually, I prefer it isn't. You do what I say, when I say, you do nothing more and nothing less. Five hundred the first time. Seven fifty the second. If there's a third, we'll discuss it then. Are you in or not?"

"I'm in," I say. He pulls out two $20 bills and leaves them on the table, buying our two beers each and leaving a very nice tip. We walk outside the Fourway Bar and he points to an undistinguished-looking blue Ford Focus.

"You drive. I'll tell you where to turn." He hands me a single key.

We drive south on Route 41, until we get past the shopping area and the stop lights thin out.

"Right at the light," says Neil. He wants me to turn north on Redford Avenue next. I know this area pretty well, it's what comes from living in the same town for all 36 years of your life. The traffic is dying down from what passes for rush hour here, which means three cars ahead of me at the stop light. I turn, and there's no car ahead. So I get to the 35mph speed limit.

"Right at the next light, then a quick left." I know this area better than pretty well. Bill lives in this neighborhood. He'd had Laura and I out for drinks a couple of times, and once or twice for dinner. Back in the day. Somehow, I'm not surprised when, after the right and the quick left, I hear Neil say "go up about a block and a half and then slow down." There's a small compact car ahead just braking and turning into a driveway. No turn signal. Most people wouldn't notice that, I probably wouldn't, except I'm pretty sure it just pulled into Bill's driveway.

"Pull over now," interjects Neil, "and shut off the engine." I do as instructed, pulling over just before the side street past Bill's house. I give it about 3 minutes before I raise my hand and start to ask a question.

"No, we just stay here for a while. I'll tell you when we move and when it's OK for you to speak."

"Let's go around this block."

I start the engine, go up to the stop sign, turn left and follow the street as it curves around in a long, sweeping, 180-degree turn to the right.

"Right at the stop sign, then pull over and park on the right."

We settle into our seats again, the dusk settles into the sky and it begins to look more like night than day. I look straight ahead down the street, and occasionally turn my head a bit to the left and move my eyes down the opposite side of the street. No way am I glancing over at Neil. So I stay focused. This is the time of night when I'd be getting home from a long day at the office, ready for a quick Jack and a hug and some chat about homework assignments before dinner. It's getting easier and easier to shove those thoughts out of my head. So I shove them out. I try my damndest to listen hard enough to see if I can hear the grass grow but no luck.

"Get out of the car. No, first, turn off the interior lights completely so when you open the door there's no light. Go across the street, walk up on the sidewalk to the third house on the right. I want you to walk slightly slower than normal, go past the house and see if you can see anyone inside. If you can see anyone, turn around and come back like you forgot something. If you can't see anyone, walk past the house and go into their yard. I don't want anyone to see you, so check out the lights of all the houses you walk past. If anyone can see you, turn around and come back. If you can, I want you to go past the corner of the house, into the back yard. Peek into the window that's back there. Stay there and look in if you can. When you've seen something, keep walking through the back yard, into the back yard of the house in back. Walk to the sidewalk, turn right and circle back here. Got that?"

"Yes."

"I want to know absolutely everything you see so think carefully about everything you see. Remember everything. Got that?"

"Yes."

"Now go."

I'm undecided if I'm happier to get out of the car and away from Neil or petrified of becoming a peeping Tom. I knew when I said yes at the Four Corners Bar that there was some likelihood of doing something on the other side of the law. But I need the five hundred, so I forget all that and walk and peek at the houses along the way.

I know the third house on the right. It's my ex-boss, Bill Hanlow's house. I know what's around the back side of that house. There's a beautiful deck, a great outdoor grill, and behind a high privacy fence, a hot tub. Laura, Bill and his wife Beth and I had wine out there one evening last summer. Just wine that time, no grill, no dinner, no hot tub.

I meander across the street and onto the sidewalk. I unzip my jacket, not because it's warm outside but because I am. The first house on the right has no lights on, ditto for the left side of the street. The second house has a light on in the front room, but the drapes are drawn. I can't see inside. The second and third houses on the left are dark.

My breathing slows to nearly a stop as I walk past Bill's house. The animus inside is ready to well up as I look at the field stone borders from the sidewalk to his front door. Any one of those rocks would easily destroy that large picture window and I'm tempted. But I swallow it. Since there is only the obligatory light in the front room hidden behind the drapes, I know I'm headed for the back yard.

The trainers I'm wearing don't make any marks in the grass as I walk through. I hope. The grass is longer than I keep mine, but then I freeze in panic. I hear voices. It's Bill and a female. I don't know Beth's voice well enough to know if it's her or not. But Neil will want to know so I walk as lightly as I can get my 185 pounds over three-and-a-half steps until I'm right next to the privacy fence. It's a two-sided fence, extending parallel to the side of the house and then turning back towards the house and across the first 10 or 12 feet of the deck to make the enclosure private on three sides. There's a big sliding glass door that opens out onto the deck from the side of the kitchen.

So now I'm able to hear voices. They are coming out of the kitchen and onto the deck. I hear glasses clink, and Bill's voice says "Let's get into the hot tub. I'll hold your wine while you get in, then you hold mine." Without moving my feet, I lean forward and twist my head to see if I can peek in between the stained cedar boards of the privacy fence. There's about a quarter-inch gap and just the tiniest knot hole. I hear the woman's voice say "Here you are and here I go." By luck, she steps just into my view as she moves her left foot into the tub. She's naked.

She's nice looking, speaking quietly and looks to be a bit modest. It's not Beth. It's Carson.

8 I like Thursdays

Thursdays I have something productive to do. When Laura leaves for work, I switch off the radio and take my second cup of coffee, the small one, into the living room. The coffee is just enough caffeine to get me through checking the job boards and my email. I pull my weekly report together along with the receipts, invoices, checks and other paperwork, stuff it into a 9 x 12 manilla envelope, and head off to Dr. Joseph's.

These meetings never take more than 20 minutes, as I go through last week and pick up this week's work. It's simple, almost mindless work, the kind of thing, once mastered, I've always found relaxing. After the first two weeks, I settled into a routine that rotated me from a five-minute pickup on Monday, home to do the actual work on Tuesday and back to the good Doctor's office on Thursday. It would have been easy to do the work on Monday and bring it back mid-afternoon the same day, but this fills out my week. And JoAnn seems to like the routine that Kay set up.

I'm hesitant to ask how Kay is doing as I don't want to lose this job. The $85 a week keeps me in gas, a fun addition or two to the Thursday dinners I make with the girls and, so far, the occasional special at the Fourway.

JoAnn greets me as I come through the door. Again, I'm the only one in the office.

"Kay called yesterday. She said she's feeling better, but

thinks it'll be a few more weeks before she wants to get back working. Are you OK with continuing on with us?"

"Oh, yes, sure, absolutely. Long as I can help," I reply. I think briefly about resumes and business cards and quickly push that out of my mind as Dr. Joseph appears in the doorway.

Fourteen minutes later, I'm back in the car, heading for the Hy-Vee to think about extra ingredients for tonight's hot dogs. I run out of ideas before I get to the store, so I drive on a bit to Riverside Park.

I walk along the paved bike path that doubles as a walking path. It's not much of a river, maybe thirty feet across and shallow enough in spots that I can see the sandy bottom. I'm unsure when a creek grows up sufficiently to earn river status. It's peacefully quiet here. There's a fresh, spring-green tint in the shoreline bushes and the sycamore and maple branches stretch out over the river. The water flows fairly quickly in spots and pools in the wider stretches.

I'm not used to the long expanse of the days. I want to be busy, to produce, to move forward, to have something to do. I need a paycheck. Our savings balance goes down every week, to the point where I hate to look at it. Laura and I both made decent money, and together we made a nice enough income. If we wanted to go out for pizza, we did it. Now it's grocery-store frozen. I wonder what cable extras we can eliminate. I like seeing spreadsheets saved, and moving from step to step. The river flows on, over and around the rocks and the weeds and I'm one of those rocks, or maybe one of the tall water weeds gently waving in the current, being sinuously directed here and there with no ability to influence the direction or the speed. My roots keep me here, and I wave uncontrollably as life, like the water, gently flows by, going somewhere I'll never go.

Jan, Jess and I are almost finished with our movie when Laura gets home. We hug, exchange a brief kiss on the lips.

"Tea or wine tonight?" I ask.

"No, I don't think so. I just need to relax a bit before we go to sleep. Girls, off to bed with you."

They scramble off to bed, leaving Laura and me alone. It's not quite comfortable between us, and although I'm unsure of the barriers between us, I feel them. We used to enjoy a few calm moments together these evenings, with both of us tired, when we'd simply sit, turn the TV and screens off, sometimes with a glass, sometimes with a bit of soft music, but just as often, with nothing, just listening to the small sounds of night, the furnace or the AC running softly, the occasional car driving by. The comfortable time I feel like I'll never know again.

"I think I'm done being an accountant," I blurt out.

There's a bit of fire in her eyes when she straightens up and turns towards me. "What? What do you mean?" she demands.

"Laura, I have done what I can do. I've done the online search, I've done the on-the-street sales, I've tried to turn myself into a sales person, I've tried to find a job, I've tried to start my own accounting business. There's a single client, $85 a week, and that's temporary until Kay comes back. I don't know if I've done a good job or a horrible job at finding work, at creating income, but I do know I've done what I can do."

Her face softens as she reaches out and takes my hand. "I know you've worked, and I know your work ethic. I know this is hard for you, it's not what you do best. And I know you've tried. How did you come to this conclusion? Are you ready to give up?"

"Give up! Jesus!"

I make the mistake of raising my voice, dropping her hand and standing up. Three mistakes in quick succession that I'll regret for the next several days.

"What do you think I've been doing for the last six weeks?"

"I know you've tried everything you can. I really do. You've worked hard."

"I don't see other options. There just aren't other accounting firms, every store and manufacturer have the finance and accounting covered, there is no place for me."

I want to describe that water weed waving in the river, but the words don't come. I'm suddenly exhausted beyond what I can stand, and I collapse onto the couch. At the far end. As far away from Laura as I can get and still be in the same room.

We sit this way for what seems like an hour, but then, time has been an unkind friend to me lately.

"I stopped at the bank today to get some cash, and there was a sign on the ATM that they are looking for tellers. I went in and applied."

"A bank teller? I can't remember the last time I was inside a bank building. Do those jobs still exist?"

"Well, I hope just this one does."

It's a cold, lonely night despite the heat of an Iowa summer and a beautiful woman in bed next to me.

Next morning, Laura is out the door, quietly, compactly, quickly and invisibly, although she did pause for a short moment to put her hands on my shoulders. Standing wordlessly behind me, it wasn't a shoulder rub nor a hug, but a warm gently human touch that communicated more than the words she'd said last night. I relaxed, just for a moment, while that small second cup of coffee began to cool. I was not at all prepared for my phone to ring. I turn off the radio, pick up my phone, and although there is no caller ID, by now, I'm so desperate for human contact I'll accept a call from a robot telemarketer.

Thirty seconds later I have scheduled an interview at Sunrise Bank for 1:30 this afternoon. Two days later I have a job offer and the next Monday, I start a new career as a bank teller.

Just a hair's breadth over minimum wage. I do training for two days, and gradually ease into the public contact. I learn the banking business from the inside, how to balance, when to shift, how to be polite to the occasional jerk. The drive-through window is where the best teller is stationed, so to provide the fastest service possible. They can work on two cars simultaneously; I'm pretty slow with one at the indoor line. I aspire to be good enough to be assigned to the drive through. But this work is simple, repetitive; I put figures down, double-check, establish eye contact, say thank you and move to 'next please."

The evening of my second working day, I call JoAnn and Kay Johnson, pack up all my materials, update JoAnn's flash drive, and take everything over to Kay's house. She's feeling much better, offers me a cup of tea which I decline, and seemingly looks happy to accept Dr. Joseph's accounting work back. More needlepoints, I think.

On my tenth working day, a Friday, my first paycheck

shows up in my bank account. It's much less than the paydays from Hanlow Accounting, but it's more than unemployment. There's a satisfaction glowing inside me I can feel as I drive down Maple Street towards home. Laura and I get there about the same time, and, as I had planned for the past two weeks, pretend to have a sudden brainstorm idea.

"Hey, how about we all go out for dinner?" I think I'm so extemporaneous, so spontaneous, until my pipsqueak Jess pipes up.

"Oh, feeling flush are you now, Dad?"

She has me right where she's always had me. Totally unprepared and baffled at what to do next.

"Oh, yes. The entry-level, low-guy-on-the-Sunrise-Bank-totem-pole is incredibly flush for this one night. Tonight, we dine at the exquisite El Maguey restaurant in beautiful and historic downtown Stillwell. We shall be overwhelmed by the garish yet tasteful bold colors of the tables and chairs. We will appreciate the photos on the menu, rather than trying to read and order in Spanish. Mother and I will enjoy an adult slushy called a margarita and you young ladies may choose the soda of your choice."

"You are feeling flush, dear," Laura smiles at me. "I think we three ladies will retire to our rooms to change into a more celebratory wardrobe. Does Mr. Maguey know that we will be arriving?"

I'm a bit slow on the uptake, but I get the hint. "I shall inform him and the entire staff using my cellular device as soon as you all turn around thrice."

The girls giggle, turn around and head off to their rooms to change. Laura makes suggestions as to what they should wear while I make a mental note to explain thrice on our way to the restaurant.

I do feel good. The mental gymnastics to calculate my new salary compared to my old compared to unemployment have been run, rerun, and re-rerun until I can recite them in my sleep. Some things will have to give — a vacation will be a staycation, our contributions to our savings and the girls' college fund accounts will be just a few dollars, Christmas will be quite gentle, but we'll be ok.

I do feel good. Although the work is repetitive and I deal with many different people each day, it's satisfying to again have a series of tasks to complete to fill my day. The steady income gives me a sense of security and comfort I couldn't have named a month or two ago.

9 The banking business

"Arvin, before we open this morning, can I talk to you just a moment?" It's Carol, the Sunrise Bank branch office manager, who walks up to me as I come in the door 35 minutes before opening. My hours require me to be in by 8:30 for our 9 am opening, and I am punctual about being early every day.

"Uh, sure, right now?" I ask. My heart falls through my body, through my legs and feet, past my shoes and embeds itself in the double-reinforced concrete floor. I've been here before, I can't imagine why but I couldn't then, take another step, what did I do wrong, another step, feel the unease in my stomach, a step, hope I'm not going to be sick, keep moving, my forehead beginning to feel wet, one step, turn left, past Dave's desk, he's not in yet, past Doris's small office, don't look up, don't turn my head, one step, one step, calm down stomach, now I'm glad I bookmarked the unemployment website, turn left, follow Carol, turn and sit. Hands together in my lap, she comes in behind me and closes that deadly, deadly door behind her. My intestines shrivel into nothingness, my eyes widen.

"Arvin, are you happy working here?"

"Yes, very."

"I ask because you're still relatively new."

"Yes, I'm the newest one here."

"What kind of a future do you see for yourself?"

"Well, I'd like to be here for a very long time."

"Do you enjoy your work here?"

"I like numbers. I like setting them in balance. I find it peaceful."

What in the world is she getting at, I wonder. Why can't she just come out and . . .

"We may need to shift staff around a bit."

Of course, she had to make me squirm while she warmed up to deliver the news.

"Dave is leaving. He's moving to be closer to his father in Idaho."

"OK."

Where is she going with this? Just fire me and get it over . . .

"That's going to result in changes in staff."

If I open my mouth, I'll just hurt myself. Wait. Wait. Wait for it.

"Would you be interested in Dave's position as Consumer Loan Officer? Or do you enjoy working on the floor?"

Dave's job? He stays in his office most of the time, keeps to himself, makes some phone calls and talks to people as they come in.

"Well, what precisely does his job entail?"

"Our Consumer Loan Officer works with individuals, not businesses. We work to find the best possible solution for each customer."

"Yes."

"It does pay a bit more." She mentions a sum about halfway between what I'm making now and what I used to make way back when I was an accountant.

"Are you offering it to me?"

Carol pauses, looking first at me and then at the papers in front of her. I try to read the upside down printing and give it up to establish eye contact.

"Yes," she says. And pauses again to break that eye contact. A small sigh. A tiny nod.

And then a smile.

"Yes," she says, this time with a conviction in her voice that I feel more than actually hear. "I'll have to find a new teller, but we'll move your duties around a bit. You can start training with Dave after lunch and spend as much time away from the line as you can between now and next Friday. That's his last day here. From then on, what you can't do on your own you can bring to me."

The walk down the short hall, across the lobby and back behind the counter requires about 1/100th time that the same walk took in the opposite direction eleven minutes ago. I deposit a few checks for a few customers, cash one, and when there's no line and no customer for a few minutes, ask Roberta, the other teller, if I can take a coffee break.

The grocery store brand water bottle is cold, and tastes

remarkably good going down. I'd drink a coffee, but Sunrise has only a single-serve machine with a bring-your-own policy on the coffee packets. Maybe with the raise, I'll be able to buy some of those. It's substantially less money than I was making those months ago, but substantially more than I was making last week, which was substantially more than the weekly checks from the state of Iowa.

The morning zips by, and Dave gives me a rundown on the basics of his job. He's pretty knowledgeable and I recognize it will take me some good time before I can ask the right questions and make the right matches for customers. It's numbers, I'm good with numbers, and as I walk out at 5:20 pm, I give the door frame to the parking lot a bit of a pat. My bank now.

That night Laura has class and I'm responsible for dinner, so we go out to celebrate the next night at Appleby's. We joke and laugh, the girls laughing more at than with me as usual. After two margaritas and a taco salad the size of a soccer pitch, we're back home.

We're undressing for bed when Laura turns to me.

"You're so much more relaxed now."

"Well, yes. I am more relaxed."

"I don't think I've ever known you so relaxed."

"When you say ever, how long a time frame are you looking at?"

"Ever, as in forever."

"Well, that's a long time."

"Yes. You were pretty uncomfortable when we met, a bit

awkward on that first date as you'll recall."

"Oh, I thought you liked dumping popcorn into the soda at the theater. You've always told me it was one of your favorite food groups."

"It was good for a laugh then and it appears that it's still good for a laugh now. I think the most mellow you've ever been over a period of time, was the few weeks after that when our relationship caught fire."

"Speaking of fire."

"No, wait just a bit."

"Relaxed. You also said mellow."

"I did. Arv, I'm seeing a side of you I didn't know existed. You're funnier, less uptight."

"Which side did you like better? Because I can show you front, right side, back, and left side."

I demonstrate.

"Well, you can be persuasive. But before we go on, talk to me. What's different in that multi-sided head of yours?"

I can see Laura is not going to be denied her discussion. I pull on my pajamas and sink into the side chair.

"When Bill Harlow fired me, I was completely lost. I had a series of events and steps, high school, college, Meyer Accounting, Hanlow, it all flowed from one to the next. No stops, no pauses, no gaps, no holes, just step, next step, next step. Then, after Hanlow, it was empty, nothing. I forced myself to do something I've never done before, wasn't any good at and never want to do again. It was the most awkward, stressful, upsetting, unsettled time of my life."

"That was obvious."

Just when I thought we were back in sync, there's that edge in her again. So I plow on.

"I realize, well, I do as I sit here talking to you, that there are things out of my control. Not everything is clear. Like a baseball game, you can play as well as you've ever played, and still lose 9 to nothing."

"You should coach again."

"No. Done with it."

"Why?"

"I didn't finish out last season because I was embarrassed. I was 'the guy who got fired.' It became a point of stress instead of a relief."

I surprise myself with my introspection.

"There's enough numbers and thinking in this job that I can put my mind to it. I'll have to learn some new things in the next few months, but it's in line with what I do. I can go to work and work. Then I can come home and I'm home. Between us, we make enough money to be comfortable. I want to be comfortable. I'm not interested in trying to be more."

"I like being comfortable too. I like this side of you."

Next morning, Laura goes out to make breakfast and I hear the radio come on. I shave and get into the shower when I hear a cry from the kitchen. A few seconds later, a white-faced Laura pulls back the shower curtain and pops her head in.

"Bill Hanlow was shot last night. He's dead."

10 Dead

"Dead? Shot? How, what?"

I do a quick rinse off, pull on some sweats and a t-shirt and go out to the kitchen. The girls come trooping in one at a time as I turn up the radio volume. I reach for my cell phone and type in the station call letters.

Laura's finger silences me as well as Jan and Jess. She points to the radio. There's a national feature playing and as soon as it's over and a commercial begins, she says quickly.

"I just heard the story. Jean said it was breaking news, got a call from the police this morning just before the 6 am news."

Jean is the newsperson for KSWT, our local station. Neither one of us has ever seen her but we know her voice. She's been delivering our local news for as long as I can remember. I think I can recall her when I was a kid in junior high, which would make her pretty old, but it doesn't matter now.

"What did she say? Exactly?"

"That well-known local businessman Bill Hanlow was found dead in his home this morning. That officers on the scene blah blah blah. Stay tuned and whatever. I ran in to tell you right away."

"Holy cow."

We both hate swearing in front of the girls and if truth be told, Laura swears more than I do. I blame it on her co-workers and the younger students she takes classes with, but neither of us swears. This seems like a good time for it.

"Holy shit," I interject. Once started, I stay on the roll. "I used to like the son of a bitch, but after he fired me, I stopped liking. I didn't, don't hate him, but sure don't wish him dead."

The girls have their faces in their cereal bowls. Jess looks up.

"Mom, are you and Dad arguing," she asks?

"No, no, honey," Laura soothes as she sidles over to me and puts her arms around me. The warmth and strength of her body is better than any medicine. "We just heard on the news that someone we know, the man who used to be Dad's boss, died last night."

"Did someone kill him?"

"I'm not finding anything on the KSWT or on the Stillwell Times website." I put down my phone and look directly at Jess, then at Jan.

"Jess. Jan." When I have their attention I continue. "My old boss, Bill Hanlow, was killed last night. We don't know much about what happened, that's why we are listening to the radio and I'm checking the web for more information. Someone shot him. His house is a long way from here and there's no reason to worry."

"Did you like him Daddy?"

"We didn't agree on everything and I haven't seen him in a long time. But I wish he was still alive."

"Girls," Laura chips in, "go get dressed and grab your coloring books and a toy. I'm going to take you to Grandma's today and we need to leave soon. Arvin, go finish your shower and get dressed. We need to be on time for work."

She's so together in times like these, I think as I re-enter the shower. Who am I kidding, 'in times like these?' I can't remember the last time someone was murdered in Stillwell. Maybe never. There is no time like this. Bill, the jerk who gave me a good job, one I deserved, and then dumped me, which I didn't deserve.

Jesus, I swear to myself. Dead.

I kiss the girls and jump into my car. I text Carol to tell her that I'll be there by 8:30, on time, but listening to the news in the parking lot for a few minutes before I come in.

There's no update on the radio, just the same two sentences that Laura practically memorized. I walk into the bank and tell everyone the story. Doris puts a cup of coffee into my hand and turns to make one for herself.

"I knew Bill, too," she says. "Way back when he first opened his own firm, I worked for him when he went out to see clients. He said he always wanted someone to be in the office and a live person answering the phone, so when he needed to go out, he'd call me and I'd drop whatever I was doing and go sit in a chair and read magazines. If the phone rang, I'd write down a message and give it to him when he came back. Gosh, I was such a kid. $6 an hour, with an hour minimum."

I chuckle at her memory.

"He was a bit old fashioned about some things. Everyone

in the office used their own cell phones when I was there, but there was still a land line and someone always had to be available to answer," Doris continued.

"I can't believe he's dead."

"I can't believe he was shot. Who would do that? And why?"

"Had to have been money. Bill was all about money."

Doris shakes her head.

"No, I'd disagree. Although I probably haven't really talked to him in years, I think he did care about people. Money, yes, of course, he loves - loved - money."

"He built that house about the time I started working for him, so about five years ago," I add.

"He was so proud of it. Invited all of us, the whole staff, I think there were only three or four of us at the time, and our spouses over for dinner. Beth did all the cooking, and it was quite nice."

I stop there, remembering the scene from then and the last time I peeked through the privacy fence at Bill's hot tub. And the very naked, very non-Beth getting into that hot tub with him.

"I see a customer coming this way. Gotta go."

It's a man about my age who wants to discuss re-financing his home. I dive into the numbers like a golden eagle going after a river rat.

I check KSWT over lunch and drive over to the Times offices out near the shopping district. They used to be downtown but moved out to the Stillwell version of suburbia eight or ten years ago. I dig four quarters out of the car drink holder and console to stick into the newspaper vending machine and page through today's issue in the car. Nothing at all in the print version. I check online again. It's the same story, different words in a different order. Dead of a gunshot wound, officers investigating.

On a whim, I take a quick left onto Redford, thinking to do a quick drive by Bill's house. A right and and a quick left and holy cow.

There are two TV vans with big antennas mounted on top, two other big SUVs, and I count three police cars of various designs and colors. I do a quick three-point turn in someone's driveway and go straight back to Sunrise.

Doris collars me as I take off my jacket in my office.

"Have you heard anything new?"

"Nothing on the radio and nothing in today's newspaper. Curiosity got the better of me and I drove out near Bill's house. Media and cops all over. Looks like Stillwell will make the Des Moines TV stations tonight."

"I didn't even think of turning on the TV news this morning, did you?"

"No, they so rarely have anything from here. I don't care too much about Des Moines news. I saw two TV vans, channels 15 and 23 from what I could see."

"Bit of an ambulance chaser, are you?"

"Ha! No, never did that before. Never knew anyone who got shot before."

"So how do we find out anything new? I'm glad we don't live anywhere near there."

"Yeah, was it a random thing? A burglary? Should we be afraid at home?"

"I haven't even thought about that. There is a killer on the loose, isn't there?"

"I guess we wait for the police to tell the media about it."

Laura and I watch the TV15 news at 10 o'clock that night. It's the first story on. Next morning, I check the Times website and there's the headline.

"Stillwell businessman shot dead"

And in smaller type underneath:

"Suspect sought"

There's a mention of multiple gunshot wounds.

The next night when Laura comes through the door, she doesn't even put down her bag or hug the girls before she says "I have never seen this many cop cars out. I started to notice it on my way in and I counted four on my way home. I haven't seen four cop cars in two weeks put together. They have to be looking for the person who murdered Bill. Don't you think?"

I do, but I'd rather not.

"Are we in danger?" she asks after a long pause. Jan and Jess are setting the table and taking the sandwich makings out to the dining room. It will be a casual, make-it-yourself, hot-and-humid-Iowa-summer-night dinner.

"No, I don't think so. I believe whoever did it was specifically after Bill and not anyone at random."

"Besides," I say, quieter when the girls are in the dining room banging the utensils around, "we need to keep a calm face on this. Until they find him, or her, the girls should go to your Mom's. Good for all of them."

"Right."

Tonight, 9:30 means bedtime. At 10, we watch TV15 again, with the sound low, and Lenore Goodman, the mahogany-skinned reporter with short, straight hair highlighted with slight tints of burgundy, is featured standing in front of Bill's home. I wonder what the neighbors think about all the traffic and the lights at 10:04 pm on a Wednesday night in summer. I wonder what the neighbors think about not having a neighbor. I wonder what Beth thinks about not having her husband.

Laura and I keep one eye on the hallway to be sure the girls aren't eavesdropping. When the story ends, they go to a series of commercials, then back to normal Des Moines news. I imagine the reporters and camera people in front of Bill and Beth's packing up their gear and heading out to go back to their TV stations and eventually home.

"Let's take a glass of wine outside."

We go. Laura picks up a wineglass. I pick up another and the three-quarters full bottle. I put it back down, reach into the 3-bottle wine rack she bought two weeks ago, and pick out a fresh bottle. One with a screw top.

The sling chairs, made out of a deep red, thick weave fabric, aren't new, but for Hy-Vee chairs, pretty comfortable. I open the bottle, pour Laura a glass and one for myself. The screw top is handy, and the bottle fits into what I suppose is actually meant for a glass in the arm of my chair.

"You're being generous with the wine tonight."

"Tonight is a four-pour night, a departure from our usual five-pour. As in, pours-per-bottle."

We sip in silence for a moment. The moon is almost full, and I'm trying to remember if it's getting larger or smaller. Waxing and waning is beyond my skill with words, but there are a few stars, a handful, one here and a couple there, that are considerably brighter than the others. Small town Iowa has some advantages, and being able to see the sky at night is one of them.

"Do you really think so?" I'm broken from my reverie.

"Do I think what?"

"What you said inside. That it was a planned, pre-meditated murder and not a random crime."

"I don't recall saying either planned or pre-meditated, but yes. I was also trying to keep our comments as non-threatening as possible."

"I know, Arv. Me, too. I just want to know what you really think."

I sip.

I ponder.

I take a healthy swig.

"All day, I've been trying to figure out why someone would kill Bill. Debts or some other money issue? Did he uncover some irregularity in a client's bookkeeping that he red-flagged, and feel a need to report it? Is it poss . . ."

"Could that happen?"

"Oh, sure."

"How?"

"You can cook books as many, no, more ways than you can cook pork. So if Bill found something that was questionable, or incorrect, he'd have a talk. That happens every once in a while. If someone did something outside the legal bounds, Bill was, I think, the kind of guy to report it. For certain sure, he would never put his or his firm's name on anything that was remotely off."

"You're sure?"

"Look, we were never great friends, but we looked over each other's shoulders on work from time to time. We'd discuss issues we found. Yes, I'm positive. He would have no part of anything illegal or even seriously questionable."

"So what else does that leave?"

"I can't imagine."

"How solid were he and Beth?"

I should have seen this one coming. I steal some think time with another good mouthful of grocery store pinot gris.

"Every time I saw them together, they seemed happy. How many times did we go over to their house?"

"The staff housewarming, I think a Christmas and then just the four of us, so three times. Dinner that Beth made each time, except I think she catered some of the housewarming. I don't know, a while ago."

"So?"

"They seemed like any married couple. I don't remember specifically any PDAs but I don't remember them arguing, either."

It takes me a moment to translate PDA into Public Display of Affection.

"Did you ever go out with him for lunch or a beer or anything?"

"Oh, gosh occasionally we'd go out for lunch on someone's birthday, but always as a group, and not frequently, maybe once or twice a year. A drink? Maybe at the end of tax season once or twice. We never had that buddy/buddy relationship."

"So who would want to kill him?"

"Lenore Goodman said — was it Lenore?"

"Who?"

"TV15 reporter."

"Ah. Yes, Lenore Goodman." "She said the State Police were investigating."

"And how do they come into the picture?"

"I don't know Arv. I'd feel better if they found the person."

I surprise myself by suggesting "I'd feel better if Bill were alive."

"I'm tired and I'm tired of worrying about a killer on the loose. Here in Stillwell."

"I wonder if the Stillwell Police have any experience at all with a murder case like this. What do you think?"

"Probably not."

The clouds begin to move in, blocking some, then more, then most of the stars. The moon has lost the hazy coppery yellow glow and is now moon white with blue shadow pools.

"It's probably time."

We stand and grab our empty glasses and the empty bottle and take ourselves and our now somewhat emptier lives back into the house.

Even the bank staff, which is most of them, who didn't know Bill or know of him are edgy the next morning. Every customer I talk to has heard the news. It's a relatively slow day, so I drive out to pick up a newspaper. I pass by a small city park and think to pull into the lot and look it over there, but then a city police car happens to drive past me in the other direction and I re-think. I peruse the news in the Sunset break room with my homemade sandwich and bottle of grocery store water.

It's Thursday, so I swing by the store to find a dinner to make. There's a palpable sense of quiet inside. A box of mac and cheese, some frozen fish and a can of green beans. I promised Laura that not only would I cook on Thursdays, but I'd buy the groceries and plan the menu to reduce her burden. Menu, I think, such as it is. A bottle of rose' finds its way into my basket, and at home, while the wine relaxes from its journey in the refrigerator, I mix the butter and milk into a mixing bowl and preheat the oven, giving the girls and I have a chance to chat.

"Are you scared, Daddy," asks Jan?

"Thank you for asking. No, I'm not scared but I'm more aware now of who is on the street and what's going on around me. I think it's important for you and Jess and Gran to do the same. Be aware of the people around you."

"Will they find the bad man?" Jess chirps.

"I'm sure they will honey, there are a lot of police out looking for him."

It could just as easily be a her instead of a him. Damned if I'm going to give voice to that thought here and now, not with two daughters.

"Did Mr. Hanlow do something to get murdered? Gran wondered if he had done a bad thing that led to another bad thing."

"That's a very interesting thought. I'm sure the police are asking questions like that of many people he knew."

"Are you mad at him because he told you didn't have a job anymore?"

"I was when he told me. And I was for a while after that. But I'm very, very sorry he's dead."

"What should we do to be careful, Dad?"

"Until they find the person, just stay with people you know. Don't be alone. But you two do everything together, don't you?"

Three hours later, I relate this conversation, over the rose', to Laura.

"Are you scared, Arv?"

"No. I'm concerned. You?"

I have a sense that there's a brooding storm on the horizon.

"Did the Hanlows have a security system? What if this wasn't a planned action like everybody thinks? What if there's a crazy person out there walking down one of our streets right now? Bill was killed inside his own home. How can we keep our girls safe when they bike over to their friends? What about my Mom? How do we keep her safe?"

"I'm panicking, aren't I, Arv?"

It takes a couple of days, but both security systems get delivered to our home and I spend most of Saturday installing them. We've always made a habit of listening to the local news on the radio each morning, and at least glancing at the newspaper when we get home in the evening, but now we pay close attention. We check out TV15 News about every other night, but the murder seems to have faded into the background.

I take a break from eating a home-packed lunch one day to step inside a chili dog place up on Wentworth Avenue. It's a tiny place in what used to be a 5- or 6-store strip, but the area is declining and there are two vacancies advertised. Moe's has been there for as long as I can remember, selling great dogs at rock-bottom pricing. I've given myself one lunch treat a week, and I plan to enjoy this one, greasy chili on the chin and a touch of heartburn included.

The Moe's Chili Dogs sign in the window used to be neon, I suspect, but I can't remember when it actually worked.

Glass store front, glass and aluminum swinging door.

I pick up my two dogs, extra cheese, no onions, just plain tap water please and head past the counter seats toward the back where there are four small booths, two on each side of a narrow aisle. Three of these are full, with people at both sides of the table, except the back table on the left is occupied by a single woman. She looks familiar but I can't place her, maybe a Sunrise Bank customer I talked to. I turn to take my tray back to see if there's a spot at the counter when the woman motions to me.

"I'll share this table with you."

"Thanks, but I don't mean to intrude."

"No, no, please, I'm almost finished. Come and sit."

I do.

"I'm Lenore Goodman." We shake hands briefly.

"I'm Arvin. Oh, you're from News15, aren't you?"

"Yes."

"Sorry to blow your cover."

"Well, if you know who I am you must watch us, so I'll say thank you for watching. That's our official thing to say when we're recognized."

"These chili dogs are just tremendous, aren't they?"

"Yes, they truly are. Today's my day off, so I can eat all the onions I want without pissing off my photographer when he's trapped in the car with me all day."

"You get a day off during the week?"

"Compensation for working every Saturday."

We do justice to our dogs, me to my first and her to what appears to be her second or third. I notice that, unlike when she's on TV, there is no News15 logo on her dark blue t-shirt.

"Not to be personal, but do you live here in Stillwell? I mean, being here on your day off."

"No, I live in Des Moines. I'm kind of working off the clock and unofficially today. The story of the killing just sticks in my brain and I want to see if I can ferret something out."

I'm not on the defensive yet, but I'm warming up my radar.

"We don't get too many murders here in Stillwell."

"How long have you lived here?"

"All my life."

"Do you remember the last one?"

"No. My wife and I were trying to recall that just last night, and we can't remember any."

"October 12, 1951."

"What? Really? How did you find that out?"

"Google."

"Stupid question. I didn't need to ask that, did I?"

"Well, don't give Google all the credit. That story was in the Stillwell Times newspaper. Google is how I found it. I talked to the current editor, and the previous editor as well, to see if they remembered a murder or had other records, and there's nothing. The current editor has been there for something like 17 years, and the previous one, now retired, was editor for even longer."

"I'm impressed that you found all that out."

"It's what I do. What do you do?"

"I work in consumer loans for Sunrise Bank."

As if on cue, I feel chili starting to drip down the front of my chin, so I get to the napkin as quickly as I can. The quality of the napkins bears a perfect relationship to the cost of the chili dogs, so I use two of them here.

"This isn't a pick up line, I can see that you're married, but do you come here often?"

"Not often, but I've been coming here for a long time. Long enough to know to grab a handful of napkins. Help yourself as needed," I suggest, utilizing the last two bites of my second dog as a pointer to the pile I napkins I brought to the table.

"What do you think the feeling is here in town about this unsolved murder?"

"I think unsettled is the word I'd use."

"What about you and your family?"

"Are you interviewing me?"

Lenore Goodman shakes her head. She looks different in person, less makeup I presume, and a little younger than I would have guessed, maybe closer to 30. Her hair is longer and has more body on the top, and is quite short on the sides, to reveal all of her ears. A single small earring in each ear, simple but a large stone. She's wearing very dark plain t-shirt that's not exactly loose but not tight either. Blue jeans. Her questions come naturally, with no antagonism but seemingly genuine interest.

"No, I'd have a microphone and a camera here if it were an interview. I'm just wondering what the feeling is here, how people are coping. Or are they ignoring it?"

"I work in a small bank branch, just a few employees. My wife and I have two young girls, so not much social interaction. I will say that I installed a new security system in my house, and in my mother-in-law's house this past weekend. Did Bill's home have a security system?"

"Bill Hanlow, the murdered guy we're talking about."

"You sound as if you knew him."

"I did. I worked for Bill at his accounting firm for five years."

"What can you tell me about him?"

"That's a long story, and although I work at a small bank in a small town, 1 pm means 1 pm, so I need to head back."

"Oh, I don't want to make you late. I'm sorry to have delayed you."

"You asked me a few questions. Can I ask you one?"

"Sure. And I'll be brief."

"Is there anything new?"

She sighs, rather heavily. "No, nothing new. The state

police have really taken over and I keep trying to talk to the detective in charge, but he doesn't return calls. I hoped I'd run into him today in Stillwell."

We get up and shake hands. We exchange nice-to-meet-yous and head out the door. As I get into my car, I realize I forgot to leave a tip and promise myself that I'll double tip next time.

11 Habit

"This has become a habit, I believe."

"Is there a rule about doing something a specific number of times that turns something nice and enjoyable into a habit?"

We discuss this as we head out to the red fabric chairs under the very mature maple tree in the front yard. I have the glasses and Laura has the wine, a blush red of some sort she bought on the way home from the hospital. We'd discussed my meeting Lenore over dinner, and I get the distinct impression that topic is going to be discussed out here among the stars. It doesn't take long.

"Is she nice?"

"I assume you mean Lenore Goodman."

"Of course."

The liquid blush in my glass is a little sweeter than I like but moving off topic is not likely to be a good idea, so I jump in.

"Yeah, I think so. If she was telling me the truth, that today was her day off and she was just here on her own hoping to find the detective, I have to be impressed."

"Was she telling the truth?"

"Based on how she looked, yes." I didn't need to see Laura's eyebrows go up to know I needed to go a bit deeper. "She wasn't wearing the formal or casual clothes she does when she does stories. Less makeup than I figured a TV personality would wear, and her hair was pulled back. Pretty informal, really. And she was at Moe's for goodness sake, not exactly the Stillwell version of a 5-star restaurant."

"Personality?"

"Decent personality, I'd say."

"No, you called her a personality. A TV personality."

"Are you suggesting that's the wrong term?"

"How about reporter." It was a statement, not a question. Sometimes I'm slow on the uptake.

"That's a better word, a better title, description, yes, thank you."

"You're holding something back on me Arv."

"I can't wrap my head around why she was here on her day off. Lots of fun things in Des Moines on a Wednesday, not so much here. And if the state detective isn't returning her calls, isn't the story dead? I didn't get the impression she was looking for the murderer but for information."

"That's her job. It's what she's paid to do. Speaking of which, what kind of car did she drive?"

"Uh, uh, you know, I'm not really up on the make/model/year thing with cars. Customers tell me what they own and what they owe and I look it up online. Are you wondering if she drives an expensive car?"

"No, I was wondering if it had a TV15 logo on it."

"Hmm. Subtle. I don't remember which car she went to, but there was no logo on any of the cars in the lot out front."

We sit and sip for a while. Muggy is an insufficient description for an Iowa night in mid-summer. The old saw that you can hear the corn grow on a quiet night is a lie, but I do believe I can hear myself sweat. I begin to think the blush red is great for Laura, but I'd be into my second lawn-mowing beer right now if I had any. Call it sensible replacement of body fluids.

I keep on wondering through the first glass and into the second. Why was Lenore Goodman here on her day off? Why is she here when the state police detective isn't? Why isn't Jean from the local radio station on this? What about the newspaper? Which is the North Star? Neither have had a mention of the story this week. I wonder if the detective wears a police uniform or is in plainclothes. I wonder where Orion is. Is that the big dipper? Is that faintly blue light a planet or the International Space Station?

I jump slightly and almost spill my half glass when Laura pops in. "Space Station. Definitely the Space Station."

"Did I say Space Station? Because I was wondering that exact thing just 3 microseconds before you said 'Space Station.'"

"No, you didn't say anything. What do you think?"

"I think two thoughts. One, yes, it's the Space Station. We could look it up online and get its position based on our location and time of day and be pretty sure, but the hey with that, you and I agree, and that's good enough. Two, tomorrow night, I'm shifting to beer."

"Not fond of the blush?"

"It's OK, but I need more volume to replace the liquid I sweat out."

We sit in silence a few more minutes and watch as the last of the light fades away. A dead Bill and a loose murderer are as far away as the ISS when we get up and walk into the house. I take a quick shower to rinse off my body and have to put a towel around me to go back to the living room where I forgot to turn on the alarm system. We sleep the sleep of the semi-content, a bit of tossing but as close together as the heat will allow. Laura hates air conditioning and keeps it off as much as possible.

Next morning, I get up a bit early as I've promised the girls I'll make pancakes before I take them to Laura's Mom's house for the day. I'm adjusting the batter to the perfect texture while the griddle heats, listening to the morning chit-chat on KSWT. The morning host and Jean, the newsperson, do a little back-and-forth for no discernible reason that drives me crazy, but I turn it on because once in every six or eight months they stumble into something that's actually funny. Today they're talking about the minor league baseball team in Des Moines.

"They beat the Bills last night 3 to 2 in 11 innings," Mr. Host says. But then he pauses, and I can visualize him looking at Jean who's either right across a desk from him or in another room with a large what appears to be a picture window dominating the soundproof walls surrounding them. This is the mental picture I've created and they destroy.

"Speaking of Bills, Jean, remember Bill Harlow, the

businessman who was shot a couple of weeks ago? What is going on with the investigation?"

Jean may or may not be prepared to answer this question, but she seems to be ready to talk.

"I talk to Police Chief Dawson almost every day, and I do ask him that question. As we know, the State Patrol are responsible for investigating this tragedy, with the Stillwell Police supporting as they are needed. The detective in charge is working diligently to bring the perpetrator to justice."

Mr. Host jumps back in. "So, nothing new. Is that right?"

"Nothing they are sharing. I don't remember another murder here in Stillwell since I moved here all these many years ago. Do you?"

"Oh, let me think. Nothing comes to mind immediately. Let's go to some wake-up music while we put our memory caps on."

Yeah, I think to myself, they are hard to listen to at times. But it's the only local radio station in town and they have a newsperson. So, there's that. I think I've done my due diligence to follow this story in the media, and yet I know as little as I knew a few hours after it occurred. I've now heard from two media sources that the detective in charge is not updating them, or even communicating with them. Is the detective on vacation?

Pancakes made and eaten, dishes mostly done, Laura off to work and class, the girls and I jump into the car for their day of Gran and my day of work. I'm a human question mark until I reach the door of Sunrise.

12 A reason to worry

Friday is our relaxing night. Laura gets off at 5 pm, my life as a banker ends promptly at 5 pm, she picks up the girls, and we make a fun easy dinner. Tonight, it's pre-made hamburgers from the Hy-Vee, so I change out of my bank suit and tie, slip on shorts and head to the kitchen. Laura and the girls come in, and I start the grill while Laura changes out of her hospital gear. I pour a wine for Laura and a beer for me. After burgers, we play a couple of board games and the girls go off to bed, a bit early for a Friday night, but that shows that Gran has done a good job of tiring them out today.

This evening we take iced tea on the red fabric chairs and we watch the late sunset with our hands touching.

"It's just about 10. Catch the late news or go to bed?"

My inclination is to choose the second option, and I can't quite guess what Laura's preference is.

"It's been a very relaxing evening and we've got a nice weekend in front of us with no particular plans. I kind of hate to spoil the mood with the news."

"Me, too," she replies, "but maybe your friend Lenore Goodman has something interesting. Let's catch the headlines and then go to bed."

I take her use of 'bed' rather than 'sleep' as a hopeful note and we head inside. The male anchor reads a teaser that's also on a ribbon at the bottom of the screen.

"A suspect has been arrested in the murder of a Stillwell businessman. Stay with us for details."

One hundred and twenty seconds, plus a flashy graphic introduction later, the story comes on. They cut from the two anchors at a desk to Lenore, standing in front of the Stillwell Police Department, then to a photo of the suspect with his name, George Watt as a caption. I have no idea what Lenore says. I can feel my eyes grow as wide as the watermelon we had for dessert, my body goes cold, my brain ceases to function and my stomach starts to send that watermelon back where it came from.

I recognize the photo in half a heartbeat. I don't know the name George Watt, because I know him as Mr. Greying Hair, "Neil," the guy who bought me drinks at the Fourway Bar.

The guy who had me scope out Bill Hanlow's house. So he could murder him.

I feel a dull repetitive thumping in my left rib cage, and look over to find Laura's elbow jabbing back and forth into my ribs.

"Arvin, are you awake? Are you all right? Are you sleeping?"

The blood comes back into my brain. I gradually become aware of my arms and then my hands. The legs and feet show up in a few seconds.

"Are you OK? What is wrong?"

"No. I mean yes. I'm fine. I just went . . . I need to stand up."

"You're acting like I've never seen you act, Arvin." She stands in front of me. "Give me your wrist." I stand and hope I'm not too wobbly while she takes my pulse.

She drops my hand. "You're a little elevated, but not much." I watch as she turns off the TV, switches off the lights and arms the security system. She walks toward our bedroom, stops and turns to me.

"Are you coming to bed or are you going to sleep standing up tonight?"

Laura ducks into the bathroom to do her nightly routine while I sit on the bed. We change places and I wash my face with cold water. Twice. Then once more before I open the door and lay down on Laura's right side.

The news has the opposite effect on Laura that it does on me.

"Are you feeling OK? As soon as that story came on you just became mesmerized. Aren't you glad they finally found him? I think I exhaled as soon as they said arrested and jailed. I was so worried there was a killer out there, stalking around. We can all breathe easier now, can't we? Mom will be so much more relaxed; I hope she watched the news too. George somebody, the owner of a company in Medina, how odd. Do you know the company he owns?"

"Arv?"

"Arvin."

"ARVIN!"

"I'm sorry, yeah, OK, yes, it's good."

Laura rolls onto her side, and puts her left hand on the right side of my head. Gently but quite firmly she turns my head to face hers, our noses almost touching. She taps the side of my head with her forefinger.

"Arvin, what's going on in here."

I have no idea what to tell her. Nothing? Everything? Create a story? I'm not in a creating mood just at the instant.

So I wing it.

"I'm just so surprised. This came out of nowhere, just like the shooting. One moment everything is fine and dandy, and the next wham, it's different. One wham, Bill Harlow is dead, then nothing, nothing, nothing, nothing, nothing, nothing, then wham, they find this guy and arrest him."

"You don't act terribly happy that they found him."

"Oh, I'm happy alright."

"Do you think I should call Mom and be sure she knows? She's probably asleep."

That's a continent I don't expect to visit anytime soon.

"Sure, I think she'd actually sleep better if you did call."

She picks up her phone and as she's talking, I try to get my brain engaged and my thoughts organized.

I do a bad job at this.

Laura and her Mom chatter for a while as I sort through the oatmeal in my cranium. She finally taps out the call, puts her phone on the nightstand and rolls back over to face me.

"I wish you'd tell me what you are thinking."

"Baby, I'm just numb right now. It's too much on top of too little."

"Tell me more."

I get a small chuckle out of that and think we might take this in another direction. The thought doesn't last.

"This, tonight, is so sudden, like Bill's death was so sudden. I wish I'd reached out to Beth like you suggested, but I was still pissed off at him. I was still somewhat pissed off at Bill until Lenore Goodman showed the photo of this guy." 'This guy' being the best my oatmeal can conjure up at the moment.

"Then, all of a sudden, all of that pissed-off-edness just slid out of my mind." I don't say what it was replaced by.

She's good at this, my Laura, she just nods ever so slightly and raises her eyebrows.

"And now maybe this is over," I verbalize. I don't verbalize the 'not for me' that belongs there.

"Where is your head? You had a lot of questions a little while ago. Any answers?"

It's my attempt to divert the conversation.

"If there's such a thing as a surprise level, it's a 10. On a safety level, I've gone from a 4 to a 9. I'm safer, the girls are safer, Mom is safer, you are safer."

Uh huh, I think. Yeah, OK, right.

"Probably some business thing, a disagreement of some

sort, a deal gone bad, who knows. Arv, you knocked on the door of a ton of businesses down in Medina. Do you remember this George schmuck?"

"I've been trying to remember his name or his company. Did Lenore Goodman say what company he owned?" A second discreet attempt at a small diversion. I hope sufficiently discreet.

"If she did, I don't remember."

"If it was a retail store, I left a business card. If it was a manufacturer or a professional business, I left a resume. I actually didn't talk to that many people. I don't remember any Georges." All of that is, actually, true.

"Well, we don't have to worry about it, do we?" She snuggles a little closer than I actually feel totally comfortable with. This doesn't happen often; usually I can't get close enough to her. Tonight, I just lay flat on my back, feet straight out, arms flat on my chest, brain flat, emotionless, clueless. It's not long before Laura drifts off to sleep, with only the soft whisper of her breathing next to me. That's when my mind finally clicks into gear. Right then, at that moment when the panic hits.

I desperately don't want to wake Laura. So when I begin shivering, I concentrate on breathing in and out. Slowly. I vaguely remember going to a few meditation classes in college, and count forward and backward with each inhalation and exhalation. When I shop shaking and can feel only my heartbeat, I begin with an inventory.

1. I lied to Laura about not knowing Neil/George
2. I worked with a murderer
3. Scratch that, I worked for a murderer
4. He paid me $500 cash

5. That makes it some sort of legally binding thing
6. I helped to commit a murder
7. I helped to commit a murder
8. I helped to kill Bill Hanlow
9. If I tell Laura she'll walk out on me
10. If I don't tell Laura and she finds out she'll walk out and divorce me immediately
11. If the guy from the Detective Bureau is any good, he'll find out about me
12. Are George and I the only two who know the truth about the role I played?

Then I go to the potential outcomes.

1. George is guilty
2. George is not guilty
3. George will be found guilty and will spend major time in jail
4. George will be found not guilty
5. If my participation comes out, I'm fucked
6. If my participation doesn't come out, it will depend on George
7. The state patrol detective bureau will be all over this
8. Will George tell them about me?
9. Does George know my name?
10. Does the bartender at the Fourway, who's name I've forgotten, know me?

I have no idea what to do.

I notice a bit of light coming in around the bedroom curtains. The police can't be coming after me already. They just can't. George and I didn't share our real names, he has no idea who I am just as I had no idea who he is. But the light doesn't change, it remains steady, so I move as slowly as my body allows, and get out of bed. As I stand, I glance at the alarm clock. It shows 6:04 am. That's not police car headlights, it's daylight. I haven't slept a wink. I get up, go out to the living room, flip on the computer and make a pot — a full pot — of coffee.

I hit the "Incognito" button on the computer web browser and go into the state legal statutes. I find the right section and run quickly through the few lines of text when I see Laura drifting sleepily out of the bedroom towards me. I bang out of the window and go the weather tab. Then I raise my head to look at her. Her hair is mussed, she has no makeup, she's wearing an old long-sleeved cotton shirt of mine, a red, black, blue and white weave pattern with the sleeves rolled up and the top several buttons unbuttoned. I'm going to have one hell of a time lying to her.

"Hey, baby, you're up early. This is a Saturday."

"I know, just couldn't sleep."

"What are you looking at?" "Just the weather." I point to the screen as evidence. "Wondering if it's a good day to mow the grass."

"You look like you didn't sleep well. Your eyes are all red. Let's go back to bed."

She reaches out for my hand. I take it and bring it to my lips, pulling her closer as I do so.

"I didn't sleep a wink last night. Not a wink. No way can I sleep now. You go back to bed; it'll be a couple hours before the girls wake up."

"It would be better with you."

"You need sleep, and I can't sleep. Go."

She turns and mumbles something I can't catch. We've never been ones to close bedroom doors unless we have company, so, with our bedroom door open I can't really tell when she can no longer see what I'm doing. I get back to the state website and spend a few minutes reading and re-reading the law. The analysis to date, that I've been working on mentally since about 10:35 pm last night, does not point to a positive, happy outcome. I'm sitting in front of the computer pondering the hide-and-avoid-the-maximum-pain strategy versus the confess-and-get-massacred-by-everyone strategy when out of our front window I see a vehicle stop in front of our house, pause, and then move on.

I glance down at my sleeping shorts, figure no one else is awake at 6:41 am on a Saturday and head outside to see what the heck. The car stops at the next house, right in front of the mailbox, an arm comes out, and puts today's issue of the *Stillwell Times* newspaper in the yellow plastic mail tube. After I exhale, I go grab our copy and see Mr. Greying Hair/Neil/George Watt's photo on the front page.

Back in the kitchen, I dump a healthy dollop of the cheap bourbon I keep for Laura's Mom into my coffee, fill the mug, and wander back to the living room to read the front-page story. First, I shut down the computer, then I unfold the broadsheet.

Medina Businessman Held by State Patrol for Murder of Stillwell Accountant

by Times Staff

Forty-three-year-old George Watt was arrested yesterday at his office in Medina and charged with the murder of William "Bill" Hanlow. Ten days after Mr. Hanlow's bullet-riddled body was discovered by his wife, the suspect was placed in

the Polk County Jail without bond. A charge of first-degree murder has been filed.

Hanlow, 47, was shot three times with a 9mm handgun, which has not been recovered. The Iowa State Patrol Division of Criminal Investigation has been investigating the case since Hanlow's body was found. Detective Chad Lance did not immediately return a phone call to provide a comment. Monday's initial court appearance is expected to be followed in the next few days by a preliminary hearing or a formal arraignment.

Watt owned and operated Watt Metal Forming, a manufacturer of aluminum extrusions primarily used in the automotive and farm implement industries. According to sources, about 30 people work at the factory, which is located in the Norton Industrial Park on the southeast side of Medina.

There's a small photo of Bill next to the photo George Watt/Mr. Greying Hair/Neil. No mention of Beth. My coffee mug is empty and I'm staring into space when Laura comes out of the bedroom. I'm afraid to look at her. I can hear her in the kitchen pouring her coffee, and think maybe I should hide the newspaper. I can't even make that decision. I simply sit, the one most burning question I've ever faced in my life searing my heart and my head — do I tell her?

Of course, the second most burning question is do I tell the ISP Detective?

My gut feels like a cement mixer, slowly churning round

and round. The coffee isn't settling well in there, and I'm intermittently nauseous. I can't focus my vision on the newspaper, or on the family photos we've mounted on the walls. Laura takes what seems to be a half hour getting her coffee. I don't want to see her. I want to be invisible. I want to hide.

"Hey, babe, good morning," she says as she runs her fingers gently over the shoulder of my t-shirt. I try to smile while staring straight down at my lap. It's a miserable excuse for a smile, and I know she can't see it.

"Are you done with that paper?"

I wordlessly hand it to her and pretend to take a sip of my coffee. The cup hides my face and gives me something to do without speaking.

She's a fast reader, Laura is, and she's ready with a question faster than I can blink.

"This isn't much of a story, really, is it? I expected much more, about evidence and how the State Patrol narrowed down their search. There's no drama in this. I thought it would be more like NCIS maybe. Wait, maybe it is like that old TV show — just the facts, ma'am just the facts. Do you recognize this photo of Bill? It looks like he's at some kind of event."

"He was a member of every service club in town, the Chamber of Commerce, Rotary, a couple of others too. Always going to one or the other for lunch. Said it was a business thing. He deducted the cost of memberships so it probably amounted to free lunches for him. I think that photo looks like some award ceremony. He hung plaques on the wall."

I'm astonished I can get this many words out.

"Makes sense, I suppose. I heard the girls when I got up, they'll probably come out soon and tell us they're hungry. Have you eaten anything for breakfast?"

The fact that life is going on, a normal, regular day with normal, regular activities is surprising to me. I have issues larger than breakfast.

"I don't feel well."

"Did you get any sleep at all last night?"

"No." That's the truth.

"I closed my eyes and tried to nod off here, and that didn't work either." That's a lie.

"Do you want to go back to bed? I can make pancakes for the girls."

I just sit. She comes over and does the fingertips-on-my-shoulder again.

"Arv, I thought finding the guy who killed Bill would be a good thing. We're safer with this George guy in jail. It's closure. Assuming that he actually did this, then we can turn the page, right?"

I almost tell her. The words are forming and I feel my lips moving, but there's sufficient adrenaline running now that I'm able to choke something else out.

"I really expected to be interviewed by a detective for the past few days. You could make a case that I had a motive for murder. Obviously, I didn't do it, I was here with you and the girls that night. But the newspaper, the TV news, even KSWT never said the time of day when Beth called the cops, or the approximate time of death."

"Are you relieved?" She can be so gentle.

"No." She has no idea.

"Maybe a shower would relax you." She can be so thoughtful.

"That's a great idea." I try to smile, try to look at her, but as I glance up at her face, I feel tears forming in my eyes. If I look at her, I know I'll tell her. I go right to the edge and I don't know which words I use until I actually hear them in my own ears.

"I'll take a shower."

I alternate between hot as I can stand and cold as I can stand. It may be the longest shower in the history of Stillwell, and just when that thought comes through my brain, I feel the water start to get cold without me adjusting the tap. I turn the hot up all the way and it still gets cold. I register my first accomplishment of the day; using all the hot water from our 2-year-old water heater.

"Daddy has his lawn-mowing clothes on," Jess exclaims as I walk through the kitchen to the coffee pot on the far counter.

"Hi, Jess. Hi, Jan." No cute nicknames today.

"Thanks," I'm able to squeak as I try to return Laura's fingers-on-the-shoulder gesture. I'm immediately sorry I did that, as she stands and gives me a massive hug. The water starts to form in my eyes again.

"Good shower?"

"Every bit of hot water we have."

"Dad, you were in there a long time," adds Jan. "You always yell at us when we take too long."

"I don't yell and I was trying to see if there is any benefit an adult could get from a shower as long as one of yours." Interestingly, it's easier to talk to the girls than to Laura.

Which I can't do. If I tell her . . . If I don't tell her . . . Will she find out anyway . . .

The lawn will provide an answer, so I go out to make it shorter.

I don't mind mowing. There's an honest visceral pleasure in the noise of the gasoline engine and a satisfaction of cutting the edges first to form a perfect square or rectangle, then using the back-and-forth technique to create small incremental progress with each turn. It's not unlike taking a stack of receipts, invoices, checks and notes and pulling out the numbers one needs to create a spreadsheet that may not tell a story but does present a picture taken at a moment in time. The best part of mowing is the trimming, cleaning up around the trees and Laura's gardens, moving the red fabric chairs just enough each mowing to preserve the view of the stars through the tree branches yet not block the sun so much that the shade from the chairs will kill the grass. I'm a master at this. Taking a lawn that needs attention and turning it into a field of smooth green gives me a feeling of satisfaction, proof of some basic skill set.

I lie. The best part of mowing is not thinking.

"How are you feeling Arv?" she asks as I come in.

The bitter hollowness inside me that the grass had filled is emptied instantly.

"The movement helped but I'm still a bit dizzy. Do we have any lemonade?" I don't dare look at her.

"If we do, it's in one of those frozen cans. Mom will have some I'm sure. You remember she invited us over this afternoon for lawn games and hot dogs. Right?"

"Oh. Yes. I remember. I forgot there for a minute, but I remember now."

"Do you want something to eat? Maybe you should take a nap."

"Food might be good."

"There's two pancakes left. I put them in the fridge. I finished the coffee."

"I'll try the pancakes." I go into the kitchen and take them out. Laura and the girls go out to inspect my work in the yard. I hold one pancake in my left hand and put my right hand on the small table we pretend is a kitchen island. In four bites the thing is gone, but I stretch the second one out to a full six bites.

I wash my face and hands and decide against another shower. I hear the girls coming back inside and I lay down on our bed. Crosswise. Shoes and socks and Cyclones baseball hat still on.

"A nap might be a good idea," I hear Laura say. "You best take those grassy shoes and that smelly hat off, though. I'll wake you up when it's time to go."

I do as instructed. I consider stripping down to my underwear and actually getting under the covers but dismiss this as too much like work. I find, if not peace, if not bliss, sufficient rest that my eyes close.

In a couple of nanoseconds, Jan and Jess come in and poke my side, tickle my feet, throw my hat on me and eventually succeed in waking me up. I stand up, go to the bathroom, and then back to our bedroom where Laura is checking the fit of her new summer top. I'd check the fit of that shirt on her too, but wisely look away and pretend to be considering a clean shirt and pair of shorts myself.

"Feel any better?"

"Some, but not great."

"Is this a physical or a mental malady?"

She's good, my Laura. I have to stop calling her 'my' because after this, she may not be my anything.

"Both. Mental to begin with, but no sleep turned into physical."

"Why don't you stay home and sleep. We'll make it a girls-only cookout and you can catch up from last night and relax. Get some alone time."

"Are you sure? Is your Mom counting on me doing the grilling?"

"Jan can do the grilling and you know it. It'll be good for her, good for us, good for you."

"OK, then. I think I will go back to sleep."

"I love you." She kisses me lightly on the lips and I close my eyes as she walks out the door. I lay back down and close my eyes and hear them slipping on their shoes, getting the dogs and buns out of the fridge and going out the door. I sleep until about 5, when I can almost smell those dogs sizzling on Lorna's gas grill.

I grab a pre-made deli sandwich and a jug of iced tea at the Hy-Vee and eat it sitting on an old patio chair on our back patio. We hardly use this patio and I can't remember the last time I sat in this chair. The kitchen is saturated with family objects and memories and the dining room doesn't feel like mine right now. The red fabric chairs I repositioned perfectly this morning aren't mine; they belong to Laura and I together. I don't belong in any of those spaces.

I have to tell her.

Laura isn't a violent person, but she will go ballistic. Divorce is the most likely outcome, but I might wind up in the state pen for a few decades, maybe the rest of my life, so divorce would be a good thing for her. I hope she can stand me long enough because I need, desperately need her help in answering one question; Do I turn myself in to the State Patrol?

Thinking of Jan and Jess, my tears fall as I predict what they'll think and how they'll remember me. I sit there sighing and whimpering like a baby the first time its mom leaves it overnight with someone else. I'm sitting there, elbows on my knees and head in my hands when I hear a car pull into our driveway.

From here on my life changes dramatically. I had thought that getting fired, not finding work, and making a new career constituted a big change. Damn fool.

13 Something to tell you

"Laura, we need to talk. I have something to tell you. Let's go out front."

Everyone is back, they've shared the story of Jan only "slightly burning" two hot dogs, the girls are watching a movie on TV, and the sun is approaching the horizon.

"I think that's good, Arv. Do you need a beer?"

"No, but you might want a glass of wine."

I get the raised eyebrow, but she respectfully pours herself a four-pour glass and we head out to the front yard and the red fabric chairs.

"Hear me through and know I'm not proud of this." She nods, which means that I have to go on. That I've started now on the end of our marriage and our family.

"A few weeks after Bill fired me, I was feeling really low. I happened to drive past this bar . . .

I tell her the entire story, leaving out no detail, and ending with the state aiding and abetting law under which I can be tried and punished as a principal. When I'm done, the silence envelopes us like the darkness that's fallen. I'm talked out, spent, humiliated, breathless, lifeless. Laura doesn't move, her wineglass upright on the lawn next to her chair. Untouched.

Suddenly, she turns to me, pauses, and stands up. She starts to point at me, pauses again, puts her hands on her hips. Then it's a staccato barrage of lightly tempered emotion and action.

"If you had a place to go, I'd kick you out. You don't and we — I — don't have money for a hotel. I'm taking the girls to Mom's and staying there. You are not to come to her house, you are not to call, you are not to visit, and if you happen to see any of us somewhere you will turn around and go the other way."

"You didn't tell me what you did with the $500."

"I paid both car payments, in person, at the bank. I kept out $40 in cash for Thursday night dinners."

"I'll verify that online tonight."

"You stay out of the house until we are gone."

"I can't believe that you placed all of us in jeopardy for $500. But you did. You can possibly save our marriage by extricating us from this mess. I don't know how you can do that without spending time in jail . . . no, I don't care how you do it. You got yourself in this mess, and me and Jan and Jess and now my Mom as well. You get yourself out. You get all of us out. You do it legally and above board. Then we'll talk. I don't want to fucking see or hear from you until then."

She quickly turns and runs into the house. I hear her voice telling the girls to get their backpacks. The living room lights come on, I see both bedroom lights come on, and a small girl's shadow comes to the window. I can't tell if it's Jan or Jess. I think I make eye contact, but then a larger shadow comes and the two merge together into a hug. They disappear into the darkness of the hallway. I walk out near the street, and look up into the maple tree. I sit down at its base, my back against the trunk, facing the street.

I realize I'm used to the hollowness that overcomes me and turns off my brain. I've felt this before, on the drive home from Hanlow after Bill fired me, on my way back with George Watt's $500 fresh in my pocket. And then again, most of the day today. This is different. Then I was filled with a nothingness. Now it's a vacuum.

The car doors open and close, the brake lights go on along with the backup lights. I sit and feel the car back down the driveway. Then the car is in the street, stopping, turning, going forward. I watch until the tail lights become brake lights at the corner, then the turn signal comes on, the brake lights go out and the car and my wonderful family disappear.

Twenty-five minutes later I'm standing in the kitchen nursing a glass of water. Neat, no ice, from the tap, cool but not cold. A car pulls into the driveway and as I peek out the window the back door of the house opens and Laura comes in. I put down my glass and open my mouth to speak.

"Don't say a word to me." Laura points to the front door, with a fire in her eyes that I've never seen. Maybe it was in those eyes when I was telling her my story, but I couldn't look at her then. It's killing me to look at her now.

"Get out of the house. I forgot my books and notebooks and I don't want to see you while I collect them."

I walk out the front door, close it behind me, and stand there looking out over the yard, past our red fabric chairs to the maple tree. It takes Laura maybe three minutes to gather

her school materials, then I hear the car door close and the car, the books, and my only reason for living back down the driveway towards the street.

The car stops half way. I see the trunk lid open a bit, and Laura gets out. Determinedly, she stalks across the lawn to the red fabric chairs. She takes the one nearest the driveway, the one she always sits in, folds it without disturbing the still-full wineglass perched on the ground just a few inches away, takes the chair back to the car, puts it in the trunk, closes the trunk, backs the car out and drives away. I don't know the scientific name for "less than a vacuum" but I can describe it in detail.

14 A personal day

A quick and easy phone call to Carol to ask for a personal day on Monday. My to-do list was carefully thought through, written down, torn up, written down, re-ordered, torn up, re-written and committed to memory yesterday. Today is all action. My second call is to the State Patrol. Detective Chad Lance is not available, but I get his voice mail. Then I hit 'send' on the email to Lenore Goodman at TV15 that I wrote last night. It's 8:07 am and my to-do list is done.

Riverside Park has one visitor this morning, and as I get out of the car, I wonder vaguely why this is even a park. Why is Stillwell a city? The meandering river is flowing gently today, considerably shallower than it was on my last visit. A dark blue, uncomfortable metal bench invites me to sit, and I accept. As I pull my phone out of the pocket of my jeans it rings and I deftly manage not to drop it. It's a number I don't recognize but I answer anyway.

"Hello," I manage to choke out. I vaguely become aware that I haven't spoken since telling Laura my story on Saturday night. I repeat "hello" again to reassure myself that I can.

"Arvin, this is Lenore Goodman from TV15. I'm returning your call." She's more business-like than I expected, but then, this is a business call. Serious business.

"Yes, and I appreciate that. I hoped you'd remember me from Moe's Chili Dogs."

"Yes, certainly."

"Well, I wonder if we can get together for a cup of coffee or a lunch or something."

"And your reason, Arvin?" There's a somewhat softer tone in this question, but it's not warm.

"Well, I find myself in a situation and I'd like to talk with you about it."

"What kind of a situation?"

"I really want to do this in person."

"Arvin, I am not interested in a date."

"Neither am I. This is serious, and I'd really like to talk with you."

"I have two stories to do today, then write and help edit. I probably can squeeze out 10 or 15 minutes mid-afternoon. Can you come to Des Moines?"

"Yes."

"OK, there's a Denny's on Highway 27 as you come into town. Let's say 3 o'clock."

"Great. Thank you."

I get to Denny's at 2:40, and order lemon pie and iced tea. Lenore Goodman comes in wearing a dark blue conservative length skirt, some sort of black heels and a collared white shirt with the TV15 logo on the chest. She's in full makeup now, carrying only her phone in her hand. Figuring there's an excellent chance she doesn't remember what I look like, I raise my hand. She nods to me and sits.

"Arvin, I'm sorry, but I'm really in a rush. Can we do this in 10 minutes?"

To save time, I start with the end, the really hairy part. The part about aiding and abetting, charged as principle, murder part.

I end with "my wife is the only other person who knows."

"How did she take it?"

"Not well. She moved out as soon as I told her, and took our daughters. She's living with her mom."

In response to an upward tilt of the left side of her head, I add "We don't have the financial wherewithal to afford even a cheap hotel, or that's where I'd be."

"And you want me to do what?"

"I tried to get ahold of Officer Lance, but he hasn't returned my call."

"Why would you want to talk to him?"

"To tell him. To confess, if that's such a thing."

"Who is your attorney?"

"Attorney? I don't have an attorney."

"You did what you said you did, which may or may not have led to the end result. And you don't have an attorney."

"Do you think I need one?"

"You need to call an attorney before you finish that pie."

I look wistfully at the pie. Probably not on the menu at the

State Pen.

“Who do I call?”

Before she can answer, I ask Lenore another question.

“Did I make a mistake in calling Officer Lance?”

“You can’t un-ring that bell. If he calls you back, you really, really, really need an attorney before you talk to the Patrol. He may not call you back. I’ve interviewed him a couple of times, maybe three, and in my opinion, he doesn’t work as hard as he might. But if he does call you, do not, and I mean do not, talk to him without an attorney.”

She pauses, looks at my pie, and reaches for her phone.

“Can I get you some pie or coffee or anything?”

“No,” she says, tapping and scrolling. “I really have to go. These stories won’t edit themselves.”

“Pah,” she puts down her phone. “Calvin. Calvin. Calvin. Can’t grab his name right now.”

“I have to go. If it comes to me, I’ll call or text you.”

“Is he here in Des Moines?”

“I really don’t know.”

“Thank you. Sincerely. Thank you.”

Lenore stands and looks at me. “Arvin, eat your pie. Then call an attorney.”

She heads briskly for the door. I see her get into a car — no logo — and drive off. Twenty seconds later, I get a text with the name Calvin Jenkins and a phone number.

I get through right away. I mention Lenore Goodman, Bill Hanlow, and that I'm concerned because I may be an accessory to the murder. I start to explain what happened but he stops me.

"No, I don't want to hear any more. You need an attorney. You need one as soon as you can get one. This happened in Stillwell, correct?"

"Yes."

"Is that where you live?"

"Yes. But I'm in Des Moines right now."

"You are? Good. I'll text you my address. Come over in . . . 45 minutes."

He does and I do. I'm early, in fact.

Calvin, is a large, imposing man. He's about my age I'd guess, maybe a bit younger, but at least 6'4" or 6'5" and somewhere north of 200 pounds. He looks like he might have played sports and like he still could. My right hand disappears into his, and I feel if not hear my bones crack. But his smile lights up his office, which is as neat and tidy an office as I've ever seen. The largest iMac I've ever seen is on his desk, along with a coffee cup the size of a small lake. Bookcases cover the three walls that aren't windows, filled with law books but also what seems to be a sizable personal library of fiction. I pick out several titles that I've read, back when I used to read, before the girls came along.

"I'm Calvin Jenkins, thank you for coming in so swiftly. So, you know George Watt?"

"Yes, I met him at this bar in Stillwell. He and I . . ."

I get cut off.

"Just answer my questions and say nothing else. Until we have an attorney/client relationship, I don't want to know anything you shouldn't be telling me."

"OK."

"What was the nature of the activity that leads you to believe you may be an accessory to the murder of Mr. Hanlow?" He had to glance at his iMac to pick up Bill's name, but I give Mr. Jenkins credit for being prepared.

I think of the best, most succinct way to explain. I go carefully and slowly.

"He promised me a sum of money, in cash, to do a job for him. That's his word, not mine. It would be one night, just a few hours. He did not describe what the job would entail. I assumed somehow that he would tell me what to do, and, no, wait. He had me drive what I think was a rental car to a neighborhood, then explained precisely what I . . .

He interrupts me again. "What made you think it was a rental car?"

"He gave me just the key. No ring, no fob, nothing else on it. I've never seen a car key used like that, like someone just took it off the ring, like you might do at a valet parking place."

"OK, go on. He's telling you what to do."

"Yes. I'm to go to this particular house and walk on the left side of it through the yard, then through the yard behind it that goes with the neighboring house, come back and tell him exactly what I saw. It was Bill's house that he wanted . . ."

Mr. Jenkins large hands come up and stop me. "Who is Bill?"

"Bill Hanlow."

"The murdered Bill Hanlow."

"Yes."

"When did you do this job?"

"About two weeks before the murder."

"You said Bill."

"Yes."

"Did you know Mr. Hanlow?"

"Oh, yes, I worked for him in his accounting firm for over 5 years."

"Past tense, worked, correct?"

"Correct, he fired me about a month before George hired me for this job."

"So, you were to trespass on your old employer's house and report back."

"Correct, but I didn't know any of that until we got to the neighborhood. He, George, just told me to park down the street a bit and gave me directions which house to go to."

"Did Mr. Watt know of your relationship to Mr. Hanlow?"

I pick up on the increased formality of the names, but at this instant, I'm working on short answers.

"I don't see how."

Mr. Jenkins leans back a bit in his chair.

"Mr. Miller, you need an attorney." He mentions an hourly billing rate, plus expenses, and requests a retainer that's about double my current monthly income. About double my current monthly income before taxes.

As I empty my lungs and replace the air with a fresh, full intake, I see a photo of Mr. Jenkins, alongside a beautiful woman who I take to be his wife, and a very young child, maybe just a few months old. I had a photo similar to that of my own, with Laura just after Jess was born on my desk for years. I think of Jess and Jan and Laura and it's easy to go from here.

"Can I use my credit card?"

He does some tapping on his keyboard, asks for my driver's license, asks about my current address and a couple of other questions. He taps a single key and I hear a printer whirring into action, then there's a small square white gizmo on the desktop. He walks me through the contract and asks if I have any questions.

I do have just one, but I don't ask it because I figure I have to be the one to find a way to pay off my rapidly melting credit card. Mr. Jenkins can't help me there.

We shake hands and he goes back around to the other side of the desk.

"I'll take some notes while you talk, if that's OK. I'm pretty good at keyboarding, but if you talk too quickly, I may ask you to slow down."

"No problem, Mr. Jenkins."

"Just Calvin. Once we work together, it's just Cal or Calvin."

I start to relax just a hint of the tiniest bit.

"Now," Cal says with a smile as wide as his entire face, "give me an overview of your relationship with Mr. Hanlow, and then tell me about Mr. Watts. And this time, don't leave any single little thing out."

I start with the Fourway and the promise of a free drink, run through to Bill hiring me, and by the time I get the story to the $500 in cash in my hand, I'm talked out.

Cal isn't listened out yet.

"Have you seen or heard from George Watt since then?"

"No. I've only ever seen him at the Fourway and I haven't been back since."

"Describe the Fourway to me."

"I'd call it a local, I guess. I figure the name came from the fact that it's on a corner with 4-way stop signs. There's some parking on the street beyond the yellow stripe, maybe two spots on one street and three or four on the other. Small gravel parking lot, that's where most people park, I think, space for eight or ten cars. Two doors, one in the back up a couple of steps, you walk past the wait station and the kitchen to get into the bar. Front door is in the center of the building on the other side. If you walk in that way, there's a table, maybe two, on your left, then the bar. A row of booths on your right, and maybe two or three tables between the booth and the bar. Classic red and chrome bar stools, kind of high, but seemed to be in good condition."

"Impressive description."

"I went there so I could erase my mind, simply stop thinking altogether. I suppose I looked around a bit."

"Your local?"

"No, until I got fired, I'd never been there. So, maybe I was there four, tops five times.

"Does your wife know about the Fourway and George and the $500?" Cal asks.

"Yes. I hadn't told her anything about the bar or George until I saw his photo on the TV news. Not one of my proudest moments, you know, nothing I especially wanted to brag about to Laura."

"So, this would have been this past Friday when you told her. What did she say?"

"Saturday, I couldn't screw my courage up until Saturday night. She was calmer than I thought she'd be. Told me she was leaving, that I was to stay outside the house in the front yard until she packed up the girls and her things and left to go to her Mom's."

"Girls?"

"Jan is 11 and Jess is 9. She told me she doesn't want to talk to me until I fix this."

"Well, Arvin, I'm not sure that this situation is one that will get fixed as easily and cleanly as it got broken."

"So, what kind of trouble am I in?"

"Well, you certainly trespassed on Mr. Hanlow's property.

There could be a voyeurism charge, but I don't think either of those are likely to be pursued. You're clear on the identity of the woman in the hot tub, this Ms. [checks his notes] Carson."

"No, Carson is her first name. Carson Rhodes. Yes, I'm sure, I worked with her at Hanlow."

"On the other side of the ledger, you did this while in the employ of Mr. Watt, for which you were compensated, and related specific information to him. The fact that you did not see a security system or cameras at Mr. Hanlow's, and that you specifically related this information to Mr. Watt, could have proven valuable to him in perpetrating this crime. If, in fact, he did commit this crime, which has yet to be proven in court."

"So, you're saying I'm in serious trouble."

"I won't soft peddle it, Arvin. You could be. It depends on how the State Patrol investigates and how the Prosecuting Attorney wants to proceed. And on how thorough they are. The only person, besides yourself, of course, who can place you at Mr. Hanlow's home that night is Mr. Watt. Is that correct?"

"Yes. So, what do I do?"

"I'll recommend that if, and I do mean if, Detective Lance returns your call, that you not answer the phone and let it go to voice mail. You can always say that you changed your mind about the information you have or thought you have."

"As I understand then, in essence, a confession, which is what I thought to do, is not a good idea."

"It's a great idea for your conscience, but legally, not quite so much."

"What can I tell Laura?"

"That you've hired me, and that I am earning that fee you deposited."

He pauses and looks at me. Leans back a bit in his chair, and I see his eyes go the photo of he, the woman and the child.

"I really feel for you, Arvin, being in this spot with no hard answers, with a ticked-off wife and not able to love and hug your daughters. I'd be a wreck myself. I promise you to work as hard and as diligently and as smart as I can on your behalf. That's the truth, and it's the only promise I can make."

I debate with myself for the entire drive back to Stillwell about calling Laura and telling her what I'd done today, to see if she'd come back home. To see if she'd even answer my call. Hard, diligent and smart are good and wonderful words. But they're soft words, while State Detective and Prosecuting Attorney are hard words.

Mind-emptying, muscle-numbing, hard words.

I don't call.

Next day, after work, on a whim I drive over to Medina to check out George Watt's factory, Watt Metal Forming in the Norton Industrial Park. I simply drive by — it's past 6 pm and there are no cars in the parking lot. It looks familiar to me from my days in Medina handing out business cards and resumes. This would have been a resume place, on the smaller side and somewhat more run down than many of the neighboring buildings. This with a single-story brick office section connecting to a two-story blue metal-sided factory area behind it. I estimate the parking lot could hold maybe 20 cars, but I can't see behind the factory portion of the building, beyond the chain-link fence topped by loops of razor wire. There could be more parking back there, I suppose, for the factory employees. Maybe I was here, maybe not. Many of these factories look identical and trying to remember this one or that one is more than I can force my brain to engage.

The access road takes me, after two loops, back out to the main road to Stillwell. I stop into a smallish grocery store along the way to pick up my dinner. My dinner for one. I hope I never get used to this.

I toss a couple of canned items, some bread and deli meat into a basket and head up the aisle to the cash register. This happens to be the alcohol aisle, and I linger. I look at the brown bottle of Jack and it looks very inviting. I wonder about making a martini or a Margarita at home. For a store of this size, they appear to have a good selection of booze. I check out the gin and vodka, and compare to the tequila and bourbon. Next, I look at the proof ratings of each, run a couple of numbers in my head and decide that the vodka martini presents more bang for less buck. We, by which I now mean I, don't have an extensive collection of stemware, and lack the classic martini glass. We do have wineglasses, which are larger. I grab a plastic bottle of a lower-priced brand of vodka, the large size.

It's two days before I hear from Calvin. We trade calls, as I don't want to have these conversations even in the relative privacy of my private office in a" bank. We trade phone calls and voice mails, and I reach him at the end of my day.

"Arvin, I want to give you an update on what I've found. Detective Chad Lance is in charge of the investigation into the murder, as you know, and I've reached out to several sources in the State Patrol. Of course, how they handle an investigation of this matter is entirely, and appropriately, up to them. The only news of any sort that I can offer is that Detective Lance is well-known to be deliberate in his work, and is not given to discussing his tactics with other members of the SP."

"I continue to recommend that you do nothing at this time. If you can, take a screen shot of the phone call you placed to him and email that to me as a record. Obviously, if you haven't already, be sure to put that number into your contacts so that caller ID notifies you if the SP calls you. To reiterate, do not talk to him without me present."

"Do you have any questions for me?"

I want to ask about what do I tell Laura, but Calvin is an attorney, not a marriage counselor. Maybe I need to search in that direction.

"No, I don't have any questions that are answerable, probably."

Calvin, however, is ahead of me.

"Have you spoken with your wife?"

"No, although I've had that number under my thumb what seems like 87 times a day. It's just that . . . she said solve it, and there's nothing yet solved."

"I'm sure this is extremely hard on you. I'm sure it's hard on Laura and on your daughters as well. Are you keeping busy?"

Busy, he asks. Well, as a matter of fact, I ran over to Watt Metal Forming again this morning before work, just to peek at the parking lot. Probably not anything Calvin needs to know. At work, we subscribe to some online tools that could tell me more about George's company, but I haven't used them because I'm not going to come anywhere close to having an issue with Sunset Bank. I simply will not use their property and licenses for personal business. Although I'd sure love to.

"Yes, work is going well, I'm settling into this role comfortably. Outside of work, the late evenings and early mornings especially, are harder and lonelier than anything I've ever experienced."

"Have you considered counseling?"

"The thought of it, yes. Frankly, I can't handle the expense right now."

"It's outside my area of expertise, but Arvin, consider it if this separation goes on much longer. Mental health is as important as physical."

"I will."

"I'll keep you updated."

I place the phone on the seat beside me and stare at it. I pick it up and call. The copper hollowness in my stomach returns, and I roll the window down just in case. After five rings, it goes to voicemail. I'm disappointed, not surprised and somewhat relieved.

"Hi. I just wanted to give you an update on what I've done. I hired a lawyer, he's in Des Moines, and he seems really good. Really smart. I called the Detective assigned to the case, and got his voicemail. I was thinking of telling him exactly what I did, sort of as a confession, to get it out in the open. He hasn't called me back. Calvin, that's my attorney, says I should not call again."

"So, that's what I've done. I miss you incredibly. Give the girls hugs for me."

Then, softly, "love you. Bye."

Three minutes later, as I'm walking into the house, she calls me back.

"Just listened to your voicemail."

"I know it's not a solution, it's not fixed. I don't know what fixed looks like."

"It looks like not going to jail. Knowing for sure about not going to jail."

"I'll ask Calvin about that, but I don't think any guarantees are likely for a while."

"I talked to Beth."

"You talked to WHO?" I may have said that last word too loudly.

"Beth Hanlow."

Resuming my calm, I query "what gave you that idea?"

"Her husband has just been murdered, violently, in her home. She found his body. I thought she might appreciate some support. This isn't just about you, Arvin."

I have a sudden revelation with that sentence. But I also note the use of my full name instead of the shortened version.

"So, how is Beth doing?"

"Oh, we had a nice lunch. And we're having dinner

together, just the two of us, tomorrow."

"I'm somewhat surprised that . . ."

"She's actually quite nice. When we were over at their home, we got along quite well while you and Bill were talking about work."

"So, she's doing OK?" I have no idea where this is going and not sure if I care about Beth.

"She knew about Bill and Carson."

"Beth what?"

"Knew they were having an affair."

I look for a place to sit down, and see the single red fabric chair in the front yard. Not ready for that, I head for the back patio. I should clean this up, give me something to do tonight.

"How did she find out? How long did she know? Why did . . .?"

"Several months. Bill was working late one night, and Beth took him a nice dinner. Walked into the office and found them together on the desk."

"On the desk?"

I almost but not quite choke.

"Beth went into more detail that I won't repeat."

"Thank you for not repeating that."

"He told Beth that she just didn't attract him anymore that way. That Carson was very attractive and always well dressed. Something about being attentive to his needs."

"That may be too much detail."

"So, by the time he was killed, their marriage was just about over. She'd moved him into another bedroom and they hardly spoke any more. She had begun to get out and meet more people, in fact, the night it happened, she was out to a women's club dinner meeting, I forget which organization."

"Good thing they never had kids. How are the girls?"

"Mom is teaching them how to clean around the house. She's very protective of them."

"Classes?"

"I'm doing as well as ever. It's harder to concentrate."

"I wish you'd come back home."

"One more thing Beth said. Did you ever meet Carson's husband?"

"Uh, no, why? I just asked you if . . ."

But Laura cuts in quickly. "She kept her maiden name when she married. Did you know she lived in Medina?"

"No, and I don't really care. I was asking . . ."

"Her husband's name is Watt. George Watt."

It's a damn good thing I'm sitting down when I hear this.

"Arvin, are you there?"

"Do the police know of this, of their relationship?"

"I didn't think to ask that. I am planning on asking her tomorrow. Arv, I have to go, Mom and the girls have dinner ready. Bye."

"I lov" but she's already hung up.

I call her back the next day, having given her plenty of time for work, a break with the girls, and a long dinner with Beth. This time, she picks up on the third ring.

"Hey."

"How was your dinner?"

"We went to that pricey seafood place in Medina. Beth drove and bought. BMW. Starter, main and dessert. I think between the life insurance and the sale of the accounting firm, she's coming out well financially. I had a filet of sole that was just killer."

I have no idea what restaurant she's talking about, nor do I care at the moment.

"Do the police know?"

Laura chuckles lightly, "about the sole?"

I suspect there may have been wine at dinner.

"Actually, I was inquiring about their knowledge of the relationship between George and Carson."

"She said only three people on earth know . . . she, Bill and Carson."

"Now five."

"Arv, why are you so int . . ."

"Did you tell her about me? Us?"

"About our separation? Yes. About what caused it? No."

"Do you need to check in on the girls? It's late and you sound tired."

"True. G'night."

It might yet turn out that way. The late, tired and alone way.

I finally get through to Calvin over my lunch hour. He agrees with me, that this could potentially be a motive for George to kill Bill.

"We can't play detective here, Arvin," he tells me. "Let me spend some more of my time and your money to review a couple of statutes. There's no purpose to be served in spreading personal information where it has no need to go. Yet this information could and maybe should have an impact on the investigation."

"What should I do?'

"I don't think there's anything you can do right now."

"I'm thinking of giving Carson a call."

"Be careful there, Arvin. If you want to get back with Laura, that may not be a wise step."

"Nothing like that, Laura is my number one and only. I think there's more here than we know."

"That's Detective Lance's turf. I caution you to be careful. If it's just a friendly check-in with an ex-colleague, that's up to you."

"I appreciate your concern."

I make one more call before I call Hanlow Accounting and ask for Carson. She's out for a few days, but I get her cell from the receptionist when I identify myself and say I just want to tell her hello.

We set up a time to meet on Saturday morning at Riverside Park. It's public, but not drinks or even pie and coffee after work. Laura would probably understand my seeing her, but I'm taking no chances.

I have other plans in Medina for Friday night. Dinner with Lenore Goodman and her partner.

I'd tried to make reservations, but the upscale beer-and-burger place Lenore suggested doesn't take reservations. Being free as a baby bumblebee, I get there early enough to wait for a high-top. The place is darkly lit, a darkness that's enhanced by the dark stain on the pine table and the deep, gloss black metal holding up the leather seats, backs and short arms of the chairs. The bar area alone can maybe seat 40, and there's about 55 people huddling around. I pass on trying to find a free bartender and begin memorizing the menu.

I'd promised Lenore that I only wanted twenty minutes of work-related discussion, and that I'd buy. She demurred, and I asked if she knew someone who could join us. Lenore said Friday was typically special time with her partner, but OK as long as we could talk about happy subjects after my 20 minutes. The starters are what I might pay for a splurge of a meal and desert these days, and the mains go into the next category above. I cringe thinking about the mounting balance on my credit card, and how close I am to the limit, but there's enough headroom. Just. I'll figure out the money later.

I'm seated and planning a gentle-as-I-can-be-on-my-card evening when Lenore walks up. She greets me with a hug, and introduces me.

"My partner, Linda Lu."

Linda is a slender woman with jet-black hair accented by several streaks of various shades of grey. She could be in her late 20s or mid 40s depending on how much of those colors are real and how much come from a salon. Impeccably dressed in a soft yellow blouse the color of the inside of a lemon peel, blousy pants that match the black of her hair and billow as she walks. Lenore is showing off a strikingly short dress in a pink and blue polka dot pattern, with a lower-than-I-would-have-guessed neckline.

After greetings, we order two starters to share, me with a beer and they with a glass of pinot noir each. We start to get into a discussion of the restaurant's decor, but Lenore shuts that off and demonstrates her ability to lead a discussion.

"Let's get the business out of the way so we can relax and enjoy the night. I've been working late a lot of Fridays and Linda and I haven't done this in a while."

"I apologize, and I'm honored to be here with you both."

Linda chimes in. She's dropped the light social chatter as deftly as she handles her glass of pinot.

"Lenore tells me you've had an interesting experience recently and that you might have something new to share. She updated me on the way over, so, what's new?"

I pause for a solid swallow of my draft All-Day IPA, and get on with it.

"So, I spoke to my wife on the phone last week, and she,

unknown to me, reached out to Beth Hanlow, Bill's wife. We knew each other socially when I worked there, and it seems that Beth and Laura had an affinity for each other. Anyway, and I have to ask this question first, can we keep all of this confidential?"

"Yes, of course," says Linda.

"Depends on where we go," says Lenore. "They pay me to be a reporter."

"OK, good, fine, I'm comfortable." Well, slightly uncomfortable but I continue anyway.

"It turns out that Bill Harlow and Carson Rhodes, a CPA who works at Hanlow Accounting, were having an affair. I know Carson, she was there for a year or so when I was, but I didn't know that she kept her maiden name when she married. Not that it matters. But the guy she's married to is named Watt. As in George Watt."

I take another hefty drink of my beer to let that settle in. Then another. The two ladies look at each other as if they are thinking the same thought. I'm about to take another drink when Linda says one word.

"Motive."

"Yeah, that's where I was going," I contribute.

"How well do you know this Carson," asks Lenore.

"Does Linda know about my uh, trespassing?"

"Yes." Under other circumstances, I'd accuse them of harmonizing.

"Then I know her well enough to have seen her naked."

Damn, the server said this was a lower-alcohol beer, but I think she lied. "Just once, briefly, through a gap in a fence and a small knothole."

My comment shreds the tension related to our discussion, and as we finish our drinks, order dinner and another round, I peek at my watch.

"I have two minutes left. And I want to throw two other facts out. First Hanlow Accounting is up for sale. Not surprising, but still. Two, Watt Metal Forming appears to be closed. I've driven by several times, and while I can't do that during the 8 to 5 hours that most factories are open, I've seen no visible indications of any activity."

"What do you make of it, Arvin?" asks Linda.

"I'm out of my depth to a large degree. It's very, very common for a business to close or to be sold after the death of the owner. Special knowledge, customer relationships, whatever, a million reasons. To close a factory while the owner is in jail, I can't say I have direct experience with, but I would think there's a plant manager or a sales person who could step in and keep the place afloat. I found one business listing that said the company had between 50 and 100 employees and sales between $10 million and $50 million. I could look up more in-depth information on some tools at the bank I work at, we use them daily, but I'm not comfortable doing personal work with my employers' tools."

Lenore tips her head about 3 degrees to the left, her eyes open slightly and peer if not through my head, then at least through the first 3 layers of skin.

"Arvin, I'm impressed. Call me cynical, or maybe it's my experience with lots and lots of bad things and worse people, but you are one in a hundred. The other 99 would be all over that."

It's Linda who breaks in.

"As scintillating as this discussion is, we set a time limit, all three of us together, and we are just now at that time limit. Arvin, that beer looks too light to be a craft beer. Have you tried one of their barrel-aged stouts?"

I'm back in my car completely full and with a new appreciation for barrel-aged anything. A 4-ounce sampler was enough to get me to sit up and pay attention. Linda even bought dinner, beverages and starters.

"It's been four weeks since we've been out and if you, Arvin, hadn't been here we'd have spent the entire dinner discussing why we work so long and so hard and never take enough time for ourselves. This was fun."

15 Carson

Next morning, I'm up and mowing the lawn while the dew is still heavy. While I mow and trim, I'm setting up an outline for my meeting with Carson. Carson, who kept her job while I got fired, because she was fucking Bill. The imbroglio stew in my brain has cooled over the months, but maybe just enough to be a consistent simmer. I've only known a few married people who I know for sure cheated on their spouses, a line I've never crossed and feel strongly about. I suppose some people have agreements for other marriage arrangements.

Still, having her husband taken to jail for a murder of the guy she was sleeping with can't be something one gets over quickly. Or ever. I begin to feel an emerging sympathy for and empathy with Carson; her lover is dead, killed at the hands of her jailed-and-suspected husband. Whatever she thinks or feels for both of those men has to be layered, complicated, confusing, emotional, frightening. I don't know what to expect when I see her at the park.

I shave, shower, heat some water and make a pot of strong black tea. I pour it into two travel mugs, one for each of us.

"Hi, Arvin. I was glad you called. I think we have some things to talk about."

She's wearing dark grey trainers with short neon green socks, a pair of tightly fitting, rather short running shorts and some kind of exercise top with neon green and black and white swirls and whirls. Stylish tortoise shell sunglasses and a full brim straw hat against the Iowa sun.

She accepts my tea with a quiet, gracious "thank you," a tone I don't remember from the workplace. We stroll slowly along the path, past the first couple of blue benches and head for the top end of the trail.

"I can't imagine going through what you're going through," I throw out. "It has to be petrifying."

"That's a good word, I suppose." She sips. We stroll.

"I figured you would be so pissed off at me when Bill fired you instead of me. I worked on Mercury, the account we lost, it should have been me. We, Bill, I, nobody did anything bad to lose it, the account just went away like some do all the time."

She stops walking.

"Did you know we were seeing each other?"

"I do now, didn't then."

"I'm sorry. You were — are — a good accountant. You didn't deserve to lose your job just because I was fucking the boss."

I'm beginning to appreciate not only her honesty but her vocabulary.

We start strolling.

"I felt terrible. I did not know that Bill was going to do that. If I had, I would have had him fire me instead of you."

"Do you think it would have changed anything?"

"Would Bill still be alive and would George not be in jail? Maybe. Possibly. Probably."

"I don't follow."

"George and I had issues. Well, in my mind, he had issues that I couldn't solve." She pauses.

"Arvin, do you mind if I talk to you? I haven't told this to anyone and it might help to get it out."

"I think we both could use some healing."

"George and I got married three-and-a-half years ago. We'd only known each other seven months. It was kind of a whirlwind. Maybe it was just infatuation. We bumped into each other — literally — at a bar. I just picked up my glass of wine, turned to go back to my table and he walked right into me. He had an Old Fashioned and it went right down the front of my dress. I mean right down; I was wet from the inside out. I'd gone out with a couple of friends from college, and we all went into the restroom to see what we could do to dry me and clean me up. One of them went out and came back with two fresh napkins, nice cloth ones. It was very embarrassing. Once I was as dry as I was going to get, we went back to our table. George was holding the table for us, and there were fresh drinks in front of our chairs. We laughed and talked, my friends went home, George and I had dinner. And coffee with dessert. We didn't drink ourselves silly. George wasn't a big drinker. He did like to eat. Gained some weight that way."

"The next day we had a date, went to a movie and ice cream afterwards. So innocent. Well, for a while it was innocent. It was less than a week before we wound up in his apartment.

He's nine years older than I. The metal forming company was booming. He obviously had money, the Caddy SUV, and his apartment was impressive. Knocked out, actually. He bragged how he'd hired a designer to do it for him, every stick of furniture, the curtains, the paint colors, appliances, everything was so impressive. I was struggling to make the rent and the car payment every month, had just taken a big step to get my own one-bedroom apartment, first time I hadn't had a roommate."

"It got physical then, and it went on that way for long enough that I thought I was in love. Maybe I was. Maybe I don't know what love is."

"We got married. Just a small ceremony. My parents are both gone, and my only sibling lives in Toronto. I never met any of George's family. I asked several times early on, and he simply said "no family." Just those two words. A year after we got married, we went out for our anniversary. Went to Chicago for a night, a suite in one of the hotels just off Michigan Avenue, dinner at an expensive restaurant, the whole deal. I asked him if he'd ever thought of starting a family. He just looked at me, kind of cold in his eyes, and gave me those two words, "no family" again. I asked again when we got back to the hotel, and it almost ruined our weekend. I never brought that subject up again."

"That should have been my first hint."

We reach the end of the path, and have a short conversation about this being either the end or the beginning of the path, and mutually agree that the beginning is upstream and the end is downstream.

"Am I boring you?"

"No, no, I have nothing at all in front of me today."

Or tomorrow, I think to myself.

"The other clue I never picked up on was his financial dealings. It would have been natural for me to do his books; I was doing exactly that for the big farm equipment dealer just south of town. We were married, I said, I can do it nights and weekends. You don't have to hire or pay me, I said. He just said no, he had someone who did the heavy lifting when he needed it, but he did most of the financial side himself and wasn't going to give it up."

"He did very well with the metal forming business at that time. He wanted to build a house, so we, well, he, found a lot in that Deer Meadows subdivision on the west side. Do you know the place, Arvin?"

"No, no idea, sorry. I'm pretty much a Stillwell guy."

"He bought the lot, we picked out a house plan and he hired the same designer from the same furniture store that had done his apartment. The most work I did was helping her with the theme and colors for the master bedroom. I signed on the mortgage, but that was really the extent of my involvement. He paid all the bills. Whatever money I made was mine to do with as I pleased."

I try to give her a break. "Was he the controlling type? Sometimes one person thinks they have to tell another person exactly what to do and get angry if they vary even slightly."

"No, not really. He always was the leader; he knew where to go for dinner or where our next vacation would be. But no, I think he was more interested in keeping me away from parts of his life."

"It wasn't like I just took a sip of coffee — or tea — one

day and realized how he had divided his life, and my life, into clearly separate segments. The feeling grew as if from a seed and as I talk to you, it continues to grow. Or maybe it's clarifying in my mind as I talk to you."

"Most people, I think when they see each other at the end of a work day, have an exchange, you know, 'how was your day?' "good, but short, I have to go in early tomorrow.' 'Oh, what happened?' 'Well, this customer called and was all bent out of shape . . ." Just sharing normal stuff about what you'd done all day. Early on, we did that, but as his business slowed down, he just wouldn't discuss it at all. By the time I started working at Bill's, I knew nothing about Watt Metal Forming."

"To my knowledge, he never had a staff Christmas party, or 4th of July cookout or any kind of social event for employees. He had a couple of people who had been with him a while who were managers I guess, but I never met them."

"One time, it was a Saturday, he was working at the factory. I was bored, so I decided to go see him. I stopped off at the sandwich shop, got sandwiches and drinks, and took them to his factory. The door was locked, but there was a doorbell. It took a couple of minutes for him to answer; had his car not been in the parking lot, I'd have left figuring he was gone. When he came to the door and saw it was me, he had this shocked looked on his face, briefly, so briefly I hardly knew it was there."

"He was clearly pre-occupied. He asked me why I was there. He asked that question when I had a bag of subs and two drinks in my hands. I had to ask him if we could have a sandwich together. It was an eye-opening experience, this first real at-work experience of him."

"We were the only ones in the place, and we sat in a small office to eat. Not George's office, a small one that appeared to be unoccupied. We were eating the cookies when his phone rang, he looked at it and said 'I have to take this. Stay here.' Then he went back, I presume, to his office, although I couldn't see around the corner."

"I sat there alone for what I think might have been 15 minutes. I looked at my watch, gave him another ten, and got up, peered around the corner. I could see him in his office, with a phone headset on, sitting in a chair with his feet on the desk. His back was almost directly facing me."

"I started to go towards his office, but noticed that the door was closed. Now, there were obviously just the two of us in the building, so by closing the door, I figured it must mean that he didn't want me to hear this conversation. That's when I decided that I didn't know the question to ask him, but I knew the right answer wouldn't come from him. I turned and walked down the hallway, past a washroom and through a door that opened out into a manufacturing part of the building."

"I've not been in very many factories. There were huge dark green machines in rows and what looked like the carts at a garden center with pieces of metal on them. It didn't look very busy. I walked over to one of the machines and looked at the controls. Big buttons with numbers and letters, maybe a dozen of them. This was not a new machine, it looked years old, with accumulated dirt and grime and some of the numbers and letters on the buttons were partially worn off by use. I looked around and thought that if the business was booming, or even doing reasonably well, the area should have been, well more crowded with more machines and more carts."

"So, I glanced at my watch and saw I had been gone for just

three minutes. I went to one side of this big room to where I saw a single door in the long wall. That part, that wall I mean, looked newer than the rest of the room."

"Do I sound like I know what I'm talking about, Arvin? I'm not familiar with factories."

"I think you're telling me what you saw. And what you saw is just as accurate as any factory expert's opinion because it's your truth. And I get the impression your visit to George's factory isn't really about metal forming."

"You know, if he was capable of sharing, he would have given me a tour. He would have told me about those huge machines. I think those old things would have a story to tell."

I nod.

"Anyway, I go through the door into the next room, and I can see that it's a new wall because on this side there are all these pieces of lumber and wires running every which way. It's a rectangle shape, and on the opposite wall straight across from the door, almost at the far end, is another doorway. I walk over there, and it's not as complete as this section. There's another, smaller room, maybe a third the size of this one and then to my right is still another room, about the same size at that, with what looks to be plumbing pipes in the floor and part way up the walls and a row of faucets that are above my head."

"By this time, seven minutes on my watch, I figure I better get back to our lunch room, so I head there. I go back through both doors and turn the corner. I get a few steps down this hallway and see George coming around the corner heading for our lunch room, too."

"I see that shocked look on his face again, this time for just an eye blink longer than when I rang the front door bell. He takes a few steps toward me and I see anger, real anger in his eyes."

"Where did you go? What are you doing?" he asked me.

"That was the angriest I'd ever seen him. Maybe, even to this day, the angriest I've ever seen him."

"I just went to the restroom. Those were large drinks, and I drank every bit of mine."

"'Oh,' now he's cooler. But he puts his arm on my shoulder and leads me back past our lunch room to the front door."

"He said he had to work, and did everything except push me out the door. I went to go back home, but decided against it, called an old school friend and we met and had a glass of wine. George didn't mention anything when he got home that Saturday evening, and neither did I."

"You must be bored, Arvin, I've done all the talking. How are your wife and girls? You had the cutest photo of the three of them on your desk."

"They're good. Actually, we're not getting along too well right now. I did something which seemed small and insignificant at the time but suddenly blew up in my face."

I wonder whether I should tell her my experience with George and she and Bill, but think the better of it. I've told too many people and I want the whole thing to go away.

"Do you want to talk about it? Honestly, I can listen just as good as I can talk."

Uh-huh.

"Actually, listening to you takes my mind off Laura and the girls. This is a good break for me. Keep going," I encourage her.

"You know, the three-and-a-half years we've been married seem like 35 years. I know I look decades older."

She doesn't, but I'll let it slide.

"That incident happened about, let's see, a year, maybe year and a half after we got married. He changed. I don't think it was the sub sandwich I brought but I do think Watt Metal Forming was going through some tougher times then."

Carson stops walking, turns to me and puts her hand on my forearm. She looks into my eyes and just at the instant I start to feel uncomfortable, she says "Arvin, I had thought I was living the dream. I had a handsome, successful husband who I loved, a beautiful house, the Audi, and a career. And then it just started to go downhill."

"Do you ski?"

"Ski? Like downhill or cross country?"

"Either one?"

"Nope, not me. I'm just a boring Iowa kind of guy."

"George and I went to Colorado that winter. Took lessons, did the apres-ski thing, that was the best part. Anyway, we were there four days. I think he spent more time on the phone than on the hills. Always went for a walk or paced in the hallway. I never heard a word he said on the phone. I didn't even hear him say 'hello Betty' you know, use a name. He seemed to be in another place mentally."

"And we never slept together there. We didn't have sex; we

didn't even share the same bed. He'd gotten a suite, with one of those couches that pulls out into a bed. He slept there and I had the big bed all to myself."

"When we got home, that continued. He took the second bedroom. Two days later, he'd moved all his clothes, everything out of our bedroom and the closet and the bathroom. He never touched me, well, like you know, again."

"And he started to work all the time. At least, he was gone all the time. We'd always had coffee together in the morning if not an actual breakfast. That tapered off to zero. We'd usually have dinner together almost every night unless one of us was working late. I can't remember the last time we had dinner together, even on holidays and weekends."

"Didn't you talk about it, confront him?"

"I did, once. He referred to it as 'the confrontation' for, well, he still probably does."

"I tried, I really tried to make it work his way. But one night when he came home after I was in bed, I went downstairs to talk. It didn't go well."

"We just divided then, living in the same house but not together. As George and I moved apart, Bill and I moved together." A long pause.

"Arvin, I'm sorry. My personal relationship with Bill should have had nothing to do with you. I'm sorry you got let go."

But I was, and there I went and here I am. I go back mentally to my outline for this discussion, remember a few of the points and ignore the darn thing altogether.

"Carson, your business is your business, and your personal

life is your personal life. I wanted to talk to you today about George, not to pry, but to try to get some handle on why he might do what he did."

I let that settle, then add, "Assuming he did it."

"Are you asking me whether murder was in his character?"

"I wouldn't have phrased it that way, but yes, I suppose so."

"Not murder, no. But being a complete and utter prick about something, yes. Not in the beginning, not when we were truly in love, in fact, maybe not even after we stopped being in love. He changed, he became gruff, he gained a lot of weight."

"Did he know about you and Bill?" I think I need this answer. I hope I can live with it.

"Yes."

"When did he find out?"

"About the third time Bill and I got together, so well over a year ago. I'd come home late, like, after midnight. George straggled in while I was putting my makeup on the next morning. We argued, I asked where he'd been keeping himself. I thought if I spit it out, he'd follow suit. He did. He asked who I'd been seeing, although he didn't say it quite that way, and I told him. He turned and walked away to his bedroom and I heard him lock the door. As if."

"So, he had a reason to hate Bill."

"Yes, I suppose so. But he never acted as if he cared. Arvin, I've done all the talking. How are you doing? Tell me about Laura and the kids."

I give her a simplified, shortened version, leaving out the cause of Laura's leaving. We promise to stay in touch, I retrieve my travel mugs and we get back into our cars. When I shut the car off in the driveway, I look out at the single red fabric chair. But I drink my drink on the back porch.

16 A customer from Watt

That was Saturday. On Tuesday, a customer comes in asking to re-finance his home. He's carrying a 9 x 12 manilla envelope that looks like it's seen some use. Lost his job, factory closed, needs to reduce his expenses, will be hard to get a new job that pays the same, yada yada yada. I've been doing the consumer bank thing just long enough now to actually know what to do.

I pull up his info on my screen and figure we may be able to help him out. Give him a list of the pertinent paperwork I will need. He pulls up the manilla envelope.

"I think I have most or all of that here."

"Great, it's unusual for someone to be as prepared as you."

He smiles and we go through it. I start with income and ask for his wife's W2. He hands me two, with hers on top, and when I finish importing and scanning that, I flip to see his old W2. It's from Watt Metal Forming.

I input that, and as I wait for the scan, I ask, just to be friendly and to dispel any tension in my customer, "How long had you worked at Watt Metal Forming?"

"Over five years."

"That's a long time in this day and age."

"Longest job I ever had. Mr. Watt said he hated to see me go, gave me three weeks' severance. Said that was the best he could do."

I mutter something as I wrap up his application. I'd love to be able to talk to him, Lyle Mattern by name, but sure not going to do it in Sunrise.

"I was the last one."

"I'm sorry, I was inputting the last of your information. You said . . ."

"I was the last one, the final employee to go. It's shut down now. I mean, of course, with Mr. Watt being in jail it would be, but he let me go five or six weeks before he, uh, got into, uh what he got into."

"Yes, that's a terrible thing, a horrible thing. It affects so many people."

I need to talk to Mr. Mattern outside this office.

"What else do you need from me?"

"From my end, nothing. Here's what happens next." I explain about my role, the various tasks I will initiate, and that it goes from me to the Branch Manager, then to the Regional Manager.

"Mr. Mattern, I can't promise anything but from what I see right now, I think we can save you over a hundred and fifty dollars a month."

He perks up at that.

"I'll let you know if I need anything else, and I'll keep you posted on the progress here on my end."

I sit down that night at home, which I now refer to as house, with my frozen dinner and a vodka martini. I want to talk to Mr. Mattern, but there is no way in an Iowa corn field I'm having any kind of off-the-record chat with him. I catch the 6 pm news, take another beverage out to the back patio and hit 'recents' on my phone.

Lenore picks up almost instantly. I explain.

"Let me kick that around," she says. "I'll get back with you tomorrow."

She does. I explain.

"I think he may be interesting on the periphery, but not sure that he's going to be crucial to whatever we are trying to do here. I can ask a few people about other companies, but frankly, I'm not going to spend a lot of time to chase down this lead."

"Just thought maybe . . ."

But Lenore interrupts. "George's arraignment is scheduled for Thursday. I'll be there."

She walks me through a bit of the legal process and tells me it's scheduled for 3 pm. Suggests I watch the 6 pm news.

Thursday is the night when I used to make dinner with or for the girls. I've tried each week to set something up, always leaving a voice mail on Laura's phone. A voicemail that hasn't been returned. I do this again, using my most remorseful, sincere voice, but get the same voicemail box.

Sure, I have a date with the TV tomorrow at 6 pm. I also have a martini, also on the back porch.

At the Hy-Vee, I consider a can of corned beef and an egg,

but after recalling 'breakfast for dinner,' reconsider and go with 3 frozen burritos for $1.97. I pull them out of the microwave, drop some ice cubes into a tumbler, go easy on the ice and generous on the tea, and flip on the TV15 news.

There's a photo of a portly George in a grey jumpsuit and the announcer simply reads the words that appear on the bottom of the screen.

"Man accused in murder drops dead in courtroom."

I actually spit iced tea out onto my pants, bare feet, and almost all the way to the TV.

The co-anchors go back and forth and finally cut to Lenore Campbell, who is standing in front of a sign that says Iowa State Courthouse. She's talking into a microphone that she holds in front of her.

"Yes, Ralph, I did see this happen. Judge Arlen T. Bookhouse had just read the charge to Mr. Watt and his attorney. He asked, 'How do you plead to this charge,' and Mr. Watt started to open his mouth to make a reply, when he collapsed there onto the floor. He hit his head on the table, and lay crumpled on the floor. The entire courtroom was in shock, Judge Bookhouse told the bailiff to get a physician. It was chaos."

"Lenore, not only did you see this, but TV15 photographer Carl Wiess was there as well."

"Yes, Carl was just a few feet from me."

We hear the voice of Ralph Williams, the anchor, but Lenore remains on camera. "TV15 has decided not to show the video of Mr. Watt collapsing onto the floor. The image may be disturbing to some of our viewers."

Lenore takes over. "It was disturbing to all of us. The emergency paramedics came in very quickly, by my watch in just 4 minutes, from the fire station just two blocks away on Second Street. They cleared the courtroom of everyone except the bailiff, I believe four police officers and the 3 responding paramedics. We stood in the lobby of the courthouse just outside the courtroom. At 5:02 pm, a cart carrying Mr. Watt was wheeled out of the courthouse, down the steps (the video switches to the gurney being carried down the steps) and taken to St. Elizabeth's hospital."

"Lenore," (we go back to anchor Ralph), "the covering, that is, the blanket or the sheet covering Mr. Watt's body covered his entire body including his head. Our News15 team reporter Sam Mince is at St. Elizabeth's Hospital."

We go off to Sam at the hospital, who is waiting for a word from the Hospital Spokesperson. The rest of the local news follows, with the briefest of recaps just before 6:30. "Stay with News15 for updates as they happen."

Some game show comes on, I turn it off and look at half of one burrito and some diluted tea without ice.

I consider calling Lenore, I think I should call Calvin, and I really, really, really want to call Laura. None of which I actually do.

At 9:17 pm, I get a text from Lenore. "Pronounced dead." I turn on the TV, and those are the words going across the bottom of the screen, 'Pronounced Dead' but the program is still on. I watch the 10 o'clock news. Lenore is still at the courthouse, Sam is still at the hospital and George is still dead.

It's too late for me to call Calvin, but I do just before 7 am. I tell him it's hard for me to respond from 8 to noon and 1 to 5. He replies a few minutes later, and asks "who knows?" "I think everybody knows by now" I reply. "No, who knows about you."

I don't run out of fingers counting the people who know about me. About me and George. About me and George and Bill and Carson.

He asks me if Detective Lance has reached out to me, and I type in 'no' just as I go into the branch office. I try, and fail, to lose myself in customer service, questions, answers, a couple of spreadsheets and the endless forms of daily bank life.

Carol, Doris and I go out for lunch to a little taco restaurant that's close enough to walk to, although we don't. Most of the lunch talk is related to courtrooms, heart attacks, criminals, and then we drift off to TV shows and movies about courtrooms. It's banter, but keeps me highly occupied and away from my phone.

I call Calvin as I get into my car at 5:03 pm. Thankfully, he picks up.

"Calvin, I'm a little stressed out here. Sorry I wasn't available until now. Do you know what's going on?"

"I'm sure there will be an autopsy and probably a formal inquiry. He's deceased, as odd as this case is getting, who knows?"

"What does that mean for me?"

"If George is the only person who can positively place you at Mr. Hanlow's house 30 days before the murder, then I don't think there's anything that anyone can do against you. If Detective Lance knew about your scouting mission, he'd need Mr. Watt to confirm and explain it and demonstrate how he used the knowledge you gave him in perpetrating the crime. Even if George told Detective Lance about you, you are not going to incriminate yourself. I can't think of a way for anyone to corroborate your being at Mr. Hanlow's home in advance of the shooting. I'm not ready to say you are safely out of the woods, but I am ready to say that you are in a much more favorable position today than you were yesterday."

I exhale. Apparently, somewhat loudly.

"I'm sure that's a weight off your mind and body, Arvin. You should sleep soundly tonight."

"Should I call my wife Laura and ask her back?" I'm choking a bit as I say this.

OK, I'm choking a lot. Fact is, I'm surprised that Calvin understood what I said.

"I'm not as familiar with family law. I have not met your family. Yet I think, here, a phone call and a discussion are appropriate and in order."

"Thank you," I say. "I think I'll do that right now."

This time, Laura picks up.

"I'm assuming you heard the news about George Watt."

"Yes. What does it mean, Arvin?"

"I just hung up from a discussion with Calvin, my attorney. He said no one can corroborate my being at Bill's house. There were only the two of us, and George is now dead. That leaves just me. No one else can prove I was there."

"What if George told the Detective before he died?"

"If I understand Calvin correctly, that goes back to the corroboration issue. It can't be proven."

"I've missed you, Laura. And Jan and Jess. A lot."

"We've missed you, too. The girls always ask about you. Every day."

"Come back home. This is about as fixed as fixed can be."

"Are you sure?"

"Are you skeptical?"

"Let's say cautious. I want to be sure because I don't want this to happen again."

"I've learned my lesson, if that's possible. If you are cautions, maybe you should call Calvin and hear it for yourself."

"I'd feel better."

We hang up, I text Calvin, and 20 minutes later Laura calls me back. The phone hasn't left my hand.

"He made me comfortable."

"Will you come back?"

"Yes. Give us some time to pack."

I run out to buy ice cream although my credit card is getting worriedly near my credit limit, and splurge on two half-gallons. My family — what a glorious word — pulls into the driveway about 45 minutes later. The car barely stops before the back doors open and the girls spill out and run up to me. I try to pick them both up at the same time, but it doesn't quite work, and we go tumbling in a heap onto the small patch of lawn between the driveway and the house. I'm prone on the ground with Jan and Jess bouncing on top me when I put my head up to see Laura coming around the car.

She's wearing a pair of multicolored tights I haven't seen before, what appears to be a pattern of flowers in every color imaginable. A sea green top with very short sleeves, and if my eyes don't deceive me, a bit of eye makeup. She doesn't wear eye makeup often, rarely actually, but I quickly focus on her mouth.

Her smile. Then her hands on my shoulders and down on my shoulder blades as our bodies come fully together. We stand like that for what seems like 20 seconds. It could have been half of one second.

Then Laura suggests we go inside. I pull out the ice cream and everybody gets three scoops. I take another scoop for seconds.

We bundle the girls off to bed and pick up the rest of their stuff from the car. I promise to pick up what they didn't pack from Lorna's tomorrow morning. Tucked way in the back of the trunk is Laura's red fabric chair. I pick it up and look at it.

"I never took it out of the trunk."

"And I never sat in the other one."

"Maybe we should."

"We should."

I take the chair out as Laura finds the wine and glasses. She brings out two glasses at the five-pour level. I'm standing, not sitting yet, as we gently clink glasses and drink. Then we sit and look through the maple tree limbs at the dark, dark blue sky and the darkly grey fluffy stratocumulus clouds.

But that's not where my eyes stay. Nor do Laura's. There's so much I want to say, so much I need to say but I don't want to waste this feeling, this peace, this calm, this centered-ness that all I do is stare and occasionally, very occasionally, take a sip. Laura notices where my gaze is finally.

"You look hungry."

"Ice cream and wine for dinner tonight."

"You are one heck of a chef."

"And you are one heck of a woman."

"I have a lot to say, a lot to tell you Laura. But maybe tomorrow or the next day. Right now, I want to savor this."

"I want to listen to you. Listen better than maybe I've done for the last 12 days."

She finishes her last sip.

"But that's for tomorrow."

I finish mine.

"Tomorrow then."

We pick up our wineglasses, join our hands, and walk inside our home.

Saturday is typically Laura's study day, and this one is no

different. I make breakfast, the girls and I get the rest of their stuff from Gran's. The four of us sit and I help Lorna feel more comfortable with her alarm system, which she has continued to use.

That evening, there's an unusual chill wind, so Laura and I slip on sweatshirts for our nightly discussion.

I feel as if I owe Laura the chance to relax a bit, so I begin. I tell her about Calvin Jenkins, how much Lenore Campbell has helped and do a much-shortened version of Carson's story. It's still just light enough that I see her eyebrows go up at the mention of Carson's name.

"You've been busy," she says.

"I missed you and the girls."

"I've gotten to know Beth Hanlow pretty well. We've gone out for dinner a few times."

"Hers' wasn't the happiest of marriages either. They met in Iowa City, Beth was majoring in social work and Bill working towards his degree in accounting. She had planned to stay for her master's but when Bill proposed and got a job here in Stillwell, she threw herself into the relationship."

"She got a job at the high school as a counselor. They tried to have children, and had a miscarriage. It was early on, so they kept on trying but with no success. They both went to doctors here, and in Des Moines, but neither really wanted to go through the process and procedure. And investment. Those choices are expensive."

"Bill started his own firm with a handful of accounts he took from the old Applegate company when it went out of business. Worked out of their first house, blah blah blah, rented some space, so on so forth. Beth can talk. Once she gets into her second glass of wine, you just listen and nod."

"Carson was exactly like that. Talkative, I mean. We drank iced tea on our walk."

"She said Bill seemed to change as his business got more successful. More prideful, more into moving up the social ladder. Traded up houses twice more before they built the one she has now. She's not living there, by the way, she's renting a place out on Butterfield Road in that new complex. It's nice, tastefully done. Said she just couldn't go back to the place where he was killed, and anyway, the state was all over it for almost a week, looking for evidence and so on. Didn't do a great job of cleaning up, either, Beth had to hire cleaners to come in and do that."

"What I thought was interesting was that his interest in her cooled just like Carson said George's did. Nothing significant, no big fight, no disagreement on life decisions, just a slow sliding away. He started to get into all those social clubs as a way to attract business. Said many nights he came home and wasn't interested in dinner because he'd had such a big lunch."

"He took me out to a couple of those from time to time," I interrupt. "I thought the food wasn't too good, but there was plenty of it. The country club was a popular spot for those."

"That's what Beth said too. Said Bill always said 'it's a great way to meet people.' She thinks that's where the affairs started."

"Affairs as in plural affairs?"

"Yes. I don't know any names, but wouldn't recognize them anyway since I don't go around in those circles. And no what you might say about hard evidence, all she could claim were just the occasional late nights at work when he came home with a different smell on him, or bourbon on his breath. Said he did like his bourbon."

"Did you know Beth was on the payroll?"

"What? At Hanlow Accounting?"

"Yeah, a few years ago Bill asked her if she'd ever thought about not working. By this time, she was at the Boys and Girls Club as, I dunno, Social Director or something. Working with both kids and adults in programs, helping to get funding, stuff like that. Said she liked the work well enough, but it paid beans."

"So Bill said he could bring her onto the firm as Secretary. She could do the women's side of his service club thing, get into the clubs that wouldn't take members if they belonged to certain other clubs."

"They do that? Like an exclusive, if you are in A you can't join B, kind of thing?"

"That's my understanding from what Beth said. Never been to a single meeting at a service club. Sounds like I never will."

"So he offered her a job working for him. Not with him, mind you, for him. Beth made a big point of that, it really seemed to get under her skin. He set up these places to go to, people to buttonhole, the words to use, the whole thing. Like she was his puppet and he was the puppeteer. The first six months, he paid her just under what she had been making at Boys and Girls Clubs, but then when they both seemed to think that it worked, he gave her a raise to something more than she had been making. Always had to be in control."

"She didn't do much else. I don't know what a corporate Secretary does, do you?"

"Records, meeting minutes, that kind of thing. Policies and procedures."

"Beth said it got to the point where she almost felt Bill was pimping her. Putting her in these places and with selected people. Men and women, however."

"Was there more than, say, meeting and accounting discussions going on?"

"She didn't allude to any, and I can't see it. Not that I know her well. But, now my words and not hers, Bill enjoyed using her as a utensil, a tool to do his bidding. So, she's leaving."

"Leaving?"

"Putting the house up for sale, although she thinks it will take some time to sell and she won't get what it's worth, due to its history. Seems there's even a place on the real estate agent contract about disclosing such occurrences. Bill had a hefty life insurance policy, the business was doing well and will sell well, plus the house. She's moving to Oklahoma City where her sister is, and interviewed for a job with a counseling service. She's not rich, but the income from her job will be fun money for her. Her basics will be covered with ease."

"You learned a lot."

"She's nice. Feels free and likes to have fun in a low-key, classy way."

By now, it's completely dark and we're both getting sleepy. But we're pretty well caught up. Getting completely caught up will take some time. We head inside to get started on some more of that catching up.

It's beyond beautiful to get and give a kiss in the morning. I'm triple-conscious of that now, as I get a sloppy one from Jess, a shy one from Jan and a long, very unhealthy one from Laura now two mornings in a row. This is repeated on both Saturday and Sunday, with Laura's coming earlier in the morning than those from the girls and lasting considerably longer. And being more complex and nuanced.

A few days later I get a "call me" text from Lenore, and after the 6 pm newscast is over, I call.

"Arvin," she gets right down to business, "we should get together."

"Sure. What's going on?"

"That's an in-person discussion. Dinner? I can meet you in Medina Wednesday night."

"That can work. I want you to meet Laura, too."

"You guys are back together? Arvin, that's great!"

We settle in for dinner, although Linda can't make it and Laura has to leave early for class. We talk socially through a drink and starters and then Lenore gets down to business.

"Have you heard anything from the State Patrol?"

"Not a whisper."

"From Detective Chad Lance?"

"Zero."

"Well, I finally got him to pick up my phone call."

"Do I have to wait or ask you or what? Your smile has some meaning that I don't know."

"Arvin," she says as she takes my hand in both of hers, "he's dropping the investigation into Bill Hanlow's death."

"Really? Wow! Should I order another drink?"

"I have an advantage on you, because I've known since Monday noon. Think about what this means."

I order that drink, then start thinking.

"I think I'm clear."

"Yes, I think so too, but you need to talk to Calvin on that. Soon, like today or tomorrow."

I take a sip, then a drink. A real drink. I haven't had a vodka martini in a while, and it's damn good.

"Do you see any negative in this, Arvin?

Well, it tasted damn good for that moment there.

"Noooo, I can't think of one."

"I'm going to give you an exercise here, because a thought has occurred to me. I told Linda about this, she agrees with me, but maybe because I gave it to her. I want to see if you come up with the same thing on your own."

"I have no idea what you just said."

"Why would the State Patrol, or particularly Detective Chad Lance, stop an investigation into a murder, which was quickly followed by the death of the accused person, apparently by natural causes?"

"Because George killed — Jesus, he shot Bill three times in his own home. Then George died. Although he pled not guilty, he had to have done it. There are no clues any other way."

"I'm sure you are a good accountant. But you'd make a terrible reporter."

"Oh, thank you. For the first part of that."

"Technically and actually, he didn't plead at all. He was standing, addressing the judge to do just that when he collapsed. I saw and heard all of it."

It hits me then that she saw George die. Maybe he deserved to die on some level, but Lenore didn't deserve to watch it happen.

"Lenore, I'm sorry you had to see that."

"The Four Roses bottle wasn't. But I never heard anything about evidence. Did they find the gun?"

"I think I watch TV15 extensively so that you tell me those kinds of things."

"They never released that information, Arvin. I asked Detective Lance point blank and he told me they had the murder weapon, that it had been found at Watt Metal Forming and that the slugs recovered from the body and Mr. Hanlow's home had gone through ballistics testing and proved that it was the murder weapon. Oh, and that George Watt's finger prints were the only prints found on the 9mm pistol."

She sips her iced tea. "I had to ask four separate questions to get those four answers. Then I asked him if I could use that information, he paused and said 'I guess so' and hung up. I wrote a story, cleared it past my news director, she took it past our attorney, and we had an exclusive that ran on the 5 pm tonight."

"Darn nice work, Lenore. Congratulations." We all clink glasses and drink. Laura has already stayed 13 extra minutes, and will be late for her class. The ladies hug, then Lenore goes back into her interrogation mode.

"Remember, Detective Lance had whatever other evidence they recovered from the house and from Watt Metal Forming. So, now answer my question, Arvin."

"Uhh, your question . . ."

"Why would they drop the investigation?"

"It's open and shut. The guy who did it died. Why proceed?"

"Why stop this soon?"

"I dunno. Limited resources or something. Police dramatically under staffed. Political stuff. Not sure that I care. In fact, I don't think I do care."

"Or because Detective Chad Lance is lazy. Or maybe he had something to hide."

That catches my attention. I encourage Lenore to elaborate.

"I don't have anything, it's just my gut."

"Well, I'll keep my ears and eyes open. Although, honestly, I think this is a dead end. Bad choice of words, it's closed. It's certainly closure for me, for my family, for Beth Hanlow and for Carson, George's wife. I'm glad you got an exclusive story, if that's what you call it. I, we, Laura and I, do like watching your reports."

"Aw, that's nice, thank you, Arvin."

"Did you set this up just to tell me? Or to prevent me from seeing your story?"

"Yes, I did want to tell you in person. I'm glad I got to meet Laura; she seems terrific. And the same story will run tonight on the 10, probably will lead."

"That means it's the first story they do?" She nods a 'yes.'

"I promise to call Calvin tonight or tomorrow. And thank you, I got answers not from the police, but from my favorite TV reporter."

"Stay in touch, Arvin. And if something further comes to you, call me. I just have a feeling about this."

I'll do that, I promise. I also text Calvin Jenkins from the car before I drive back home. The girls are falling asleep when Laura gets home, and she goes to put them to bed. I flip on the TV and Laura comes out in her summer pajamas. The light, baby blue short shorts and a white tank top with spaghetti straps.

Lenore's story does, in fact, lead the 10 pm newscast. We watch the story, hug a little, watch a batch of commercials, and Laura puts her head on my chest. Our phones go off almost simultaneously.

Mine is a text from Calvin; "I think you're clear, will call in the morning."

Laura's is a call, I don't know from who, but Laura is doing some listening in between an occasional "no kidding" and "whoa" and "how did that happen." I show her my text and she gives me a thumbs up and a big smile, but returns to "a coincidence" and an "unbelievable." When I hear a "did you like him" I assume it's some friend of hers who just got asked out on a date.

The call ends and Laura looks at me with a cross between a smile and smirk on her face. I've seen this a few times before and each time, it's turned out well for me.

"That was Jannine from the hospital. She . . ."

My phone interrupts. I look at the text. It's from Carson.

"Saw the news. George knew Chad Lance."

Damn Lenore's gut anyway.

17 A few loose ends

I head out to work the next day a few minutes early, and as I sit in the parking lot typing out a text to Lenore, the phone rings. I'm a bit short of coffee at this stage of the morning, and a bit shy of sleep. My hands fly up in surprise and my fingers go loose, the phone jumps out of my hand but I manage to catch it just before it would hit the shifter. It's Calvin.

"Arvin, how are you doing this beautiful morning?"

"You know, Calvin, it is a darn fine morning, beautiful too. Are you going to keep it beautiful?"

"I'm your attorney, part of my job is to keep you on edge. However, I do want to mention to you that I want to spend some more of your money before I provide my full and complete opinion. Don't worry, we are not yet beyond the retainer you already so graciously paid. I do have some things that I want to review in context with prior cases of this nature. I pride myself on being a thorough individual and I promised you my best and complete effort. That's what I intend to do. Please give me two or three days, say Tuesday at the latest. If they've dropped the investigation and closed the case, I think you are in good shape, especially due to the nature of your situation and anyone's inability to place you at a certain place at a certain time, or of your ability to transmit information which may or may not have been useful."

I hold my breath to let all of that sink in. As I do so, Calvin fills the pause.

"I'm messing with you just a bit, Arvin. I think you're clean, but I do want to cover a couple of bases. I'll reach out on Tuesday. Until then, relax."

I promise to do as I'm told. I fire off a quick text to Lenore, another to Laura with some additional language and head inside for that coffee.

Carol and Doris are in the break room, and we have a nice exchange. They both saw the story on the news and make me promise to run out at lunch to pick up a newspaper. Mostly, they seem comfortable to know that there is no wild and crazy killer on the loose and that the killer, as they call George, met his deserved fate. I'm happy to agree.

On my way to the convenience store at lunch, I see Lenore's text.

"Not often a man complements my gut."

But there are three more texts in quick succession.

"However, it may have been right."

"I think this is beyond coincidence."

"I'd like to talk to Carson. Can you set something up?"

I'm sure Carson will be fine with that, but I hold off reaching out to her. I'd like to be there, I think, and Laura should come along.

We talk that night as we make dinner while the girls play some electronic game in their bedroom. Laura's Mom may have given the girls a treat or a present or a new outfit here and there while they stayed with her.

"Why do we want to be involved, Arv? We're free, finally, assuming Calvin gives you the green light next week."

"Because this is an odd darn thing that happened, because it happened to us, and because we, you and I, can help put the whole thing to rest."

"Isn't it already at rest? The cops are stopping the investigation, Watt is as deceased as Bill, and all is right with the world. Why keep digging up dirt?"

"This is just interesting, Laura. It happened to me, we know these people, Lenore put two together with another two and found four, and this is intriguing. It's like me trying to find that one transaction, that one entry that doesn't balance or you looking and looking for that one hint, that one symptom that changes the treatment of a patient. It's making a difference and it's realizing self-satisfaction."

"Self-satisfaction?"

"Yes, the happiness that . . . one can get . . . when one . . ." Sometimes words fail me.

"I'm as interested in satisfaction as you are baby. Sign me up. I want to meet Carson."

My morning is full of texting, coordinating schedules and mowing the lawn. I laugh when I sit down on the back patio for my post-mowing beer and the girls can't find me. I yell out and they come running. They can't believe I actually cleaned up that "yocky old place." We play a game of two-on-two baseball, they beat Laura and I 17 to 4 in 3 innings, and by 2:30 pm, we are all set for a walking conversation between the four of us for the next day, 2 pm at Riverside

Park. Laura's Mom will watch the girls.

I do brief introductions, Carson suggests we head upstream, towards the start of the path. I kick off the day's business by asking Carson to explain how George knew Detective Chad Lance.

"They actually went to high school together."

Carson, as I have come to learn, is a good storyteller, if a tad long-winded. She lets that thought sink in dramatically, as the group wanders along the river. I'm suddenly conscious of being the only male in the group. I glance down at my shorts, old sandals that I should have replaced last year, and my extremely faded green Cyclones t-shirt. Laura is resplendent in soft pink shorts that emphasize her rear end, new pink and black trainers and a white sleeveless top. She even did some extra make-up for the occasion. Carson is stylish as well, her light brown hair pulled back loosely, another indescribably colorful form-fitting top, short black running shorts and color-coordinated lime-green shoes.

Lenore, however, has gone over the top. I suspect she gets recognized everywhere she goes, so she has to look the same off work as she does when she's on TV. Her short hair seems to have more of those burgundy highlights and is shorter on the sides and more textured on the top. The dark green golf shirt has a small logo on the front, some design I'm not familiar with. Tan shorts, longer than the other ladies, but still above her knees. Serious walking sandals, dark brown with adjustable straps in what could be leather. I need to pick up my clothes game if I convene this crowd again. After I get my credit card paid off.

"In fact," Carson continues, "they were college roommates, too."

She waves off the "are you sure," "did they stay in touch," and other various comments with a simple hand gesture, then proceeds.

"I didn't know George when he was in college; in fact, I think he graduated maybe ten years before we met. He was never, ever a social person when I knew him. But one time, when we were still dating, we went out to dinner and met Chad. It was that Asian fusion place on the north side of downtown Des Moines."

"Oh, yeah, I remember that, Wok and something or other," Lenore chips in. "That was nice, used to go there myself frequently. Was sad when they closed down."

"Those seafood pot stickers were wonderful, weren't they? But Carson, please continue."

"Well, we met and had dinner. He was kinda an unremarkable guy. I expected someone more dynamic. Balding, with a pretty sizable belly, and a very messy eater. To the point that I stopped looking at him. It's odd what you remember from a simple event years and years ago, isn't it?"

Everybody nods and mumbles, waiting for the Carson to get to the point. I certainly expect a point somewhere in this story.

"We talk about his work and what he's investigating, and how hates his boss and so on. He seemed like an unhappy guy. I remember he kept steering the conversation back to me, asking me questions about high school, my summer jobs during college and all kinds of stuff."

"George didn't talk much, certainly nothing about his business or his apartment or anything. I'd expected to be the odd one out at this dinner, while two old buddies caught up with each other and told stories. But it was the opposite, like I was the center of attention."

"Then later, maybe a year or so before George died, Chad came home with him one evening. It was well after he moved out of our bedroom into his own. I stayed out of their way; George showed Chad around the house a bit like he used to do when we first moved in. They had a drink on the deck and then he left. Might have been there 30 minutes. Again, just seemed odd to me that they had stayed in touch, but kind of a remote distant relationship if you can understand what I mean."

Everybody nods, agrees, mumbles and walks around the huge pile of dog poop taking up residence in the middle of the paved path.

Lenore breaks in.

"Did you think, at the dinner, that Chad was probing your background, like maybe he'd do to a suspect in some crime?"

"That's an interesting thought. I can't say that I remember thinking that at the time, but looking back . . . yeah, maybe."

Lenore continues.

"Can you wrap your head around your husband-to-be getting his detective friend to vet you before the wedding?"

We all walk silently for a while, letting Carson think.

"Not then, but now, yes. He had me so fooled or I was so blind or he changed. Some combination and a dose of bad pixie dust maybe. What I thought at the time was him being sweet, maybe that was him testing, probing into my psyche. Seeing if he could guide me into doing what he wanted me to do."

She stops walking. Laura, walking directly behind her, almost bumps into her.

"I think he wanted to be in control of everything he touched. He never shared any business information or financial information with me. The kind of basic husband-and-wife stuff everybody shares, right?"

Carson looks into each person's eyes.

"Yes."

"Uh-huh."

"True." That one comes from Lenore, with a hint of a smile.

"Trust. Maybe that's what I'm searching for in George's character. Did he trust me? I took it, at the time, as if it was simple kindness. I don't think there was anything simple about George."

"Do you think his ego, his own sense of himself, required that he be the in-charge person?" Laura has been pretty quiet up to this point, but contributes her analysis.

"Was he like that around other people? The way you describe the dinner with the Detective, it seems like Chad just had a role to play, to perform a function, not as a friend, not as an old school buddy, but something deeper, darker, more calculated, sinister."

"He does seem to be the kind who is compelled to compartmentalize things," adds Lenore.

Then Laura stops, reaches out and touches Carson lightly on the shoulder.

"How are you doing? This whole thing, the past couple of weeks has to be taking a toll on your health."

"I hadn't seen him for . . . six days, maybe a week, before he was arrested. So, do I miss him? Maybe the way you miss a cast on a broken bone when you finally get to take it off. But miss him like I wish he was here? No. Hell, no."

"I don't know why I stayed in the marriage, why I didn't get divorced two years ago. I could see it was going nowhere, but I did like that house."

I feel it's time for me to make some contribution. So I ask Carson a question.

"What happened when he was arrested? Did they put him in the back of a squad car? They must have had a search warrant to find the gun, right?"

"He was arrested at the factory, so I wasn't there. That one phone call the accused gets? It wasn't to me. I suspect it was to that LA lawyer that represented him at the arraignment."

"Carson, don't the cops have to have your permission to get into the factory?"

"I don't think I have any rights to any of that property or the business. I know I never signed anything."

"Carson, I don't want to pry. Did he leave a will?"

"Not that I know of. I went into his bedroom Thursday night, after a bit of wine, for the first time. He always kept the door closed, I never bothered it, and actually, I was somewhat surprised that it was unlocked. I poked around but there was no desk, just a wardrobe, the walk-in closet. Clothing. I started to go through that, said the hell with it, had some more wine."

"Do you know if the State Patrol took anything else from the factory besides the murder weapon?" Lenore is in full reporter mode.

Carson seems not to notice. Or care.

"I have no idea. His car was in the back parking lot, I peeked around through the fence, thought about bringing it home. But I couldn't figure out how to get back there, and anyway, there was just me. I didn't want to have to leave my car there, with no other driver. When I got his personal stuff back from the police, besides his clothing, it was just his wallet, cell phone and keys. I tossed them back in the envelope and it's laying on his bed."

"What about the factory? What about his employees?"

Carson just shakes her head and looks at the ground.

"I know one of his ex-employees." I briefly explain our connection, and look to see what Lenore's reaction is.

"I think he could help answer some questions, but Arvin, you shouldn't talk to him. Carson, do you know this Mr. Mattern?"

Another headshake.

I look at Laura, and manage to catch her eye. I glance over at Carson, then back to Laura and try to twist my face into a question mark without anyone noticing or me not being able to get my face back to normal. My view of Carson has changed dramatically in the past month.

I look back to Laura and make a small gesture, putting my open hands out in front of me, briefly, very, very briefly. Laura nods slightly.

So I dive in.

"Carson, this has to be extremely hard on you, and there are a number of loose ends. Would you like some support to run some of these things down?"

"If the son of a bitch had just walked out the door, I'd have felt better. But no, he has to kill Bill, he doesn't give me a clue about his factory or his business. If there's no will, all his property is mine, I know that, but what the process is, I have no idea."

"Well, Carson, I think here's what we can do. Laura and I can come over and look through his things at home, that may be easier for us than it would be for you. That's the personal side."

"On his business side, Lenore, can you see what you can dig up on Watt Metal Forming and maybe reach out to Mr. Mattern? I truly need to stay away from him due to banking regulations and policies."

Lenore pulls her upper body back at an angle away from me, tilting her head back just a degree.

"Look at you Arvin, taking charge here."

"Just trying to help out," I say, looking down at my worn and somewhat dirty sandals.

"No, good for you for being so generous," Lenore adds.

"Yes, that would be nice." This from Carson.

We're just about ready to get back into our cars, Laura and I to follow Carson to her house, when a middle-aged woman walks over to us.

She's possibly overdressed for the day, has to be upper 80s and typical Iowa humidity. I'm ready for the car A/C, but I pause as she strides purposefully up to Lenore. Mid-to-late-50s, greying hair, a simple and not unattractive blue-green conservative dress in a geometrical pattern with short sleeves, short white socks and walking shoes. Serious walking shoes. White. All white, with lots of arch support and no graphics. Tiny white earrings in a design I can't identify. She walks directly to Lenore.

"Are you Lenore Goodman from KDMI?"

"Yes, I am."

"I'm Jean Davis from KSWT, the local radio station here in Stillwell. I watch you a lot." "Oh, thank you."

"I watched your reporting on that awful George Watt story. I watched it many times, actually."

"Oh, well, thank you again," Lenore replies in a voice that sounds like a recording that's been well used. "It's always nice when someone comments on our work."

"I think you could have done a better job. That gasp, it's in the audio, that gasp just when Mr. Watts is almost on the floor, that had to have come from you. You were holding the microphone. And then as you describe that he's collapsed, face turning white and so on, your voice catches. I only do radio in this little town, but I think you could have been more poised."

"I see. How long have you been in radio?"

"Twenty-three years here in Stillwell, five in Cedar Rapids. I majored in broadcasting at Iowa Central." Her shoes are really out of proportion to her body, and might add two vertical inches to her overall height.

"You must be very good to have remained in radio for all that time. And you must have seen a lot of changes."

I can't stand the excitement of this discussion, so I get into the car and fire up the A/C. Carson has already pulled out, but I'm hesitant to leave Lenore alone with Jean. They chit chat for what seems like 20 minutes, but is probably five. When Lenore waves and turns to go to her car, I walk over.

"That was really impolite of Jean."

"I agree," I hadn't noticed that Laura has joined me. I think vaguely that the car is still running and there's no one in it.

"I get that all the time," Lenore says. "Noticed, I mean. Critiqued, not so much."

Laura and I mutter something about KSWT.

"Do you know this person? Jean, Jean something, right?"

"Know her, no. Listen to her every morning though. She doesn't look at all like I expected her to."

"No one in radio does, Arvin. Is she the only newsperson at the station? Is she any good?"

Laura dives in this time.

"As far as we can tell, yes, she's the only newsperson. Mostly the news is some banter between her and, what's-iz-name, the morning host. We call him that because we have no idea what his name is."

"Does she go out into the community and gather news or does she just sit in the studio?"

"She does the local stuff, the school board, when the new Walmart opens, reads the scores of the high school sports games. When the school board wanted a tax increase to build a new school and when the mayor was found passed out drunk in his car one morning, yeah, Jean is how we found out."

"What do you think of her, professionally speaking?" Lenore is not going to let this go. "Do you think she does a good job?" Laura and I look at each other and I think how happy I am that she's back in my life. So, I smile.

"In a little itty-bitty town of this size, you don't have to be good. You just have to be."

I let that roll around before adding an amendment.

"When that school tax discussion was going on and when the Mayor had to get up and apologize and write a letter that was printed in the Stillwell Times, yes, it's good to have local media. Because you and TV15 just aren't going to cover those stories all the way over here, 60 miles away in a town of 25,000, are you?"

"No disrespect intended," adds Laura.

Damn, she's good.

"And none taken," explains Lenore through a huge smile that shows her excellent and bright white teeth. There's a reason she's on TV and not on radio.

"But you're right, Arvin, look at the towns without any media. You're incredibly fortunate to have both a newspaper and a radio station here. Those stories you mentioned have impact, and you're right again, we are not going to cover them because they don't impact the majority of our viewers. But here, there're dammed important."

We are interrupted by Carson, who drives up, lowers the window on her Honda, and says, "It's hot, I'm thirsty, let's go."

We wave goodbye to Lenore and jump in the car to follow Carson. The A/C was working overtime, and we actually have to shut it off for a moment to let the car warm up.

Carson sets out three glasses and pours three iced teas. With actual ice.

"I have some sweetener here if anyone wants sweet tea."

We decline, drink, and head upstairs to George's bedroom. Carson stays in the kitchen, something about crackers, cheese and finger sandwiches.

It's a good-sized room for a second bedroom. Laura and I talk softly about the house (all brick), the size of the kitchen (might need an intercom in the kitchen), the garage (three-car size, for two people) and wish that our bedroom was the size of this. With a walk-in closet and an ensuite bathroom. We make jokes and conjectures about what the master bedroom must look like while we go through the massive, Henredon armoire that has six columns of drawers from the floor to my waist, and three huge doors that provide storage for hanging clothes above. I haven't owned sufficient clothes in my entire life to fill this baby.

Neither did George.

Drawer after drawer is empty. There are three drawers with clothes, underwear, shirts, socks and a few t-shirts. Behind the doors in the armoire are unbranded golf shirts and several pairs of chinos of various mid-tones. A couple of belts and three pairs of shoes; the dress black shoes are covered with dust. One section has a selection of seasonal coats, with a battered fedora, a stocking hat and two pairs of winter gloves. It's a disappointing survey, so we grab the envelope from the bed and head back downstairs.

The crackers are on a platter, the cheese has been diced into cubes and Carson is working on the finger sandwiches, when we go back downstairs. Non-sweet tea glasses refilled, we try to make sense of George Watt.

"Carson, you are so nice," remarks Laura as she places a chunk of medium cheddar onto a Triscuit. "You've taken some real blows and you're a strong woman."

We settle in around the kitchen island and take our choice of one of six available stools. Laura is on the corner of one long side, around the corner to her left is Carson, while I'm ensconced on Laura's right side.

"I don't think I'm strong at all. I'm living in a house I don't want to live in, dealing with a factory I don't want to deal with, doing a really shitty job at my job that I love. I'm a mess."

Laura reaches out and touches Carson on her right forearm. Carson looks at Laura and wraps her arms around her. They embrace for what seems like a long time and when they finally break off, I see wetness in Laura's eyes and full-on tears on Carson's cheeks.

"You two are the only ones who've been nice to me," she says through those tears and a light sob. "You listen and seem to care. I'm such a mess." She breaks down and cries, head on her hands.

"I need to get through this. I want to be on the other side of all this."

"You will, you will, Carson. Go ahead and let it out. Release is good."

They embrace again, Carson's head on Laura's shoulder.

"We'll do this for you, won't we Arv," Laura turns and looks at me.

"Of course, we will," I reply without knowing at all what I am agreeing to.

"You tell us what has to be done, we'll do it,' reiterates Laura. "Do you have any place you can go to get away, somebody to visit?"

"No," Carson says as she wipes the tears away. "I don't want to think about George, his car, his factory, his business. I don't want to live in this house. I don't want to think about Bill."

"We can do that for you if you want, Carson," Laura says gently. "You need some time away."

I find some tissues, the ladies wipe their eyes and we settle back into the finger sandwiches. Carson goes off to the bathroom, leaving Laura and I to chat quietly.

"Did you just volunteer us to close up this part of Carson's life for her," I ask?

"She needs help, Arvin, and doesn't have anybody. Her husband who killed her lover just dropped dead with more loose ends than we even know about. No one can face this alone. You can do the financial and logistical side and I can help on the emotional side."

"Are you sure this is a good idea, Laura?"

"You two are my heroes. I don't know what I'd do without you," says a newly brushed, cleaned, re-made up, very composed and smiling Carson as she turns the corner from the stairway and comes into the kitchen. "I brought paper and a pen. I can make a list of everything I know and the things I'm going to have to find out about."

Two hours, the entire box of Triscuits, most of the cheese and two batches of finger sandwiches later, we have a list.

Monday to Friday being the standard banking work week (I'm lucky to have no Saturday morning duties, actually), it's Lenore who gets busy immediately. She calls me Tuesday evening.

"I called and called Detective Lance, got no response, so I went over his head and reached out to the Director of the Division of Criminal Investigation. She called me back in less than half an hour."

"I explained that I was doing a follow-up on the death of the suspect in the Hanlow murder. She expects to get a report on the autopsy late this week or more likely late next week. I pushed a bit; she won't provide an opinion as to what the cause of death was. If there is any doubt, there can be another autopsy ordered. To the best of her knowledge, all of George's possessions were returned to his wife, in person, by a member of the Patrol. She'll verify that and get back to me if that's not the case. Other than the pistol, nothing was taken from the factory."

"So, we wait on the autopsy, then, I guess," I reply. I'm flying blind here, but Lenore isn't.

"Actually, we got along pretty well, for a phone call,"

Lenore continues. When I thought I had all the info I needed, I suggested that had Detective Lance been so forthcoming, I would not have had to bother her. She essentially apologized to me for having to push as hard as I did. Said — here's a quote — 'Detective Lance is unlikely to do anything that isn't specifically required. That's not how I'd prefer my staff to operate, but there it is.' Then she said I could call her anytime I wasn't able to get what I needed."

"How do you read that?"

"Well, Arvin, I got the impression that the two are not the best of friends. I know when Director Jimenez was appointed, there were some grumblings from the staff. There had been a female director a few years ago who didn't last, and I don't recall another minority in that slot. So that could be some of that 'good 'ol boy' network coming out."

"Does that really still exist?"

"What planet are you living on, Arvin? All the time. Everywhere. It's not just systemic, it's the foundation on which the police department is built."

"Lenore, help this rookie out. What did you learn?"

"Detective Lance may not be the most ambitious boy scout in the pack. Or the smartest."

"How do you get from A to B on that?"

"If you are running the investigation into a murder, in addition to three, four, or maybe five other investigations, you're a pretty busy guy, aren't you? Do you think you would be too busy to actually do an on-site investigation of a murder in a small town 73 miles away?"

"No. No, I think I'd make that a priority."

"Do you know if Carson has seen Detective Lance?"

"Oh, gosh, Lenore, yes, remember, she said they knew each other."

"And that she'd seen him once before that. Twice, excuse me, but not three times."

"You are a reporter, aren't you?"

"It's just logical math."

"OK, so he hasn't been on-site. Lenore, is it legal or ethical, there's a word that's not coming to mind, but should he be in charge of investigating the murder of someone he knows?"

"Conflict of interest."

"Who knew that they knew each other?"

"Carson and whatever friends they had from high school and college."

"But there's another angle here. Let's climb out on a fairly small and dangerous limb. You don't really want to drive an hour-and-a-quarter to some small town to do on-scene work when there's something else to do? I'd like to confirm with Carson that she hasn't seen him. Bottom line, as of right this instant, lazy is probably the most likely, most kind label I can put on him."

We agree to meet next Sunday for updates.

On a whim, I search the Sunrise Bank data base for George Watt, and find nothing. No big deal, there are other banks around, but I wonder who did his business and his personal banking work? I make a note to ask Carson about the home mortgage.

Saturday morning, after leaning on Laura's Mom yet again with the girls, Laura and I drive over to Carson's house to pick her up. Carson has the keys to the factory and to George's car. Our plan is to get his car out of the back lot, then the ladies are off to lunch. I'll stay and scope out the factory.

It's a nondescript entryway made of dark brown metal and large glass windows. Dark glass windows, to the point it's all but impossible to see in. I use one of the two keys, the first one works, we walk inside and I find a light switch.

This particular factory doesn't look familiar, but then again, I didn't take notes. My purpose those months ago was to get in, find a human being, and talk or leave a resume. But I did learn that exit signs are usually correct, and I follow a few back a short hallway, ladies trailing behind me. We are strangely quiet for we three. I'm looking for a door that will take us out of the office and into the factory, and then another door there that will lead to the exterior of the building and the parking lot in back of the building.

At the end of the hall is a door, and finding it unlocked, I go through, wishing I'd brought a flashlight. I stick a foot in the door and grope around for a light switch. The ladies lag behind me and I hear some whispering as I find a switch and turn it on.

It's a very large room. There are two rows of huge, dark green machines with cutouts on one side and an array of large buttons. The room goes maybe 200 feet to my left and 50 more to my right, and about 100 feet back. That's where I head, the small door with an exit sign.

The lighting isn't bright, certainly not bright enough for workers to work in, but plenty bright enough for me to see. I get to the door, stop to look around for cameras or an alarm system, but don't see any. I make a mental note to check the front door for the same. The ladies come up behind me as I open the door.

There in the parking area is a slightly dirty but otherwise pristine white Jaguar SUV. It has a subtle style that Ford and Chevy don't, enough to make me stop and appreciate the lines. I'm no car guy, but this one is nice.

The engine turns over instantly and the sound is, true to its name, is more a purr than a rumble. I flip on the AC and unlock the chain around the gate. We all climb into the SUV, I drive through, put it in park and re-lock the gate.

Carson speaks first.

"I think this is the first time I've actually been in this vehicle. He got it, late last fall if I recall correctly. I remember he pointed out the front window, said he'd bought a new car, that was it, so when I saw it, I'd know it was him, not a stranger. He was cold, cold to me. I probably wasn't much warmer to him. This is pretty nice." Laura and I smile, nod and say approving things without going gaga over George's taste in vehicles. I drive back up front to the main parking lot. As the ladies get into our car, and I lock up the Jaguar, I ask Carson about security systems, alarms, cameras, anything.

"None that I ever knew of. If something goes off, all I can say is when the police get here, have them call me so they know you're not a burglar. Although those machines would be hard to take out of here, even for this white thing. And Arvin, take anything you want from here. I have no idea if there are computers or office equipment you could use, but help yourself."

"I'll look around, and thank you, that's quite generous. Lenore found out that they found the gun here, but they didn't take anything else."

"I suppose they had the key to this on George's key ring, which, by the way, I didn't so maybe they'd have put things back afterwards?"

"I guess we'll never know, and it probably doesn't matter. I'll go through here, you two have a fun time together. Do you want to take the Jaguar now?"

"No, Arvin, you keep it, you might want to use it to take stuff to your home. I'll pick it up there tomorrow."

We say our goodbyes and I head back inside the office area, checking and rechecking for any hint of cameras and alarm systems. Nothing.

I start in what I assume was George's office. Spartan gives this space too much credit for decorating. There's a rather large, outsize metal desk that looks like something out of a World War II movie, metal painted a color similar to those huge machines out in the plant. A well-used-and-somewhat-abused brown swivel and tilt chair that might easily be as old as I am. Arms are worn and what is supposed to be the cover is ripped, the left one showing the base metal through the ancient foam padding. Two four-drawer upright metal filing cabinets, one a slightly lighter shade of green and one off-white. The fluorescent lights mark the only openings in the drop ceiling, which might have been white at one time. A long, long time ago.

The most interesting object in the room is a new iMac sitting on a really tiny little table which George has used as a return on the left side of his desk. The table is more stable than it seems it should be, and is sufficiently deep for the keyboard. I hit the on switch on the back side.

While the computer boots up, I sit in his chair and look at his domain. No pictures (oh, yes, I remember Carson emphasizing the 'no family' mantra), no artwork, no wall calendar. I lean back a bit in the chair and think that, if any office in existence today would be the home of one of those 1950s girly calendars, the ones with the overly colorful and optimistic girls with plenty of cleavage, this would be the office.

Time to get to work. I open every drawer of the desk and every drawer of the filing cabinets. Nothing is locked. No flash drives, no externals, no DVDs, CDs. I half expected to find a few 1.4MB floppy discs, but no.

Damn iMacs always seem to take forever to launch, so I get up and wander down the hallway. I count three more offices on this side of the hallway, three on the other side and a single smaller office around the corner next to a unisex washroom. A total of 2 tables, 4 desks and 3 chairs in all. Not even a coffee pot.

The iMac is up and running now, so I take a look. He was a tidy guy, George was, as there is a total of four folders on his desktop. One of the standard Apple backgrounds is the desktop image. If George had been an architect, he would have been either a minimalist or a brutalist.

The folder named $ is the first one I open. Because, you know, I was an accountant and now I'm a banker.

18 Heaven is a spreadsheet

I drive the Jaguar home a few hours later than I intended, the iMac carefully laying on the floor behind me. I dip back into the life of a father and husband, with hamburgers on the charcoal grill, two really cold, really bland beers, washing the dishes, and another game of family baseball. Kids 12, adults, 1, game called after 3-1/2 innings due to a disputed safe/out call. Pitcher's hand is a tough game to umpire.

Laura and I retreat to the red fabric chairs in the front yard after the girls are in bed. It's been a long day for both of us.

"Carson is really happy that you're doing all this coordination for her. She's planning to pay you. You keep track of your time and she'll pay you twice the hourly rate that Bill was paying you. I don't know how you feel about that."

"Well, I hadn't considered any payment, thought we, not just I, but all of us are just helping out a friend when she needs it. I do have a bit of a nut on my credit card from Calvin's bill, so let's think about that. Tell me what you two did today."

"We went shopping, as much as you can do that in Stillwell. Around the square and out to the strip by Appleby's. She's selling the house, has set up some appointments with realtors. She's thinking of buying the Hanlow Accounting business. Wants to stay in town."

"Oh, and we're all getting together for a picnic tomorrow. Here, we're hosting, everybody is bringing something."

"Who is everyone?"

"Carson, Lenore and the four of us. I thought about asking Beth, but putting Beth and Carson together is probably not a great idea."

I mull that over while we watch a shooting star. As much as we've sat out here recently this is the first one we've seen. We chit chat for a few minutes before Laura asks about my day.

"It's an office set up that might have come right out of the 1950s," I lead. "I found two things of interest. One, there was a copy of my resume in a filing cabinet. Which I found a bit strange because George was not a man of paper. I didn't go through every drawer in every office, but that was in one of the filing cabinets in his office. I did not check out the factory, and we should do that at some point. I brought home — ah, rats — I brought home the computer from his desk and it's still in the SUV. Forgot all about it when I pulled in and saw the girls and the soccer ball flying around."

"You were gone quite a while for not having done much digging. Snooping. What are we doing, anyway?"

"I've felt that way too. We're helping Carson clean up this mess so she can move on with her life. That computer has only a few files on it."

"Not much help, Arv?"

"I think it might be a lot of help. George wasn't a paper guy but he was a spreadsheet guy. I bumped through a lot of spreadsheets."

"How do you feel sharing a language with a murderer?"

I choose not to pick up on that. Laura continues.

"No wonder you were gone so long. You must have been in heaven, the way you love spreadsheets."

"Do you want an overview now or do you want to head inside and go to bed?"

"Hmm, which of those two offers is most appealing?"

I open my mouth to start with the verbal overview of the spreadsheets, but Laura stands up and holds her hand out to me.

"Bed," she states firmly. I don't argue. We go inside.

Next morning, after I install the iMac in our living room, the girls and I take the Jaguar out to buy charcoal and soft drinks. The girls get a kick out of it and someone needs to pick Carson up anyway. She's waiting outside for us; we pack two bags and a large box into the back and she hops into the front passenger seat.

She chats to the girls as I drive. I look over at her and she looks somehow different than I remember from a few months ago. I can't label it happier, considering all the hell she's been through, but somehow younger. She has her shoulder-length light brown hair pulled back loosely, a conservative light pink t-shirt and off-white capri pants, which pair nicely with brown leather sandals. But it's in her face where I see the difference. Is she younger than I thought? I push the line of reasoning away as we pull into the driveway.

The girls bounce out and help take the bags into Laura in the kitchen. I grab the heavy box, then go back for the charcoal. Lenore and Linda pull in and climb out. It's apparent the ladies have certainly dressed for each other today. Lenore looks like she's ready for a poolside wine tasting in Beverly Hills rather than hot dogs on the grill in small-town Iowa. White sandals with two straps and open toes. A short white skirt in some crinkly material, short enough that I look again to be sure that it's a skirt and not shorts, topped by a strappy top with blue, red, pink and orange patterns that might be based on flowers, but most certainly shows more cleavage than anything I've seen Lenore wear before. Linda is wearing a simple dress that goes down to mid-calf, with a single diagonal stripe, magenta on the top and orange at the bottom. I grab two of their bags and follow them in before I notice that Linda's dress has an asymmetrical slant at the bottom that matches the stripe, and the short side is split very, very high on her left thigh.

Lenore introduces Linda all around, we open the large and heavy box from Carson to find, surprise, there is wine, bitters, a bottle of simple syrup and a bourbon I've not heard of, but looks expensive. Carson takes orders and starts making Old Fashioneds, Linda dices up some oranges and I pour wine.

I forgot to put on some music, and I look over to Laura to catch her eye and see if I should break and do that. This causes a fresh review of my favorite person ever, and yes, she's clearly joined the crowd today. I didn't know Laura owned blue jean shorts at all, much less shorts that short, and although the yellow sleeveless top goes nearly up to her neck, it hugs her torso the way ink hugs a magazine page. She's barefoot, a look and a comfort which we do a lot at home, but she's done her toenails in a lemon that seems a perfect match for her top. I forget all about music.

It's crowded in the kitchen, so I head out to fire up the charcoal. I fill up the chimney and grab some newspaper to use as a fire starter. I remind myself I need to pick up my sartorial game, although I am sporting a tan collared golf shirt that I'm pretty sure I bought since Jess was born. Lenore and Carson come over.

"Was there anything on George's computer, Arvin?" asks Carson.

I answer with another question.

"Was George a computer guy or a write-it-down guy?"

"He was pretty good with a computer. He'd write something occasionally, back in the day he'd keep the grocery list and there were times I bought the wrong thing because I couldn't read what he'd written. But I'd say mostly computer."

"I have it here," I continue, "because there are a lot of spreadsheets on it. I opened a few of them yesterday and actually, they are pretty sophisticated. Not bragging here, but I know my way around Excel and he had a pretty good knowledge of formulas. Funny, in some spreadsheets, he'd have a tab marked "notes" and those, from what I've seen, are entirely text, no numbers at all."

"I've heard about people who do that," Lenore chimes in. "Like the salesperson who's so used to PowerPoint they do everything in it. Some people even use it to draw diagrams."

"I want to spend some time getting into those. Someplace, there has to be a banking relationship, credit cards, maybe even a will, don't you think?"

"Arvin, do you want to see his financials and tax returns?" asks Carson.

"Yes, that would help me track down a lot of loose ends. Do you have those?"

"No, he hired Paul Applegate to do his year-end work and tax returns. I know because we argued about it. I thought I should do his accounting, that we should do that together, but he would have no part of it."

She stops and takes a second drink of what I believe is her second Old Fashioned.

"No frickin' part. We were islands."

Lenore puts her arm around Carson.

"Not anymore, Carson. You're your own continent now."

We watch the charcoal begin to turn grey.

"I'll get those files from Paul," says Carson.

"I'm meeting Mr. Mattern on Tuesday," says Lenore.

"I'm in spreadsheet heaven this week," I say. But I add, "and I want to check out the plant, especially if we don't find anything. Anyone want to come with?"

The two look at me as if I had just asked them to grab a fistful of charcoal.

"No, nope, never mind, I got the factory, that's me, Mr. Factory Inspector Guy. You know, seriously, I think it is an interesting place. It's like time froze there two generations ago."

I tell them about the furniture and chairs as I pour the now glowing coals from the chimney into the bottom of the grill. It's true, I am much more interested in this building than anyone else. We head back inside where Jan, Jess, Linda and Laura are all congregated at the small table in the kitchen, dicing, cutting, mixing, tossing and telling crazy stories of other summer cookouts when they were nine and eleven.

Linda's homemade potato salad is a huge hit, more popular even than Carson's Old Fashioneds. Laura, with help from Jan and Jess, has made her baked beans and those are the second item to go empty. Remarkably, I get my hot dogs done perfectly, slightly charred from a very hot grill yet not overdone and dried out. Lenore brought two flavors of ice cream, a strawberry something-or-other that has a very recognizable flavor of shortcake, as well as a chocolate caramel that might be the richest ice cream ever.

"A little bitty local place a block from the station downtown," she says in answer to my question.

"They make four flavors at a time, and most days they only have two or three available. I did a story on them the week of their Grand Opening last summer and they've never let me pay for anything. I kind of hate to go there, I don't feel comfortable getting anything for free, but for this event, and for these two girls (pointing at Jess and Jan), nothing but the best."

I start to go in to do dishes, but Linda, Lenore and Laura seem to have hit it off well and they shoo me out. Carson and I pick up some of the plates and utensils and napkins while the girls run off and kick the soccer ball around.

"I want to pay you for your time Arvin," she states.

"That's really not . . ." I try, but am unsuccessful.

"I want to partition my life too, and the first step is I need to get George out of it. So the more you do, the happier I am."

"You do look happier. Are you?"

"Yes. I'm not saying I don't struggle, and that from time to time I think I flirt with depression, but when I get this shoved behind me, I have a new life ahead."

"That's really good. I'm happy to help, and that's . . ."

Nobody can say I'm not trying.

"I'm thinking of buying Hanlow Accounting from Beth. Her attorney has given me all the financials going back five years. I have your payroll records buddy. I'm using your raw salary divided by 2,000 and doubling that number. You tell me how many hours you spend each week, and I write you a check. Mileage at the IRS max, too, any expenses, add them in."

"Carson." I give her the look I give to the girls when they do something they know they shouldn't, like leaving their toys outside overnight.

It doesn't work on Carson either.

"I'm paying you because it's worth it to me. Bill was paying me a good salary, maybe a bit too good."

She pauses there, and I look, but I don't see her blush.

"George may or may not have had life insurance, he may or may not have had a business worth anything, but I'm pretty sure he owns that factory. And he paid off our house two months ago. I called the bank and asked about the balance and payments. I was surprised."

"Oh, they are sending me a copy of the release on the mortgage."

"OK," I say. "As you think of things, make a list or text me. I probably will do most of this in the evenings while the girls are gaming or watching TV. I'll go to the plant on Saturday. Hope I remember to take a flashlight."

"Which I will pay for."

I resign myself to this fact, and the two of us go back into the house. We ask about one more dessert or a lemonade, but there are no takers. Hugs all around, bags and dishes collected, Linda and Lenore get into the car, Carson into the Jaguar, and Laura and I head to the red fabric chairs. We watch the girls practicing their shots and goal-keeping skills, trading off roles.

"They are such nice people," Laura sighs. "Fun, smart, good to be around. Linda's potato salad was killer, wasn't it?"

"Speaking of killer, you sure dressed the part today. You always look good, but today, wow, is that a new outfit? And your toenails."

"You were in spreadsheet heaven and Carson and I had to find something to do. I haven't had a pedicure since I turned 15, that was my birthday present."

"Nice shorts."

"On sale at Kohl's. Carson had some coupon thing they do, and she wanted to go there."

"The top, too?"

"Yep. Top, bottom, three pair of new underwear because

these shorts are a little lower waisted than I what I was wearing yesterday and they showed."

"She did promise to pay me, but I still have the credit card to pay off."

"Carson gave me her coupon. Everything you see," she says and waves her hand dramatically from the top of her head to her waist, "and something you don't, $21. The pedicure I paid cash for, $20 with a tip."

I stopped listening at "something you don't."

Monday night I dive back into spreadsheet heaven. George was good in Excel, not quite as sophisticated as I may be, but clever for guy who . . . then it hits me. I don't know anything about George except what Carson told me and those visits to the Fourway.

There are 67 files, and of ones I've opened, they all have many spreadsheets. I copy all of them onto a flash drive, recopy them on the iMac, and then when I open each, save it with an invented suffix. I want to maintain the originals in two separate locations, just in case there are ever any questions.

George was big on spreadsheets, not so big on folders. I sort by name, then date, trying to find some pattern or meaning. There is a file for each of the last six years, so I start with the earliest and the most recent and compare. There are spreadsheets for Plan, Proforma, Actual and then a string of Scenario sheets. In the earliest year, there are names, such as Scenario Big 3 or Scenario Small. The most recent year, the current year, the Scenarios are only numbered.

I'm astonished when Laura comes through the door at

10:17 pm. She puts down her backpack and hugs me, goes to check on the girls.

"How were classes?"

"Review time. Next week are finals, and I want to be totally prepared."

She will be. She's been working on her BSN for three years, going part time, but I can see she's even more anxious now to put the school behind her and get that new assignment she's been talking about with the hospital. The money would be nice, but reaching an objective she's had since Jess was born would be even more satisfying. Not mentioning being done with school, notes, backpacks, books, pens, and late nights and early mornings studying.

"You've done well in every class you've taken. A 4.0 is hard to do, yet you've done it."

"These two classes, and two next semester, then I will have done it. How are George's files looking?"

"Like they are going to take a long time. Step one is to discover what's there, then organize. He's helped me by giving me what I think are all of his own financials, beyond what Applegate has. Sometimes that outsider adds or covers up facts. You know, well, I know, there's a story in there someplace and I just need to tease it out. What about you?"

"I'm done analyzing collapsed veins. Let's get some sleep."

Saturday morning after I make waffles, sausage and frozen orange juice, I'm off to Watt Metal Forming. I stop at the HWI and pick up what is advertised as a Tactical LED Flashlight with five modes. It will fit in my pocket, so $11 and 18 minutes of Carson's money later, I pull up to the

Watt parking lot.

I pay special attention to the entry way, looking for any sign of a security system or a camera, but come up with nothing. Carson won't put it up for sale until after I've inspected it and made sure I have taken anything of value out, but she has had a couple of commercial real estate agents look at it for purposes of pricing. I'm hoping to find a title, or a key to a safe deposit box at a bank or anything.

The office area is first on my agenda. I spent a lot of time in George's office last week, so today I start in the last office on the left side of the hallway, that backs up to the restroom. The one with the odd door where Carson told her story about lunch and sub sandwiches.

The table in this office could pass for a desk if there was another piece of furniture for general supplies like pens, paper, cords, sticky notes and so on. One ancient armed wooden desk chair that tilts and swivels and two ugly old faded orange plastic chairs, similar to the two in the front lobby. No old computer, no waste basket, just four pieces of furniture.

The next office around the corner is the next largest compared to George's. I imagine it was used by the plant manager, as there is an old green metal desk similar to George's but in worse condition, a newer office chair with black imitation leather and what might be actual wood arms. It swivels but doesn't tilt. Two of the same ugly orange visitor chairs. However, there is a sound green metal wastebasket, empty, and a surge protector, so old that its faded from an off white to a dusty, dirty orangey brown. This office has accumulated some typical office detritus; a few reams of paper, two old printers, a variety of printer ink supplies, a couple of keyboards. No CPUs.

I check out the five other offices in a similar fashion, checking out every drawer, waste basket and, in two cases, cheap hanging cork board bulletin boards, complete with colorful plastic push pins, but no bulletins. I peek behind them, too. Nothing.

George's office chair seems like a good place to finish my second cup of morning coffee, and as I sit in his chair, my feet on his desk, I consider whether I should add some cream to my coffee. Thinking about the extra liquid encourages me to visit the restroom down the hall and around the corner, and as I use the facility, I look around and remember those old detective TV shows I used to watch as dead time in high school and college.

I should check out the toilet tank.

I wash my hands and go to use a folding paper towel from the white device on the wall, only to find it empty. I notice the locking device on the front, and go back to the second-largest office to see if there just happen to be any paper towels. The eight-inch-high stack of paper towels is banded by a light blue strip of paper with dark blue printing, identifying it as Supremo Toweling. I pick it up by the band, turn to go back to the washroom and a key falls out.

My hands are still damp, my jeans were clean this morning, so I pick up the key and head back to the washroom. I can feel my heart rate increase as I ponder what lock the key is for. I pull out three sheets from the stack, dry my hands and try to put the key into the paper towel holder.

To my chagrin, it fits.

And to my surprise, when I open the top-hinged door, I see not one, but two additional keys taped to the inside of the door. I pull them out and head back to George's office, thoughtfully putting the paper towels into the holder, closing and re-locking the door.

One key is to a newer car, with a GMC logo. The other key could be several decades old, with a L&J logo engraved on the top.

Time for me to check out the plant.

I go back through the old receptionist's area to the door to the plant and walk into the plant itself. Straight in front of me are the three rows of big green machines. I can see they take up maybe two-thirds of this room in the plant, so I start down the row nearest me. No idea what I'm looking for. Until I see the rows of excessively large and at-one-time-colorful buttons, and on that same panel is an L&J logo that matches the one on my key. That slightly faster (Laura would remind me 'elevated') heartbeat returns.

This is a large machine, old, dirty, well-used-and-probably-abused, and I cannot imagine how much it must weigh. The huge pushbuttons are on a panel that faces the front, but on the left side of the panel is a key slot. I take my L&J key and insert it into the L&J lock and turn. It doesn't budge. I turn left, right again, left again. No movement.

I count seven of these machines in the row to my right, matched by seven on the row to my left. There's still another row to the left of that, but I haven't been down that far. I go down the first row, trying each machine. No luck, no luck, no luck. The next two are some other brand of machine, so I skip to the last on this side, try the other side of the row. The second one turns and although I have to use all of my strength and a good portion of my vocabulary, the darn thing opens.

To reveal another key.

This one is a Stamtec logo, so I look for any Stamtec machines. There are two on this row, and the key fits the last one, the one nearest the door I came in through. This door opens easier and inside is a brown zippered bag from an old bank I never heard of, about a foot wide and six inches high and a half-inch thick. Inside is a printed spreadsheet, showing thee columns: Column A is about twenty websites, a couple for banks, an insurance company, some industrial sounding names I can't figure out along with Luigi's Pizza and Subway. Column B is a list of Logins and Column C is a list of Passwords.

Bingo!

Had there been a chair or a bench or a cleaner machine, I would have sat down immediately. But I put the list back in the zipper bag, and go down the following row of machines. Different sizes, shapes, colors, another manufacturer's logo on a couple and I come to the end of the row. There's a huge overhead door here, that I vaguely remember seeing from the exterior when we came here and rescued George's Jaguar SUV from the back parking lot. The door is at least ten, maybe twelve feet high and the width of at least a standard two-car garage. It's made in long horizontal sections of dirty white metal and there are chains on both sides that are connected to the railing mechanism that the door rises up on. A big dark green panel with buttons very similar to those on the stamping machines, green on the top and red on the bottom. I walk closer to look at this door and as I do, I glance to my left and backward.

Where is sitting the largest passenger van I have ever seen in my life. It's jet black, with minimal chrome and blacked out windows. It has to be twenty feet long and better than six-and-a-half feet high. I feel in my pocket for the key, pull it out and press the unlock symbol.

I'm not a small man, but it's a big step up to get into the driver's seat of this thing. The knobs and buttons aren't that much different than a car except for the plethora of cup holders. I get out and go around to the side door, the one behind the standard passenger's door. It's split into two sections, I open both and look at four rows of seats, decked out in a dark smooth surface that could be leather. It's not immaculate, but it's clean. I go back to the driver's seat, insert and turn the key without staring the engine. Over 167,000 miles on the odometer.

I settle back into the plush leather (I think?) seat and imagine who can drive a single vehicle that much. I think to check the date on the title but set that thought aside. I've explored this huge part of the factory. There's one more door I want to open before I go back home.

The wall next to the connecting door from the factory to the office area is newer. Well, I think as I approach it, it looks cleaner. I see that the doorknob has a key hole, but it's unlocked. I open, find the light switch to my left and turn it on.

The room looks like a fucking dormitory. Directly ahead of me is a blank wall, but the room opens to my left. There's a central aisle on either side of which are a series of small bunks, single beds, all made up nicely with matching blankets and sheets folded down underneath matching pillowcases. A small table on the side of each bed with a shelf about three feet long mounted to the wall at eye level, underneath which are three wooden pegs. On the peg to my left is a good quality, white bathrobe.

I walk down to the end of the row, and count six identical setups on each side of me, for a total of twelve. There are partitions between each bed about five feet high, chin level on me. It's so uniform, so clean, so perfectly modest yet comfortable looking. I turn around and walk back and I see six metal partitions like those used in restrooms around toilets, these, however, go all the way to the ceiling. I open one to find not only a toilet and sink at the far end, but a nicely glassed-in shower enclosure, across from which is a two-foot version of the shelves and pegs from the bed areas behind me. I check behind the doors to my right and then to my left. Identical. Pristine. Clean. Not homey, not for visitation or entertainment.

I walk down past the last bathroom where there's a larger space.

That's the biggest surprise of the day.

"Hello, sir," he says. "I am Alejandro. Did you come to pick me up?"

Alejandro is probably a handful of years younger than me, jet black hair, well-trimmed black mustache, maybe 5 feet 7 inches tall. He's wearing a pair of dark chinos, maybe blue maybe black, with black leather shoes and a medium-blue golf shirt. Nice, professional, serious-looking oblong gold rimmed glasses.

I soak these details up while I stumble for something to say.

It takes a while.

"Uhhhhh, take you where?"

"To the next stop. To my new place."

We stare at each other.

"I'm afraid I don't know what you are talking about."

"Do you not work with Greg?"

"Greg who?"

"No last names, just Greg."

"Who is Greg?"

"The driver of that van." He points in the direction I just came from.

"And where are you going?"

"To the next stop, the end of my journey, I hope. I do not know the name of the place."

"Where did you come from?"

"You do not work with Greg, do you? Are you police?"

"No, no, nooo."

"Is this your factory?"

"I'm working for the owner. Well, the new owner. The previous owner died and . . . how did you get in here?"

Alejandro points through the machines to the van.

"In that van with my employees, Greg was driving."

"How long have you been here?"

"It is hard to say. I think two weeks."

"Are you living here?"

"I was supposed to stay and wait for the next van. I did not have sufficient money to go on, and hope my other people will have some extra money that I can use to pay you."

"Where are you from?"

"I should not say."

"Do you have a — the proper paperwork, a visa or whatever — to be in the US?"

"No."

"Alejandro, I think we need to talk."

"Yes. Like this."

"You've been here, in this factory, for two weeks?"

"I think so. I have no calendar, no watch, no phone."

"How do you eat? What do you do all day?"

"I go out late at night, I see from the front office area that it is open outside and there are no people walking. I go out the side door, walk to the 7-Eleven store and buy three meals."

"Why are you here? I mean why did you come here?"

"That is a long story. The story ends with 'I am safer and have a better future in the US.'"

"Let's go get something to eat. We can talk over lunch."

"No, I cannot go out. I do not have, I am not supposed to be here. I would be arrested by your, by the police, and returned to my country. To Mexico. And I may miss my ride if Greg comes and I am gone."

"Give me a minute."

I make a quick phone call to Laura. Then call the Appleby's

and place a carry out order. For four adults and two kids, figuring Alejandro is going to eat for two.

"We're going to my house," I tell Alejandro. "I'm getting a carry-out order of food for you and my family. I'll pick it up, come back here and use that big overhead door to drive my car in here, pick you up, and out we go. The only time you'll be out of the car is a few steps at my house. We can eat on the back porch, no one can see you back there. Give me 15 minutes, I'll knock on that big door, you open it. I suspect it's big green button next to it."

"Why are you doing this, sir?"

"Because I'm a human being who doesn't think another human being should live in a factory."

He nods, I leave. I return and drive through the gate in the back fence, knock, the door opens, Alejandro gets in and we leave. He had figured out how to close the door behind us, so I lock up the gate and we head home.

Laura is deep into studying, so I make a quick introduction. She reminds me that the girls are at her Mom's until evening so she can study. I take the hint, she picks out the meal she wants, and Alejandro and I head to the back porch.

"You are so nice to bring me into your home, and to get all this wonderful food. I hope I do not cause you any trouble with the police or with your beautiful and young wife."

I tell him he has three adult meals and can choose two, and if he's still hungry he can eat one or both of the kids' meals. I grab lemonades and we both dig in.

"Tell me your story, how you came to be here," I ask.

"Can you assure me you are not police?"

"I don't know exactly how to do that, but no, I am not."

Alejandro looks at me for a while, smiles and nods slightly and says, "I will trust you until you prove otherwise."

"But first, I eat, I want to savor real flavor that is not from a gasoline station."

We tuck in. He goes through the large wings, medium spice, the side Caesar salad and starts in on the bacon cheeseburger, which is the twin of mine. He gets about halfway through and suggests I take the kids meals and save them for later when they return home. I do, and take the moment to refresh our lemonades.

"Arvin," he says. you are a wonderful man. Thank you so much for this delicious meal. I can pay you for what I eat."

"No, it's on me. In exchange for your story. How did you wind up here?"

Alejandro empties his lemonade, I refill it, and he begins.

19 Alejandro's story

"I live in a small town near Chihuahua in Mexico. I own a small business there. The precise name of the town does not matter for our purposes. We make different types of furniture, much of it goes into restaurants here in the US. We make 3-dimensional pieces of art, men and women and children all having fun, playing, eating, tastefully done, you understand, playful, happy. The women all are beautiful, the men handsome and the children in perfect physical condition and happy. This is very untruthful of course, but restaurant owners want to see this."

"We have a wood shop that makes this, some by machine, we have CNC, very modern, but much is also done by skilled hands. Sometimes we put cartoon characters into the art too, those are always done by hand. I understand there are sometimes copyright laws here and we want no trouble, just fun. The painting is done almost all by hand."

"I began this business with my brother nine years ago, in our parents' car port. Dad was unhappy his pickup truck had to sit outside in the sun and the rain, but I told him we do not get much rain where we live, and when we started to sell some wood working, we gave him some of our earnings."

"We work hard, my brother and I and our business grows. Soon we need help, so we hire a friend, then his friend, then a friend of someone else. My brother Raul is better at woodworking, I am maybe a bit better at business, so we split our duties that way. I took two years of college in Mexico City, my brother worked in two factories, building American cars. I pay great attention to the people we hire. Their intelligence, their character, how hard they work, of course the skills they have. Both men and women in our factory, we all work side by side to do good work."

"I hire an artist to create the designs for the tables, chairs and booths we begin making for American restaurants. Maybe you have sat in one of the chairs we have made?"

"Yes, probably. I know I am familiar with the kind of restaurant furniture you are talking about."

"Three years ago, our sales reach 12 million pesos, about . . . I think 500 thousand US dollars. We have 20 employees now, and I spend most of my day on the phone with US customers, trucking companies, and so on while Raul is the master of the factory, the receiving and shipping so every piece of wood that comes in the door is perfectly matched to the section of the furniture it will become, and each item is finished with a quality, food-grade coating and packaged so it is pristine when the customer accepts delivery. Not good, not very good, pristine, right?"

"We get more business than we can handle easily. I talk to two banks about borrowing money to rent a bigger factory building than the one we use now, buy new machines and hire just a very few new people. People are key to us; I still hire very carefully."

"We make an arrangement with one of the banks and after a few weeks of constantly working, we get the old equipment moved, the new equipment installed, our craftspeople learn the new skills and we are all very tired, very much in monetary debt but also very happy."

"The new factory is 14 kilometers away from the old one. Different area. So, everyone must learn new roads to take. Some of these roads go through some areas that are not so safe. In Mexico, we have very, very serious problems with drugs and criminal gangs. Are you familiar with our situation in this regard?"

"I am ashamed to tell you I have seen some news stories about drugs and shootings and so on, but I am not well-informed on the subject."

"Mexico is much, much different from what I have learned about the US. This is my first time here. But in Mexico, banks, police, businesses, everybody expects a little something from you. You pay this guy, you pay that lady, it's just the way things are done. If you do not pay, it can be bad. If big companies don't pay, it can be bad. Lots of drugs, serious drugs, the kind that can easily kill someone who uses them and that people are killed for making or transporting. Sometimes there are wars, this side shoots and hurts, that side shoots and kills they take prisoners, hostages like, it's very dangerous. Sometimes driving from this point to that point, you must go through some dangerous area and you can be injured or killed by accident. I think some of your cities have areas like this."

"Yes," I reply, "there are areas in many cities that are unsafe simply to walk or drive through."

"So now, the new factory, some of my people must drive through one or two of these areas each day on the way to work and back to home. My brother and I did not stop to think about this before we signed the lease for the factory, but neither did we truly know that these bad areas even existed."

"One day I am working and Raul comes into his office.

Two employees have not come in, it is late and they know we have a rule that one must call us if they are sick or have an appointment with a doctor or dentist or whatever. He says these two drive together, one this day the other the next day, to save money but also for companionship. They are good friends."

"I call both men, get no answer on a cell phone, so I get in my own car and go to their homes to see what the problem may be. I get part way there and on the road there are police cars all over, ambulances, a big traffic jam. I ask a policeman what is the trouble he says there has been a shooting, two men are badly hurt. To shorten this sad story, yes, it is true, it is our two employees, my friends, both, who are shot. One is already dead and the other dies that night at the hospital. Of course, no one knows anything, no one saw anything. But we know these people, we know their wives, their children. We know their character. Innocent victims of some stupid gang or drug war."

"Arvin, may I trouble you for some more lemonade, please? It is quite good and my voice, which I have not used for I think two weeks except to talk to Ryne and Candy, is hard. It is good to have someone to talk you. Thank you for listening."

I make more lemonade, give some to Laura, and take the rest out to the back porch.

"Who are Ryne and Candy?" I ask.

"They work the night shift at the 7-Eleven. I have not had food like you have given me in a long time. My stomach is smiling at me."

"This situation happens again, this time one employee dies. Then again, quickly, just a week later, two get shot, one badly but he recovers, and the other not so badly. He quits his job with us because of his safety. He was a very good and excellent employee, he painted the faces so well. He used all of us and our families as models, of course making us men much more handsome than we really are but our wives were quite accurate, very, very pretty. It was sad to see these people go."

"One day Raul and I have a beer after work at my house. We get philosophic in our discussion. Truly, Arvin, we each have two beers, and we talk about our lives and where we want to be and what we want to do."

"Our customers are in the US. I think there is more opportunity in the US. So, I decide to look at what options there may be for us here, in this country. Raul is intrigued but not as much as I am. I look at factory sites, suppliers for wood, visas and work permits and so on. This over many months, more than a year for certain."

"One day, I come into work and there is no Raul. This is not good, he's always in the factory early, very diligent, hard-worker, getting things ready for the day. I call him, no answer, I call Miranda his wife, no answer, so once again I get into my car and head down the road to his house. I drive just a moment, maybe two kilometers when my phone rings. Raul was in a traffic accident, he is dead. I stop by the side of the road and I cry like a little boy. It is still hard for me."

Alejandro pauses and sips his lemonade.

"This was not some stupid gang thing, this was a true accident, the other driver dropped her cigarette, it was burning her lap, she swiped it away and her car hit Raul's head on. She died two days later. Saddest day of my life."

"The day we bury Raul, I decide to move our business to the US."

"I spend several months thinking and planning and looking for the best way to do this. I cannot replace my brother's skills, but I promote a good woman to his position as plant manager. I work very, very hard, to come up with a plan. It is the US visa and work permits we need that is the biggest problem. Your government does not want to give us these documents. I offer to pay, and that is when I realize that in the US, this does not happen, but it is an honest error on my part."

"I ask the banks, the lawyers, people I know for help with this. Then one day my neighbor next door tells me about this guy he heard about. My neighbor has heard that this guy, Phil is his name, is in the transportation business. I should talk to him."

"I meet Phil at a cantina near the factory. We have a beer and a meal. He tells me that if I can get myself and my people, my employees to a certain city, which we shall not name, he can get us into a safe place in the US. He says after we over to the US there will be days of travel in a small bus, like a van, and it will be expensive. He names a per person figure. I have a second beer. I ask him if that includes getting across the Rio Grande or any paperwork. He says no paperwork, that is up to me, transportation only. That he will specify a place and time to meet near the US border, in a certain small town in Mexico."

"He says we will be driven to a place in the US where it is possible to find a job, and to live for a short time with people like us who are established there."

"He asks about my skills, we talk business and people for a while, he says he can match us with similar factory work in the US. No guarantee of jobs mind you, but in a favorable city where such work is available and where we can blend in. It takes money, lots of money. Lots and lots of money."

"I conduct a meeting with all my people, all my employees. I tell them I am selling the business and the machinery to the highest bidder, if anyone wants to buy, I will sell to them. That I am taking the proceeds and moving to the US to start a new business that will compete with this business. That any employee who wants to go, I will pay for them to get across the border and for transportation to the new place. I cannot guarantee a job for anyone in the US, not even for myself, but we will figure that out when we get there. When we have enough money, we will start the business again, we have the skills, we have the customers, we will do well and we will send for our families to join us, maybe the US rules will be different then."

"In a few weeks, we have another meeting. About half of my people want to go with me, the other half will form a company and buy us out. We discuss numbers and figures and amounts . . . Arvin, what do you do for a living, if I may ask?"

"I'm a banker, I do consumer loans. I used to be an accountant."

"Then you know more about this than I do probably. I learned just by doing. School of hard knocks."

"The harder the knock the better the lesson," I say.

Alejandro laughs.

"It is good to talk. Thank you for being such a good listener."

"I will skip the part about the border," he continues.

"Private business that benefits no one by knowing. I'll say only that Phil, the man I met in the cantina, arranged all this and that it went more or less how he said it would go."

"There are 16 who will come with me. Twelve of us wind up in a Dodge Caravan. The other four will have to wait a day or two for another van. I give the money for their transportation to the woman who was in charge of the wood carving in my factory so she can pay for the four of them.

"We are squeezed in so tight in the van that no one can move, but it's a short drive to a parking lot outside a big box store. A big dark blue van, similar to that black one back at the factory here, pulls up and we all get inside. That was late at night, maybe 1 or 2 am. There is a certain charge for this leg of the trip. As I promised, I pay it for all 12 of us. We drive well past dark to another big parking lot in a small town. I'm sitting in back and I can't see the clock on the dashboard of the van."

"We make the same transfer into that black van from the factory here, and I pay the agreed-upon cost to this driver. This is a nicer van, and this time I sit in the front row so I can see where we are going. Not in the front next to the driver, mind you, but directly behind him. He brings us here."

"Greg shows us to this room, what we call the dormitory. Everyone is exhausted from the long drive and being cramped up in two vans for two days. Greg shows us the beds, the showers and toilets, the washer and dryer and the nice bathrobes hanging by each single bed. The next van, the one that will take us to our destination, will be here tomorrow or the next day. He says one-hundred-fifty per person per day. That is not in our budget, but we are tired, dirty, our clothes have been on for three days now. I say yes and pay him."

"Actually, it works well. We all sleep and shower. Greg brings chicken sandwiches for breakfast, burritos for lunch and pizza for dinner. Greg charges us double what is on the receipts, but I pay and don't argue. He thinks the next driver will come after dark. So, we wait. No one has a phone or a watch except Greg, so it's hard to know how long we wait. At some point, he comes back into the dorm and says 'let's go.'"

"We get into his van, the black one over there, and go not far away, just a few minutes, to what looks to be a small city park. This is similar to what we did before, when we went from the other van to Greg's van, a small place with trees, some fields and playground equipment. My people and I think they chose that because there are no cameras, no security like a business parking lot."

"The next van comes up and the driver comes over. Greg and I get out to meet him and he tells me how much per person the next portion of our trip will cost. It is more than Phil had told me it would back when we met in the cantina in Mexico. I brought extra cash, but with the cost of the dorm and food, I am short. I ask for a moment, and go ask my people if anyone has extra cash. They all have some, but much too little. We can afford for only 11 of us to go. I decide to pay the money for the 11. As owner of the company, and as the one with the idea to move to the US, I feel this is the right thing to do."

"I can wait another day or two, I think, and Consuelo, my artist employee will be coming up with the next van load of people. She should have enough money that I had given her before, so I can just wait and go with them then."

"Everybody agrees, we hug and say goodbye. My 11 people

get into a dark-colored van and leave. Greg takes me back to the dormitory. He says I pay him $150 per day like before, and if I do all the laundry and make the beds up so it looks like it did for me, it will only be $100. I agree, so he takes me back to the dormitory, drops me off inside and drives away. I have not seen him since."

"Do you have any idea how long you were there?" I ask.

"Very hard to say. At first, I was afraid to go anywhere beyond the dorm. I did as I promised immediately. I washed all of the sheets and other bedding, the towels and the really nice bathrobes and put them up just like they had been when we arrived. I thought at any minute my friends would come in through the door. But I slept and spent a lot of time walking, pacing up and down the dorm. There is no window, so I had no way to know if it was day or night. I go to sleep again, and when I wake up, I don't know anything. I have to just lay there and try to look around, remember where I am and how I got there. I know where the light switch is and I go over and turn it on. I take a long hot shower and start to walk again."

"All this time, I have no food. Finally, I find my courage and open the door. That leads me out to the factory, where the big black van had come in and that we had walked through. But no windows. So, I turn and go the other way and find a door. I put my hand on the door knob and my ear on the door. Arvin, I think I stood like that for half an hour before my courage comes again. I had not heard anything listening through the door so slowly as I can I turn the knob and open the door."

"There are no lights on, but I can see a bit down a hallway there is some light. I walk as lightly as I can down past the restroom and the other room, and turn, and there I see through a window. I'm sure this is the happiest I have been in my entire life just to see some daylight. I walk right up to the window and look out. It takes me some time but I guess that it is evening sometime, not dark but not daytime either. I explore a bit."

"There are offices but only one seems used. Nice computer I am tempted to turn on, but then I think better and don't. It seems deserted. I do the same in the factory area, look over the stamping equipment, the van and so on. I find another door out there, and, knowing I am taking a huge risk, try it. I see it opens onto a parking area and there is a tall chain link gate topped with rusty old barbed wire. This is when my stomach growls so loudly I think it's thunder. The gate is locked, but there are streets on that side. I look around, I see no street lights, no stop signs from as far as I can see. When I go back to the door to the factory, I look specifically for security cameras or equipment. I didn't see any."

"Now, I am thinking of nothing but food. I want to use the back door of the factory to go out to find some food. I kept some money, not much but some, I figure I'm unlikely to be asked for identification at a store. But I need to find a key to that gate. I go back into the single office that looks like it's being used, open one drawer, there under a few pens and pencils is a key. I take it out to the gate, I'm in luck, it works. Can you believe it?"

"So now I have a way to tell night from day, I have some cash to buy food and maybe something to drink besides water from the faucet in the dorm lavatory. I have a key to use the gate, and when I leave, I can make it look like the padlock is on, and leave the door to the factory unlocked. If I need to get back in a hurry, I think I can. Do I turn on the computer and use Google to find the nearest store or not? I don't think wandering the streets of this industrial area is good, but using a computer may be a bad idea. I'm a cautious person. I decide not to use the computer, but wait for darkness and look for lights, then walk towards them."

"Once again, I am lucky. I follow this road around the curve, look for lights and go that way alongside the roadway. It feels so good to be outside that for a time I forget to be nervous. Do you know the 7-Eleven on that next busier road that way?"

I answer yes, even though I'm not sure.

"I buy one hot meal and two cold sandwiches, thinking that should last a day and surely Greg will be back by tomorrow. I look at the soft drinks but decide they are expensive, and I can drink water for free. I get a little nervous when I go to pay, but it goes well. There is a rack on the counter by the cash register, and on it are watches. I buy this very nice watch."

Alejandro stretches out his left arm to show me the watch. "Very fine piece of technology, isn't it? I think it was made for children, it's pretty tight on my wrist."

"It might be my favorite watch ever. One dollar, ninety-nine cents plus tax. But now I know the time of day."

"I eat my three hot taquitos on my walk back. I am so hungry they actually taste good. I slip in through the gate, close and lock the padlock, carefully open the door to the factory, look around, close it behind me and lock it. I go back to my bed, put tomorrow's food up on the table beside the bed and set my watch. I noticed the time printed on my receipt for the food and add 30 minutes for the walk. At 2:03 am, I turn off my lights and smile for the first time in days. Imagine how taquitos and a two-dollar watch can make me so happy."

"But my happiness decreases each day, although I become friendly enough to say hello and good evening to the two people who work most of the night shifts at 7-Eleven. Have I mentioned Ryne and Candy? They are very nice people; I think lonely and bored at night. They have no idea how lonely and bored it is here."

"It takes me a few days to think about recording days on a calendar, but then decide just to keep my receipts from 7-Eleven, with the date and time printed on them. I know for sure 19 days plus I think 3 or 4 before I began to keep a record, so I think maybe I have been in the factory for three weeks plus a day or two."

I hold up my finger, "And you saw or heard no one in that time?"

"No, there were at least three visitors. The first was a few days after Greg promised to return. This was just after I had moved outside of the dorm for the first time. I heard some people calling names, and I locked the door to the dorm. I heard some voices out in the factory, but not enough to really get any words. They weren't here very long, and after they left, I went out to the offices and saw that some things had maybe been moved, but nothing I knew was taken. The computer was still here."

"Since then, there have been two other, no three other visitors. Each time I heard something, I ran in the dormitory area, locked the door and turned off all the lights. I hid back by the laundry area. Once I heard someone wiggle the lock on the door as if to see if it was locked, but they left."

"Alejandro, why did you come out of hiding to see me?"

"Running out of money and tired of sitting there. All there

was to do was look around in the factory. I took some towels and started to clean some of the machines out of sheer boredom. Those things are very impressive. But they haven't been used in a long time, I think a few years. I keep the black van polished for Greg, but it doesn't get too dirty."

Suddenly, an idea hits me.

"What does Greg look like?"

"He's middle height, I would say, bulky, with a large torso. Big meaty hands with large fingers, silver hair, maybe mixed with some brown. Late 40s, say, but maybe some hard years."

I put up my hand to stop Alejandro and grab my phone. *The Times* will have the photo from the arraignment online, I'm sure. I find it.

"Is this Greg?"

"Yes, that's him."

"Are you sure?"

"I spent many hours staring at the back of his head, and then dealing with him several times here in this factory. Yes, I'm sure that is Greg."

"Well, I knew him as Neil but his real name is George. George Watt."

"You know him?"

"Well, yes, briefly. Knew him. Alejandro, he was arrested for murder. He died just a few days afterward, just moments after this photo was taken."

"Kaaaa," Alejandro says and slumps into his chair. He puts his right hand over his forehead and eyes. "I did not have him pegged for a murderer. What he did for us is illegal I know, but not murder. Who did he kill?"

"His wife's lover. Shot him three times with a pistol, in his own house."

"Holy mother of God. Oh, I am sorry, I did not mean to use that language, I apologize."

"No, no, no matter. I need to talk to my wife."

We both start to stand up, when Laura comes walking in the room, her reading glasses on, an oversize dark blue sweatshirt coming down almost to her knees. She looks tired and bored.

"I was just coming out to see you. There's some interesting news we have from Alejandro. You should sit down."

I get that "are you kidding me" look from her. The one where I know my next line better be good.

"George Watt was running people like Alejandro up from south Texas to here and then on to other places. He had a transportation company. George drove Alejandro here from another city and was going to hand him and some other people over to another driver later."

Laura sits down in the old clunky light blue metal garden chair that I detest but she loves. I'd cleaned, sanded and repainted it for her when she and the girls were at her Mom's. She pulls her phone out of the pocket of her shorts, giving us a nice glimpse of her leg in the process, and hits Favorites.

"Mom, can you keep the girls overnight please?"

Then she turns to Alejandro and I. "I'm really, really tired, but I really, really want to know this. Can you give me a rundown in 10 minutes before I pass out?"

I lead, and Alejandro fills in with the color commentary.

20 Sunday

"Arvin, I can give you one hour this morning, but I am taking the rest of the day to study. My finals are next week, and I am acing both of them. You need to watch the girls."

We take that hour to discuss logistics and strategy. The girls and I pick up Carson and set off to meet Lenore at a playground in Des Moines.

This time it's just Lenore, no Linda. We sit at a picnic table in the shade of a couple of huge maple trees watching the girls play on the playground equipment. It's quite a setup for them, swings, slides, towers, climbing apparatus, castle-like rooms connected by bridges, all in primary colors of blue, green, yellow and variations thereof. On a nice, cushy black foam foundation that has a spongy feel. Lenore has selected well.

I tell Alejandro's story. Then I take questions.

"Where is he now?"

"At the factory. He's very concerned about being in a public place."

"How is he getting food? Something to do?"

"I go every other day. He found a tiny refrigerator back in the plant somewhere so he can keep things cold. We offered to let him stay at our house, on the couch, but he wanted no part of it. He's concerned for us as well."

"What does he do all day?"

"I gave him a few books to read. He says now that he feels safer inside, he's exploring the factory. He knows a few things about factories, although that's not his specialty."

We settle back and watch the kids play for a few moments. Then Lenore chips in.

"I had dinner with Detective Lance Thursday night."

"The guy who won't answer his phone?"

"Yep," she replies with a combination of a smirk and a smile on her face. Lenore is a bit preppy today, in khaki shorts and a modest white t-shirt. Nice huarache sandals in light tan, matching her shorts.

"How did you manage that?"

"I called him and he happened to pick up. Don't think he meant to pick up, but he did. I just used my extensive experience and practiced guile to start a conversation. When he didn't hang up, I kept taking a small step, then another, then another. Just a chat and soon it was dinner."

Lenore tilts back as if to stretch her back. Carson and I look at her with expectant eyes which begin to probe.

"He's about the guy you'd expect, or at least the guy I expected him to be. We went to the Chophouse, at my suggestion. I figured he's an Iowa beef guy. Which he is."

She reaches down into her oversize bag and comes up with three plastic bottles of different flavors of iced tea. We each choose, and she continues.

"I have two each for the girls, whenever you think they'd

like them, Arvin, just let me know. Lance was somewhat surprised that I knew he'd gone to college with George Watt. Let's say we danced around that topic a bit. I didn't want to push too hard, but I didn't want to waste my evening and my own $150 without coming away with something useful."

"And?"

She looks at me and laughs, "Arvin, slow down. It's a beautiful day, the girls are having a ball and we can just sit here and talk. Laura needs you to give her some serious study time, so we have all damn day."

I'm properly chagrined. While remaining curious.

"I'd told him on the phone that my station manager was asking all the reporters to cultivate good relationships with news sources, so that we could do more in-depth coverage. Said I was trying to create a first-name-basis with all of the key people in state government, and he's on that list. A little sucking up, sure, but he went for it."

"Is that true, Lenore?" Carson asks.

"Close enough to be in the neighborhood. Management likes us to know people and likes us to be highly visible in the community. Not enough to pay for a dinner or even a cup of coffee when we do interviews, but still."

"I didn't ask his age, but he has to be George's age, right? He's in slightly better shape, isn't carrying around George's spare tire. Wants to make it to retirement, which is two years off, but he gets a bogey if he stays five years after that. Not a big drinker, I had a single glass of wine and he had a Manhattan. Knows his way around a menu, though. Had suggestions for starters and for my main when I told him I wasn't fond of beef."

"He works three to six cases at a time, all over the state. I asked if he was attached or had a relationship and he gave me a one-word answer: no. Has an apartment downtown, and can walk to the Patrol HQ when he wants to but spends more time outside the building than inside. Seems like a bit of a loner, I asked about partners, as in work partners, and he said he prefers to work alone. Mentioned he has a Cadillac ATS that he only uses on weekends."

"Oh, nice," Carson interjects. "I looked at those. Sleek, very sexy and very pricey."

"My impression is he's hanging around waiting for retirement, isn't going to overwork himself and sure isn't going to rock any boats. I don't think he's stupid by any means, but neither is he going to help solve global warming."

"I came out of the evening with one fact and two odd thoughts. One, not only did he go to school with George, they both went to school with Clyde Simpson, the state Attorney General. Two, he bought dinner. Now, that might be an old-time guy thing, but I did ask him out and suggested an expensive place. We were aggressive with the menu. When he paid, he paid in cash. Now, when I go to get cash at the ATM, the bills I get are fairly fresh and more or less clean. He counted out nine 20s and laid them on top of the tab. When the change came back, he dug out two more and added it to whatever the change was. Nice tipper, if he was obvious about it. But the bills he paid with weren't ATM-friendly, they were old and crinkled and somewhat dirty."

"But the thing that keeps coming back to me, that rattles around in my head at night after Linda has gone to sleep, is that as we walked out the door, he reached in the side pocket of his jacket for his keys and he pulled out a ring that had to have 15 keys on it. I didn't say anything, but why would a single guy who lives in an apartment have that many keys? I keep a separate key ring for all my locks at the station, and I can get into any room I want with five keys there. Any thoughts?"

We watch the girls run around and climb and slide. I'm vaguely surprised that there aren't more people at the park this picture-perfect summer day. I think I need to break the silence before I nod off to sleep.

"Lotta keys, used 20-dollar bills. Coming up empty here."

Lenore and I turn to Carson. Who shifts her weight on the bench, turns, then stands and walks around the table. Once, twice, thrice. She's wearing a pair of white running shorts that look a bit shorter than I think might be comfortable along with a perfectly matching white crop tank that leaves a few inches of her stomach bare. White running shoes with no visible socks. I wonder if she actually runs. I make a mental note to ask her on the drive back home.

Carson stops and puts out her right index finger. "Now, this may be my memory," as she withdraws the finger so she can put both hands in front of her, palms up, "but the last few years, I sort of remember George doing the same thing. I don't think I was actually conscious of it at the time, but now you've planted that seed in my brain. If I go back to when we occasionally went somewhere together and he needed gas, he'd always go into the station and pay cash. Who does that? Who doesn't use a card at a gas pump if you're not going inside for anything else?"

"And why," adds Lenore.

There's a pause of a few minutes. I shake my head to clear out the cobwebs.

"No idea why, but I also don't think it matters."

I'm met with two sets of eyes, one medium brown, one so dark brown they are almost black, boring holes in my skull.

"OK, I'll rescind that last comment."

We pause again. I go to fill the void again.

"What's this about the state Attorney General?' I ask.

"I have some sources who can help with that," says Lenore. "Give me a few days."

"What do we do about Alejandro?"

"What does Alejandro want to do about Alejandro?"

"I think he wants to hide. He's very nervous about anyone knowing he's here, in this country. Carson, he's squatting on your property, what do you think?"

"A dormitory, Arvin?" she asks. "How did we miss that when we were there? Are we somehow aiding illegal aliens?"

"I don't see how any human being can be illegal. They may do something illegal, and of course, there's always lying, but he seems like a very nice, educated, straight-up guy to me."

"What if the police find him in there and I'm providing aid and comfort, well, not that, but you know what I mean. If I let him stay there, he's putting me at risk."

This time, Carson is on the receiving end of two pairs of eyes boring through her skull, one medium brown and my light green.

"OK, he can stay for a while. But he has a better life somewhere. Hell, he has a better life anywhere."

Lenore and I turn the stare back on.

"OK, he has a better life somewhere. Somewhere else. How do we help him find that?"

Lenore calls the girls over for a break and a cold drink. We chit chat about summer vacation, cookouts, playgrounds, soccer. I give the girls 20 more minutes before we head back home.

"Laura has finals on Tuesday and Thursday. So, I'm keeping the girls tight tonight, Monday and Wednesday so she can study. I promised to bring home dinner tonight."

With nothing settled, but everyone updated, we go our separate ways. On the way home, I ask Carson about running.

"Yes, actually, when I got some gear and when you jumped in to help me get all of this settled, I felt better about myself, more free. I run a bit every day, even if it's just 10 minutes down the street and back. Yesterday I went to Riverside and ran, well, ran and walked for 45 minutes."

It's carryout Mexican, and while the girls are plopped in front of the TV, I scoot out to Hy-Vee for sandwich makings, bakery donuts and a pre-made salad alongside a gallon of iced tea. Alejandro is ecstatic to see me and the food, and insists on paying for it. I let him. While the girls finish their TV viewing and Laura continues to study for her finals, I pull out the brown bank envelope, open the paper and go back into spreadsheet heaven. I'm up late, way past the time Laura crashes into bed.

21 Monday

Late Monday morning I get a text from Lenore. "Can we talk tonight?" I was planning to stop off to see Alejandro after work, then take the girls out for fast food and a movie at a theater. We set a time shortly after the movie starts, something I can do quietly in the lobby while the girls are in the theater.

Alejandro dives into the pork fried rice I bring. His smile is as wide as his face, and I warm inside hoping that he is, in fact, as real as he looks, Carson's concerns now working into my brain.

"Today, Arvin, I found an interesting thing," he says over the first of two egg rolls I've brought. "I was cleaning out the van, and in the center console I found a false floor."

I look at him dumbly.

"You know, that console is maybe 15, 16 inches deep, it's really big. But I need something to do during the day, so I get the shopvac from the tool crib out there, and take it over and I discover that the bottom of the console is on an angle. Anyway, in trying to fix it I lever it up and I find two sets of keys in there. Small keys, like the one on the padlock for the fence out back. Each ring has two keys. On one, a red key and a blue key, for college sports teams, but on another an orange and green. On each ring there is piece of tape with two letters written. One is LI and the other is

MA. Here, I will get them for you."

He's back in a few seconds and puts two key rings, each with two keys, into my hands.

"What do you think this means? What are they for?"

"I don't know," he says.

"I can't imagine," I offer. "Do you mind if I take these? And I have parental duty tonight, Dad is taking two of the three most beautiful women in the world out to dinner and a show. In other words, Laura is studying, the girls and I are going to a pizza-by-the-slice place and then to an animated movie about, I think, race cars."

"Arvin, you are a lucky man. Go, enjoy your family."

I do just that. I'm comfortably ensconced, sitting on the floor of the movie theater lobby, my worn black tennis shoes almost touching the exit door. Lenore calls spot on time.

"Turns out the state AG is an interesting guy. Want to learn more?"

"Lenore, that sounds just like one of those phrases your anchors use when they want the viewer to sit through 4 minutes of car dealer commercials just so we can watch your 2-minute story."

"Teasers."

"Beg pardon?"

"Teaser is the term for those one-liners, and yes, I write one or sometimes two of them for every story I do. Stick around, Arvin, I'll teach you all about TV news."

"I'm all ears."

"Clyde Simpson is a Democrat, elected two years ago, and just squeaked by Josh Regan. Josh had been Attorney General here forever, like 20 years forever. It was a huge upset."

"OK, is your point that Iowa is beginning to look more like a two-party state every day?"

"No, I just wanted to let that sink in. Turns out he took a pretty hardline anti-immigration stance for a Democrat, and some pundits think that this strategy pulled enough Republican votes over to him and put him over the top. I didn't cover that race myself, but I know it was a big upset."

My butt is sore, my legs are cramped and I'm starting to miss the interplay between the orange car and the blue car in the movie going on in the theater behind me.

"He got extremely large donations from two men, two white men we know. George Watt and Chad Lance."

A pause.

"Arvin, these are really, really large donations. Do you remember that car that Chad said he owned, that Carson mentioned was expensive? You could buy one of those for what Chad donated to candidate Simpson. $70,000."

She pauses again to let this sink in. I think Lenore has been working on a new technique, so she can stretch a two-minute story for tonight's news out to three minutes.

"George Watt donated a hundred grand."

I'm glad for this pause.

"Where does a cop get that kind of money?"

"Where does a guy who is running a failing business get that kind of money?"

"We have good questions. Where are the answers?"

"Lenore, I spent hours last night going through George's spreadsheets. I have access to his banking information."

"Holy shit. What do you know?"

"Well, not much, by the time I got into them it was after 2 am. I can dive in again tonight, after the movie."

The red car winds up parking next to the orange car rather than the blue one, but Jan and Jess are happy and giggly all the way home, through teeth brushing and into pajamas and into bed. I make Laura some chamomile tea, and fire up the iMac.

I go to the credit card statements scan and rescan looking for oddities. I'm struck by two separate recurring charges of $39.99 each. One is at AAA Storage in Stillwell City, and the other at StoreAll in Liberal, Kansas. Google street maps shows that they are both what the names imply. I write down the local address, and add it to my list of places to go and things to do for tomorrow. Excel lets me search for $39.99. There's a two-digit number in the column preceding this one, and I add it to my note.

22 Tuesday

Blue, green, orange and red keys in hand, I drive out to the AAA Storage facility on my lunch hour. I've never been through the gates of one of these storage facilities. I drive up and down three rows and look for number 22. I take off my jacket, put it on the hook over the back seat of the car, and grab my keys.

The red one works, and I slide the door open. The concrete floored room has cheap corrugated metal sides and the ceiling is newish wood trusses with a bumpy finish on a dirty white roof at the top. To my right on the floor is a tactical flashlight quite similar to the one Carson bought for me to explore the factory. In the center of the room are three small moving boxes, and a stack of newspapers. To the right up against the side of the room are 4 or 5 more boxes, folded flat, and a roll of packing tape.

All of the boxes are identical, standard cardboard brown, with the blue and red logo of a home improvement store and printing that identifies the box as a Small Heavy-Duty model. I pick up one assembled box, and see that is taped with clear packing tape, so I take out the key and cut the tape as well as I can.

The box is packed the way Aunt Martha packs a box of Christmas presents for the girls; stuffed with loosely wadded up newspapers. I pick the box up, and it's surprisingly light. I dig through it and find a smaller box about the size of a cigar box, this one from an office supply store, also taped shut. I dig through the rest of the box, find nothing, then cut the tape on the box inside the box.

It's filled with $20 bills. Neatly laid out flat, not taped like we do at the bank, not wrapped with a rubber band, just neatly laid into piles. I pick up one of the stacks and thumb through it. All twenties, mostly older and well used. I catch my breath, replace the stack of bills, and go sit in my car. Windows up. AC on high. Music blasting.

Two-and-a-half songs later, I press Off, turn off the car, and go back into the storage room. The other two assembled and taped boxes appear identical and weigh about the same as the one I opened. I leave everything exactly where it is, fold the top of the box closed, pull down the rope on the overhead door, close the padlock, check it, check it again, get back into my car and return to work. Early. Without lunch.

Where I proceed to spend the afternoon with a monstrously upset stomach.

Today is fast-fish-at-the-fast-fish-place with the girls, and we go to the playground to kill some time. I actually swing on the swings, chase them around the tower and pretend to enjoy the longer of the three slides. I can't get past the similarities between Detective Lance's cash, George Watt's cash, and the cash I find in the storage building. I need to talk to Carson, but this topic needs more privacy than I can get with the girls. When it starts to get dark, we go home and I get the girls off to bed. I text Carson, and she calls back almost immediately.

I take the call out to the front yard, near the street. I dispense with the pleasantries.

"Carson, we, well, Alejandro found some keys in the van that's in the factory. I got into George's credit card account and found some recurring expenses at two storage buildings. Do you know anything about those?"

"No idea. I mean, I know there are such things, drive past them every day, but are you saying George had two of these?"

"Yes, one here and one in Liberal, Kansas."

"Where in Kansas?"

"Yeh, I had to look at a map too. Anyway, I went today on my lunch hour to the one here in Stillwell. I hope you don't mind."

"No, no, no, no no. I love that you're doing this for me Arvin, I have to write you a check for your time."

"Hang on. There is very little in the storage unit. Just three boxes, along with four or five others that are not assembled, some packing tape and a flashlight. I opened one of the boxes. It was filled with $20 bills."

I think I hear her sit down.

"How many $20 bills?"

"Carson, I'm a banker, used to do accounting, like you. Money takes up a big chunk of my life. I didn't count, but it has to be some thousands."

I think I hear her sit down. Or a glass being put onto a table.

"Jesus."

"I've an advantage over you, Carson, I've been thinking about this all the way since noon. If this is clean money, who owns it? I can walk through the fact that the cost of the storage facilities was paid by his corporate credit card, that the keys were in the vehicle, and that the vehicle is registered to Watt Metal Forming. I think there's a case for the fact that this belongs to the business, but I'm not a lawyer and I'm not going to play one."

"Of course, we also have to consider the possibility that George and Detective Lance seem overly fond of cash, and, well, maybe there's something here that's not . . . right."

"Legal is the word you had in mind."

"Legal is the word I had in mind and couldn't say."

"There's another storage room in Liberal."

"Help me out here, Arvin."

"Right on the Kansas/Oklahoma border. About an 11-hour drive."

"Ouch."

"Do you have an attorney working with you?"

"I've talked with Alice Norton, you might remember, we did some work for her, I think when you were still with us. I need to find some paperwork, documentation. A will and the incorporation papers would be nice. You know, I don't even know what kind of a business Watt Metal Forming is, a corporation, an LLC, who all is involved. If I was in any of it, I would have had to sign something. I never signed anything to do with the business, just the house. Speaking of the house, I'm putting it up for sale on Monday. This Saturday I'm doing an estate sale at the suggestion of Jerry Angle, the realtor. She suggested I clean out some furniture and so on before it goes on the market. I'd do better that way."

I hear another light tap on Carson's countertop.

“Like it matters. I’ll be just fine.”

“I know you will Carson, you at least have the house.”

“I’m not a house person, I’ve decided. I’m getting a condo; I’ve looked at a couple. Beth Hanlow has one in one of the buildings I looked at.”

“Yes.”

“Anyway, what’s up next, Arvin?”

“Frankly, I’m nervous about the cash. Laura is tied up this week with studying and finals, and Liberal would take up an entire weekend. I hate to go back to the storage unit here until we know something more. If that cash isn’t yours, I don’t want to put myself in a position of the owner thinking I took any.”

“No one would think that of you, Arvin.”

“I appreciate that. I can dig through some more spreadsheets evenings this week, but that’s probably it until the weekend. Then I promised Laura some make up time, she’s been working really hard.”

“I know. If you guys need any furniture, anything, come over Saturday at 8 am. Or earlier, I guess these estate sale things go nuts early. I think I can pull something out of the auction if you’d like it. I’ll give you an amazing deal.”

“Laura always has her eyes on upgrades. No promises on Saturday, but if I learn anything, I’ll let you know.”

“Thanks, Arvin. Bye.”

The words echo in my head like the Stevie Ray Vaughan version of Voodoo Child I’d listened to in the car at AAA

Storage.

My problem isn't so much if I learn something. It's what I've already learned that I don't want to know that bothers me.

The rest of that night and the following two nights are spent back in spreadsheet heaven. I uncover two more storage facility rentals, both in Des Moines. I put together a 6-year history of Watt Metal Forming, with sales and profitability fairly level, then a sharp decline for about 18 months, a modest increase, and then cratering. He's shown a loss for two years running. A single big expense late last year and another of about the same amount later this year pop out at me. I wonder where that second van is.

23 Thursday night

Thursday night I have the girls fed and a bottle of sauvignon blanc — the "good" stuff, for us — $19 a bottle, in the fridge. The girls are making homemade hummus from a recipe they found on the internet, to go with baked flour tortillas that we'll cut into dipping size when Laura gets home from her last final.

The girls want to dress up, so they manage to find actual dresses that I didn't know existed, and they pick out my suit, shirt and tie. We turn off all the lights in the house except the side door light and dining room lights. When Laura comes in through the door, Jess flips the switch for the kitchen and there is the wine, sparkling grape juice, chips, hummus and thinly sliced (by Hy-Vee) andouille sausage.

Hugs and kisses go all around. We eat, have a few sips, and tell each other what we've done for the past six days. Laura studied her head to shreds, which is consistent with how she has always done it. She categorizes her performance and how she feels about it.

"Cautiously optimistic. There was nothing I wasn't comfortable with, because I take good notes, read my assignments, do the work, and then review everything."

This, of course, for the benefit of the girls.

"But it's good to have it over, and now I have three weeks

before school starts again, and you two have two weeks. How are we going to spend that time?"

We go through various options and ideas until the girls and Laura yawn more than they talk. She packs the girls off to bed, and there's just one more thing left for the day.

We each take our half-glass of sauvignon blanc out to the red fabric chairs in the front yard. We go through a couple rounds of 'I've missed this' and 'different next summer because I'll be done with school,' and then I ask for five minutes.

"I'll give you five, and not a second more."

I do it quickly, starting with the small box filled with cash, work backward to the spreadsheets and the financial condition of Watt Metal Forming.

"Oh, and Carson is having an estate sale tomorrow. She says if we want any furniture to get there early and she'll pull it aside."

"I'd love a long sleep-in tomorrow morning, but an estate sale might be fun. The girls might enjoy going through her house. I don't know," she says as she stands up slowly, "right now I just want to sleep the sleep of the done-with-finals."

Which we both do. Sometimes, I'll go along for the ride.

At 9:17, the girls are up and making egg sandwiches for breakfast while I'm making coffee, having just turned off KSWT news, weather, local sports and all the drivel that's fit to chat about, when I get a text from Carson.

"Call me when you can."

I do.

"Arvin, do you remember that big armoire in George's bedroom that you and Laura looked through? I just sold it for $400."

"Wow, good . . .'

"No, that's not the thing," Carson interrupts. "The woman who bought it called her two big, strapping, Iowa-football-playing sons and her husband over, along with his truck, to take it home. They were taking it through the patio door out back when I noticed something taped to the back. There was an envelope. A 9 x 12 manilla envelope taped to the back of the armoire. I peeled it off and waited until they left."

"It's all here. George's last will and testament, dated four years and three months earlier, a $1 million life insurance policy on George, listing the beneficiary as Watt Metal Forming, from nine years ago. And titles to two different this year's model GMC Savana Vans. Plus, the papers of incorporation for Watt Metal Forming. The son of a bitch hid everything in one place, so simple, yet who would ever have looked there? If Jerry hadn't suggested an estate sale to me, I'd have sold the damn armoire along with the house to save the cost and trouble of hauling it out. And we'd never know."

"Have you read anything?"

"Oh, yeah. The will was dated the week after we got back from our honeymoon, when we were actually in love. With each other. Everything goes to me. The house, the business, the real estate that the factory is on."

"Holy cow, Carson, you must be relieved."

"You bet your sweet tea I'm relieved. Oh, and there's one more thing. A life insurance policy. For $500k. I'm the sole beneficiary. Not sure if it's current, it was purchased the same week as he did the will. I called Alice Norton, bothered her at home, but I'll drop this off at her office first thing Monday morning for her to review."

"What's the name of the insurance company."

"United First. I never heard of them, and the customer service number on the policy says they are closed until 9 am Monday."

"Hmm," I reply. I don't remember seeing United First on the expenses spreadsheet, or on the passwords paper, but I've gone through so much of that in the past few days it's all a blur. I can take a look to see if he paid it. Well, I can't tell if he paid it, but that's how I think he kept track of expenses, listed if paid and blank if not. What year was this?"

She gives me the year the policy was written.

"You've been darn busy for an early Saturday morning."

"Oh, I got up at 5 and started setting things up at 5:30. This has been kind of fun, making a big step to get out of here. Mostly bad memories in this house, Arvin, and now making good progress to move on."

"Hey good for you. Laura is still sleeping, so I guess we're not going to make your before-8 invitation."

"She deserves it. If you two — if you four get bored later, come on over. I have some beverages and snacks. Along about two or so, I may be looking for some company."

It's bit after 2:30 when we roll up the driveway. Hugs,

smiles, Havarti, hummus paired with olive crackers, brie on top of thin slices of French bread. The sauvignon blanc is a notch, no, two, over what we enjoyed last night. The girls check out the house on their own, while we talk about hummus recipes and wine. Carson gets reasonably tipsy, Laura somewhat less so, I stop after a glass and a half. Nobody mentions anything about $20 bills.

Sitting in a fabulous porch in a fabulous home, looking at the two beautiful ladies and our two spectacular daughters running around the yard is all I need.

As we walk out the door, Carson hands me a cell phone.

"It was George's, I got it back from the State Patrol along with the rest of his things. I wiped it and was going to sell it on eBay but why don't you give it to Alejandro? Tell him I'll cover the cost for a few months. Maybe it will be a small help to him."

24 A visitor to the plant

I'm still making trips almost daily to the plant, bringing food and something for Alejandro to do. Today, I want to ask him about other books he'd like to read. I also want to talk with him about $20 bills. I take a bit of time after work, knowing that Laura got off promptly at 5 pm and letting her have some time alone with the girls. Alejandro and I are sitting in George's old office when a car drives up into the parking lot. Alejandro gets up and heads down the hallway back towards the dorm.

A shorter, stocky man gets out of the car and approaches the main door. Short dark hair, large black mustache, black heavy-rimmed glasses, wearing a light blue t-shirt, faded blue jeans and work boots. He comes to the front door and presses the bell. I jump, having never heard the doorbell before. I wait until I hear the door behind me close, giving Alejandro plenty of time to get back to the dorm and lock the door. Then I go to the front door.

"Can I help you?"

"Yes," the man says in a thickly accented voice. "I am looking for a friend who I last saw here. His name is Alejandro Rodriguez. Do you know him please?"

"There is nobody here except me." I surprise myself by lying so easily.

"I was here with Alejandro and Greg some weeks ago."

"No, I don't . . . "

Before I can get any further, the door from the plant swings open and Alejandro comes running out.

"Dah-veed!" he shouts. They hug like lovers.

"Arvin, this is David. David, this is Arvin. Arvin saved my life and has kept me here, safely, since you left. David is one of my employees, used to be one of my employees, and came here with me. He went on ahead while I remained here."

We smile, shake hands and David makes the first move to a hug. I hug back, but David is much, much stronger than I. I get a massive, solid, chest-compressing hug.

"You cover for my boss, you take care of him, and you lie for him? I love you, man!"

"How did you find me?" asks Alejandro.

"There were 11 of us in the van, we had just left you, boss, behind. You expect us to sleep? We took careful notice of where we went, even though it was dark. We had no phones, no paper and pencil, so each of us memorized just three turns. Two new plus the last one. When we got to Wisconsin, we asked for paper and pencil and wrote it down. We were not leaving you behind, boss. But where is Consuelo and the rest? Is Greg here, too?"

"They are not here. Let's sit down and talk. We have much to talk about," says Alejandro.

"You sit, I will stand, I have been driving for seven hours."

"Where did you come from?" asks Alejandro.

The two friends talk as we walk back to George's office, where we make ourselves as comfortable as possible given the Spartan furnishings.

"We are in Union, Wisconsin. Chet drove us there and took two or three of us to different houses. In a week, we all had jobs, every one of us. Low pay, long hours, some in small factories, most in restaurant kitchens, but pay. He also told us about a factory building, so at night, after work, we look through the windows and it looks good, there is some equipment, but hard to see. We borrow this car from the man who owns the house I live in so I can come here to find you. Google maps, our notes, easy as anything. While I drive here, Pedro and Samuel are going with a real estate agent to look at the factory from the inside. Now you tell me what you have been doing."

The two occasionally slip into Spanish, and I can barely pick out a word here and there. But, as I hear Alejandro say, his life has been the Watt Metal Forming factory for over a month.

I sit back and watch the two converse. I do more watching than listening, truth be told. I've always liked Alejandro, and now to see him happy makes me happy. He's more relaxed than I've ever seen him before. I almost doze off, leaning back in George's chair with my feet on George's desk.

"Arvin, can David and I spend one more night here? Then I'll go back with him to Union, Wisconsin to start the next chapter of my life. David feels that it is safe there and had no problems driving here."

"Of course, and this is not my factory, it belongs to Carson. Oh, by the way, she asked me to give you this phone. It belonged to George. She thought it would be good for you to have. She'll cover a few months of the cost, she said, until you get on your feet."

"That is so nice of Carson. Please tell her goodbye for me and thank her. I will do my best to get a job and take over the cost of the phone. This phone is even nicer than the one I had back in Mexico. Very nice."

What a smile Alejandro has.

"None of us has a phone yet," says David. "We get together every day, not always all of us but most of us, to share and to plan. A phone is something we hope to get one to share with all of us. Maybe we can call home, call Consuelo to find out where she is. It would be so nice to call home and speak to Maria."

I make Alejandro promise to come by our house before he leaves for Wisconsin so Laura can tell him goodbye. He wants to be sure that Mexico is on Carson's phone plan before he does anything, so I call and verify. The two start putting in addresses and numbers into the phone, and laugh at how few phone numbers they remember.

While the two chat, I do a bit of mental homework, and figure I need an entire weekend to drive down to Liberal and check out the storage units there, then to Des Moines. Sooner is better than later. I call and ask Laura about the two of us going on a couples weekend, but she declines, preferring to stay home and catch up with the girls, since she was mentally absent over finals. I check with Carson on what to do depending on what I find.

David and Alejandro decide to leave the next day to head to Wisconsin. They ask again if they may stay the night at the factory, and promise to do all of the laundry and clean up so it is ready for the next group. They both also promise to pay for the overnight lodging, which I staunchly tell them I will not hear of. They want to leave early, and will come by our house early tomorrow morning.

The girls are still asleep when they get to our house, I'm in the kitchen catching the local news with Jean on KSWT and Laura is putting herself together for the day. Her Mom is picking up the girls and taking them on a school shopping trip, and has promised to buy them one outfit each.

Alejandro and David come in and sit down, I pour some coffee, Laura comes in, introductions are made, and David and Laura hit it off immediately. I make pancakes, we chat, and David invites us down to his brother-in-law's resort in Mexico.

"Well," David says with a huge smile and a soft chuckle, "he would be my brother-in-law if he would marry my sister. Rodrigo is manager of a very nice, very secluded resort near Tulum. You should go there. I will call Rodrigo and arrange it. What you have done for Alejandro is amazing and you need a vacation. Get away from all this for a few days. Alejandro says you will be a nurse soon?"

David says all this while talking directly to Laura.

I get enough pancakes together, we eat and talk about school, restaurant furniture, beach resorts and banking. I will miss talking to Alejandro, and David seems extremely kind. His English is not as smooth as Alejandro's but he works at it and seems happy to be able to converse with us. I'm embarrassed at my complete lack of any Spanish.

After hugs all around, they leave. My sadness at losing friends gets me through cleaning the kitchen. Laura leaves, and as I get into my car the phone rings. It's David, saying he has made arrangements with his brother-in-law for a weekend getaway for Laura and me. I object, say no, we can't take anything but he trumps me.

"Rodrigo is happy to do this. It costs me nothing. He manages this resort, very nice place, for a very busy businessman who owns it. Has been there for several years, and makes all decisions. But business has not been as strong as usual, so they have open rooms, two weeks, no, 9 days from now, Friday and Saturday night, you have not the best room in the hotel, that is taken, but the second best, very luxurious, a suite with view of the ocean. He will have a car for you at the airport, about a 30-minute drive to the hotel. When you get there, he will take care of you. He wants to thank you for what you have done for Alejandro and for all of us."

"I'll check with Laura, but honestly, David, I doubt we'll be able to do that. Our daughters are getting ready for school," I begin, but he interrupts me.

"Yes, she will be going back to finish her college work, daughters going to school too. This is a once-in-a-lifetime opportunity. Arvin, you work in a bank, you know the value of money and time. This room, Rodrigo says, is usually $450 per night. You get it for nothing. Take the time, the two of you. Grow your love."

I can't find a way to say no to that. I promise to call him back after I talk to Laura. I call her as we both head into our respective work buildings, and she actually sounds excited.

That night, we talk about it. I question the affordability, while my credit card debt is still sizable and when we have upcoming school expenses for three.

Laura disagrees.

"Arvin, Carson said she'd pay you for everything you are doing. You'll be gone all next weekend to go to Kansas and Des Moines. If those two days of hourly work don't cover the entire cost of the flight and our food and entertainment, it has to be close. This sounds like fun. Have we taken a weekend away by ourselves since Jan was born?"

I think about that, but it doesn't take long.

"No."

"Let's look at flights."

I fire up George's iMac and 27 minutes and a few hundred dollars later, we are all set. We'll drive to Minneapolis Friday noon, assuming we can each get a half day off. Back home late Sunday night. I overhear Laura on the phone telling her mom about the trip, and feel we've made a good decision. Despite my lack of Spanish and my concern about money, when I think of getting on a plane and going to a beach resort in Mexico, I do get enthused. Some sun, sand, time alone, and a change of pace. Authentic margaritas. I envision strolling a white sand beach, each of us wearing a long white shirt over our swimming suits, and selecting a dinner from a long, complicated menu. By the time I drift off to sleep, I'm ready to go.

25 Storage sheds

But that Saturday, I'm in the car and on the road at 8:46 am. A nine-hour drive brings me to a StoreAll near a huge beef packing plant on the north side of town. As I drive through the gate, my stomach is slightly sickened. Then I get to number 14, and it's identical to the one back home in Stillwell. Same model flashlight, same blue and red cardboard boxes, some unassembled, some assembled and taped, plus tape. I open one of three taped boxes and find the same thing as I found back home.

Carson picks up immediately, even though it's dinner time.

"Same thing, Carson. I opened one of three boxes. Haven't counted it yet."

"Oh, my god. Oh, my, god."

"I'll pack up the car, then get some dinner. And possibly a beverage."

"Arvin, get yourself a nice dinner. I mean a really nice dinner."

As we've agreed, I take the lock with me and leave the door to the storage unit open. Carson is calling on Monday to cancel all the rentals. Then I skip the Cattlemen's Cafe in favor of the El Amigo, which is close to my hotel. Turns out Liberal is about the same size as Stillwell, so I feel right at home. It's hard to get lost. On Sunday I get up early for the long drive to Des Moines. The radio keeps me company as I go along, especially the Royals game.

The Des Moines SpaceMan #4 is easy to find, and I drive up two aisles to unit 41. This overhead door works a little harder, and what's hidden behind it is surprising. I go back out to the car and grab the flashlight just to be sure.

The storage room is completely empty. I look at every corner, floor to ceiling, every section where the sidewalls attempt to meet the roof. Nothing. I drive 45 minutes over to SpaceMan #12 and find unit 78.

Same thing.

I call Carson first.

"Four storage units, two empty, two with boxes only. What the hell, Arvin?"

"Flashlights. Don't forget the flashlights."

"Thank you for that."

"I don't know, Carson, it's just over my head. I feel uncomfortable with all of this cash, and none of the explanation."

"I think we need a strategy session."

"Yes, and a counting party. Cash is dangerous. We need to count it and put it the bank. Have you talked to your attorney?"

"Not about the cash, Arvin. What about your guy in Des Moines?"

"Calvin? I can give you his number."

"Let's do this. Let's count and talk strategy tomorrow night."

"I'm not sure I can do that. I've been gone all weekend and I miss my family. Who knows, they might even miss me."

I feel good about making Carson giggle.

"Bring them over here. The girls can have the basement, we'll be in the dining room. I'll get pizza."

We hang up, and I drive on alone towards home. Iowa isn't the most exciting state to make long drives in, but at least it's getting dark. I'm tired, the road is as straight as an Iowa cornstalk, the radio is on and I need to wake up.

I pull into a Kum & Go, and for the four-thousandth time wonder about that name. Three sticks of beef jerky (one teriyaki), a large black coffee and a full tank of gas later, I'm back on the road. Just in time to take a call from Carson.

"Arvin, I want to write you a check tomorrow to get us up to date. Can you give me your time record and expenses when you come over?"

"Sure."

We hang up, and I give myself the mental exercise of going through my estimate of hours, my billing rate and the cost of the plane tickets to Cancun. My Laura is good. We'll have enough for the plane tickets, parking, gas and at least a good dinner when we go to Tulum.

I give the girls hugs when I get home, along with the tchotchkes I'd purchased for them in Liberal, a key ring featuring a map of Kansas for Jan and a pen that has three different ink colors in a barrel with "KANSAS" printed on the side. They are tired of waiting up for me and are already bored, so they go off to bed. Laura and I head out to the red fabric chairs, she with a small glass of pinot noir and I with a lemonade.

"Carson wants us to go over for dinner tomorrow night. The girls can have the basement and that monstrous TV while we count the cash. Pizzas and soft drinks are on her. Oh, and she's writing me a check, I have to get my time and expenses to her. I think it'll be a bit more than even you thought, Ms. Optimist."

"I'm really looking forward to going to Tulum, Mexico, Arvin. It's fun even to just say. But how much cash money do think is there? And whose is it?"

"I'm not going to play attorney here, but I think it's most likely Carson's since she owns the business and these, those boxes in the trunk of my car were in Watt storage units. I can't possibly think who else could claim them. Anyway, she's talking to her attorney whose name I've forgotten here in Stillwell, and she asked for Calvin's number too."

"Alice Norton."

"That's her name. You are good."

"You're just tired."

"That's true, too."

"Arvin, how much money do you think is there, in all those boxes? You dodged my question. Guess."

"I've been trying not to think about that. There might have been, I don't know, fifteen or twenty thousand in the one box I opened. If it's the same in the other boxes, it could be a hundred thousand or more."

"How did he get all that money?"

"It had to be from transporting Alejandro and his friends. Many other trips with other people in similar situations. Can there be any other possibility?"

We roll this around in our minds as I see Laura swirl the wine in her glass before tilting the glass and putting her nose way into it. Then she takes a small sip.

"Beth Hanlow called while you were gone. Wants to go out for dinner. Seems she's about ready to move out of town and wanted to get together one more time. Do you mind?"

"Of course not, go for it. I need to play catch up with the girls anyway. Maybe we'll do some Dad's cooking night menu planning for when you start school next week."

"Fun. I mean, not to say that I won't have fun with Beth. Her tastes in food and beverage are much more sophisticated than mine."

"Don't sell yourself short."

We stare at the sky hoping to see a shooting star, but no luck. My lemonade is long gone when Laura finishes the last of her glass of wine. We sit and relax a few minutes longer.

"He had to have been doing that for some time."

"Huh?" I reply.

"You were close to nodding off. But that big black van had to have been busy, he did more than just take Alejandro's group. He had to have been doing it for some time. How many miles are on it? Did he get it new? You're good with numbers like this."

"Sure, and there's another van, most likely, that I found an expense item for in the spreadsheets. Well, I found two amounts listed as transportation equipment in the spreadsheets, both of them in amounts that would have been about right for two vans. Just a few weeks apart, too."

"It might have been a big business. How much do you think he charged?"

"Alejandro didn't volunteer that information, and I wasn't comfortable asking. George built that dormitory, too, charged a hefty amount for each person to stay there."

"What's a van like that cost?"

"The numbers on the spreadsheet were in the low to mid-seventies. Seventy-two or seventy-four thousand maybe. I can check."

We look at each other.

"Later." It's not precisely simultaneous, but close enough.

I enjoy working the next day, because I can get up and go to the restroom, grab a coffee or start a conversation with Doris or Carol. Not being used to driving for two straight days is one thing, but the toll on my body is more than I expected. I clean up some older files and see we are still waiting on some information from Lyle Mattern, the ex-employee of Watt Metal Forming. I make a note to reach out to Lenore to see if she's had any success.

Once again, Carson does a masterful job. One pepperoni pizza for the girls with breadsticks and a cheese dip, iced tea, lemonade and one small bottle of Dr. Pepper each. For the adults, from a different take-out pizza restaurant, a large margherita pizza and fig pizza with mozzarella, prosciutto and, according to Carson, truffle oil.

We talk a bit about truffles and where their oil comes from, review the spelling of margherita and agree that we'll stick with tea and lemonade until we are done counting.

Between Carson and me, we become very organized and process-oriented. Laura, much to her credit, keeps track with sticky notes and goofy, funny comments that keep us engaged and on-track.

Each of the six boxes has a single smaller box inside it, packed with newspapers. The amounts are different from box to box, but when each of us has added the numbers from each box together, we get the same amount.

There in two of the smaller, cigar-box-size boxes is $420,640. Almost all of it in 20s, although there are a few 100s and some 50s.

We go through the math again. I suggest we come back another day and re-count. Laura goes to check on the girls and finds them asleep on the couch in the huge TV room downstairs, with an animated cartoon movie on.

Carson puts all of the cash into three of the cigar-shaped boxes, and those into one of the larger boxes. I help her carry all six boxes upstairs to what used to be George's room. The three of sit staring at my handwritten figures, while Carson heads to a cabinet and Laura to another one. They come back with glasses and a bottle of bourbon that looks expensive.

"Just one for me, please, I have to drive," I say to Carson's upraised left eyebrow. She asks us if we'd like ice, and Laura says yes. Carson puts a single, very large cube of ice into one of the glasses and then fills them to within 1/8' of the top. Nobody proposes a toast, but we all take a good mouthful.

And stare at each other.

She writes me a check, which is several hundred dollars more than I had thought, stupidly forgetting about the mileage. I threw the gas receipts away. With this, we'll be able to eat quite nicely on our weekend in Mexico.

Next day at lunch I leave a voice mail with Lenore asking about Lyle Mattern. On the way home after work, I stop at the Hy-Vee and select ground beef, Bisquick, a jar of brown gravy and some frozen peas. I've never made pinwheels before but tonight, the girls and I have planned an adventure while Mom is out for dinner with Beth.

We make a huge mess trying to get the dough to the right consistency. Jan boils water for the peas, Jess loves getting her hands all gooey and cold while mixing up the ground beef, egg and spices. I start to roll out the dough, but Jan takes over. Jess spreads out the meat mixture. We play rock, paper, scissors for who rolls it up and Jan wins, so she cuts the roll into slices. Suddenly, we realize the oven isn't on, so we do the preheating and sit and discuss friends they are looking forward to seeing in school. Surprisingly, it all comes together and is edible, if not fine dining.

I chase the girls out of the kitchen and do the dishes. We are just settling down into our comfy TV chairs when Laura gets home.

Turns out, Jan and Jess' favorite part of dinner was me doing the dishes.

I get a shortened version of the update from Beth as Laura and I slip out into the kitchen.

"She drove to Nichole's in Medina. We ate really well, a lobster bisque and I had chicken paella. We split a tiramisu for dessert. Two glasses of wine each, I could see she was ready for a third, but with the drive, she decided not to. I would have wanted to drive home, but she spared me asking that question."

"She's probably selling the Accounting business to Carson, Bill had a $500,000 life insurance policy that's paid out, and she'll clear over $300,000 from the house, expecting it to go at much less than appraised value. She says she has to report that someone died in the house as a disclosure on the listing. Did you know that?"

"It's in the back of my mind someplace, but nothing that I would have thought of."

"Her agent said it might take fifty thousand off the purchase price, although someone was coming back for a third showing tonight while we were at dinner. She listed it with what she said was a $10k discount, but wants out."

"Oh, one more thing. She knew there was life insurance, but didn't know the amount. Was surprised it was as much as it was."

"Anyway, she's all set to move to Oklahoma City. Has a job offer with a counseling service that she's excited about, a condo that she'll make an offer on as soon as the house is sold. I think it's a complete turn of the page for her, a new life."

"A new book."

"Yeah, that. She had one interesting thing to say."

"Do I get to know what?"

"She thought Bill having an affair with Carson was the most soulful thing he'd done in years."

"Soulful?"

"Her word, Arv, not mine. You know, her relationship with Bill had cooled way down and there wasn't much of a connection any more. They didn't do a lot together. They just fell into a routine and they became isolated and more distant. She said it was unforeseeable, yet consistent with his personality from the time they met. Psychological stuff, huh?"

We get the girls into bed and head to ours. As we lay there with our eyes open, a thought clarifies.

"Laura, I think Bill was similar to George in that regard. I mean, the separation from living as a couple, an intimate team. Not just physically but mentally, emotionally. Becoming cold, distant loners."

"Arv, let's not do that."

"No. No way. We stay in love. Forever."

"Passionately."

"I like the way you think."

"I'm so excited about Friday! Beth suggested we pack light and buy some fun clothes when we get to Mexico, that clothes make great souvenirs."

We trail off to sleep thinking of a long car ride, two long flights, a car ride to the resort, and all that time spent together. Comfort food.

26 Palm tree fronds and tequila

Our flight from Houston to Cancun actually arrives 19 minutes early, and going through customs was quick and pleasant. We drag our roller bags, with Laura also brining a large hand bag and me a backpack, into the lobby of the airport, looking for a door that would lead to the ground transportation. We are supposed to meet a driver from the Bonito Resort, figuring to look for a car or a van with a sign. We are surprised to see a well-dressed young man holding an iPad with 'Laura and Arvin' on it.

"You are Laura and you are Arvin?" he asks. We nod.

"I am sorry to have to ask you this, but may I please see your photo IDs."

We show him our passports, which he actually reads and holds up to compare our photos to our faces. A small thing, but I feel, if not comfortable, then less uncomfortable. He introduces himself as Miguel, and takes Laura's slightly larger roller bag.

"Please follow me to our bus."

Miguel could be 16, he might be 18, but can't possibly be a day older than 19. He has dark skin and short, curly dark hair. A crisply ironed white linen shirt, khaki shorts almost to his knees and dark brown sandals. We walk a few hundred feet towards the end of the airport terminal where there are a number of vans and busses. He leads us to a small white bus with a Bonito logo painted on the back and sides, about the same overall size as George's big black van that's sitting in Carson's factory, but taller, so Laura and I can almost stand up inside. There are four rows of seats, with bench seats for two on one side and for two on the other. Our luggage is safely ensconced in the back. Miguel directs us, if we please, to sit in the front row so he can get to know us. We do, choosing the bench directly behind the entry door. This gives us a view straight ahead as well as a side view of Miguel.

He tells us that it's only a 20-minute drive to the resort, and asks if we have fastened our seat belts. We have.

He chits and chats most of the way, telling us more about himself than asking us. Off to our left is the Caribbean, the first time either of us has seen it. When the length of our day and the gentle rocking of the bus begin to get to us, we make a left turn into the Bonita Resort.

Miguel brings the bus to a stop, and tells us that we can go directly to the check-in desk, and he will bring our bags. I grab my backpack, Laura her bag and we enter. We are happy to see directional signs are in both English and Spanish. The check-in desk is staffed by two young women of about Miguel's age.

There is no door barring our entry into the resort, just a wide-open place where a door could be but isn't. The two-story high lobby is dark, although it is late at night now, with dark wood desks and doors accented by tan-colored floor tiles of varying sizes. A handful of rattan chairs with comfortable-looking dark red cushions offer vistas of either the front entrance or to what appears to be the restaurant.

Check-in is swift, with both staff members, who are

wearing the same uniforms as Miguel, reviewing our passports. I have my Visa credit card in my hand when Clara, according to the name tag on her shirt, waves it off and hands Laura a card with the Bonita Resort logo on it, and another one to me. The next minute, Miguel is back with our bags and asks if we'd like help with taking them upstairs. We politely decline his offer.

"Rodrigo has this set up for central billing, everything goes to the master account and it is all taken care of. You have the VIP Suite, which is on the second floor. Would you like me to come up and help you become familiar with this suite?"

We look at each other. Clara smiles at us and comes out from behind the desk.

"Rodrigo has told me that you would be tired after a long day of travel. This is our restaurant here, breakfast is from six to ten, lunch eleven to two and dinner from four to eight. We have daily specials for all meals. Next door here is the bar. Down this hallway to your right are several shops that sell anything you may have forgotten, souvenirs, lotions and some beach clothing. Have you been to Mexico before?"

We shake our heads.

"Ah, well in here we make the best tequila cocktails in all of Mexico. My favorite is the Paloma, it is not as sweet as a margarita, but also the Mexican Sunset is very nice. Rum is not as popular here, but we make a good rum punch as well."

Clara takes us up the elevator. A short hallway to our left leads to VIP. There's no room number, just VIP on the door.

Our first house was smaller than this room.

"Here is a closet for Mrs. Miller, here is one for you, Mr. Miller," continues Clara. "The sitting room includes these two couches and chairs, and the TV remote is here. We have cable, but most programs will be in Spanish. Through this doorway is the bedroom, with matching bathrooms here on each side. If we go out through the sliding doorway from the sitting room, we have the balcony that is overlooking the ocean. We have magnificent sunrises here, and they are very enjoyable from the balcony. Or if you are still sleepy," she smiles, "simply press the bottom button underneath the light switch on either side of the bed, which opens the drapes. You can enjoy the sunrise from bed. Room service is available from 6 am until midnight, but sometimes a bit early or late. Just call downstairs and we will get whatever you want."

"May I take your drink orders to the bar? I will tell the bartender your preference and if you would like to unpack and settle in for a few minutes, call downstairs when you are ready and I will be sure your drinks will be ready for you when you arrive at the bar."

While Laura chooses the Paloma, I get into the theme and select a Mexican Sunset.

"Welcome to the Bonita Resort." Clara leaves, and we collapse on the bed.

"Words fail me," whispers Laura. "I've never seen anything like this."

"I'm a numbers guy."

It might have been a single minute or it might have been twenty.

"Here we are," says Laura. "We have sleep ahead of us. I think I'd like that famous drink, whatever it is. I should hang my clothes and freshen up before we go downstairs."

"Let's hang what needs to be hung up," I suggest. "You've never looked better since we met."

"Hmmpf."

I call downstairs while Laura unpacks almost everything from her bag, and one pair of pants and two shirts from mine. As we stroll down the stairs and along the hallway, then into the bar, I'm surprised to see just a few people, and the bar is virtually empty.

Clara was right about the drinks, they are waiting, along with a personal guide to our table, which is outside, underneath a portico, with a few huge fronds of palm between us, a strip of grass, and the ocean. Bartolo guides us to our table, holds out a chair for Laura and bows slightly as he departs.

"Do you get the impression that Rodrigo is overdoing it just a bit?" I ask as I take a testing sip. It's good, if a bit sweet, so I go back to the glass for a more nuanced, careful, intentional second taste.

"Mmmn, mine is not so sweet," affirms Laura. We're strangely silent, for us, perhaps due to the work-pack-drive-airport-change-airport-bus-hotel day we've just had. Spending all that time within elbows of each other is not unusual, but the intimacy is. I feel really close, and when I catch Laura's eyes, I feel she does as well.

We sip, and gaze, and when Bartolo comes back with a questioning in his eyes, we dutifully nod, smile, and say "si."

"Laura, upon careful and thoughtful evaluation, I think that is my entire Spanish vocabulary," I offer.

"Liar, I've heard you say margarita many times."

Bartolo is back already, and I'm impressed.

"How did he do that so quickly?"

"And so well?"

"How did we do it, Arv? How did we get from there to here?"

I'm a bit taken aback. And I don't want to go back.

"Seriously, we are in the most fantastic place I've ever seen. We're together. Really together." She reaches out and takes both my hands. We stare at each other a while. The breeze off the ocean waves the palms and the light rustle of the huge fronds melds with the sound of waves, as even and as relaxing as anything I've ever known. I'm in a trance. Entranced.

"We've been fortunate, lucky if you prefer," I finally answer. "You with two classes left for your BSN, I with a solid, stable job. All this with George, Alejandro, Carson, it all came fast and from nowhere. You have to admit, it's been interesting."

"Yes, interesting, true. Don't forget Lenore, who I really like. She and Linda are so good with the girls."

"And you haven't met Calvin, Calvin Johnson. I still have some of my credit card debt to go, but we're OK financially and . . ."

"Forget money for a few days, Arvin. I have other things to discuss."

"Oh?" Suddenly, I'm worried. Which is the perfect time for Bartolo to come over. How does he do this?

"I am sorry, madam and sir, but we will be closing for the night in a few minutes. If you like I can make you another drink or two and you are welcome to stay here in the bar for as long as you care. It is a beautiful view, isn't it, and the soft air and sounds. Very romantic," he smiles.

We take him up on his offer of one more round, and as he places the drinks on our table, I pull out my Bonita Resort key card.

"No need, Mr. Miller, we know you are in the VIP. It is all taken care of."

"Well damn," I say.

"I'll have none of that, Mr. Miller," retorts Laura in a sharper-than-necessary tone. "Let's go back to what Bartolo mentioned as 'romance.'"

"The gentle sounds, the darkening ocean, the cold of the alcohol and fruit juices, and the stunning beauty of my wife have made this one incredible evening," I say.

"Arv, you know I love it when you talk dirty."

Despite the incredibly long day it's been, we linger over our drinks. It's a different, stress-less world here. My senses are overloaded, although it could be the rum. We go back through the lobby, past a couple of small stores offering sunscreen, hats, souvenir t-shirts and swimwear. I start to walk past the elevator to the door marked 'stairs' when Laura speaks up.

"That's for tomorrow. Tonight, we ride."

I take a step backward and push the button.

While Laura is changing, I check out the button for the electrically-operated curtain. It's simple enough even I can figure it out. Press and hold until you want it to stop, but it stops automatically when the curtains are fully opened. I hadn't noticed because the curtains were partly closed, but the balcony ends about halfway through this room, so not only can one lay in bed and look out to the ocean, but there is no balcony railing in the way.

When I come out of my bathroom, Laura is standing in front of the window looking out at the sea. She's turned out the small night light, but I can see just well enough to know that she's naked.

"You look as good as that view."

"Nobody can see in here, no lights, no buildings between us and the ocean. I suppose someone on a boat out there could have a very high-powered set of binoculars though. I'm willing to take that chance. I hope you don't mind, but I opened the windows as well as the curtains. We can feel the breeze and hear the ocean, although the palms aren't as noticeable here as they were in the bar. The breeze is really like a dream."

She turns partially around, so I get about a three-quarter profile of her silhouetted against the Caribbean.

"Electrifying."

I take the few steps covering the distance between us, and we embrace.

"Electrifying, indeed," I repeat.

There's a pause the length of three waves breaking.

"Seems it's affected both of us."

"Let's both investigate."

27 Beach heaven

Thanks to the sun, we wake as just a quarter of it is visible over the horizon. I suggested Laura take the side of the bed closer to the window, and my view over her to the sunrise is beyond anything I've ever experienced or dreamed. We lay and watch the sunrise, go back to sleep, and wake up starved.

"Today is beach day," she says softly as the sunlight spills across her bare shoulders. "Do we dress for the beach or for breakfast?"

"For breakfast. Too much sun makes for an early demise, a wise lady once told me."

She chuckles, and we shower. Laura slips on some white linen pants that I've never seen before, snug at the waist but draped to flow over her legs. A lemon-yellow top that's also new, small enough to be interesting to me and just large enough to be comfortable for her.

The breakfast menu is short, but complete. We choose eggs with chorizo, potatoes and peppers. It wasn't listed as huevos rancheros on the menu, but that's what it seems to be. Bartolo is not behind the bar, thank goodness, but our server suggests a Bloody Maria, which seems like a Bloody Mary with tequila instead of lime juice. Isabel brings one for us to share together, which we do, and promptly order another.

She comes back just before my plate is empty.

"Coffee or another Bloody Maria?"

"I'll have coffee please," I say.

"None for me," replies Laura.

"Arv, while you drink your coffee, do you mind if I run into that store in the lobby? I want to get some extra sun screen."

"Sounds good," I play along.

"I'll meet you back in the room, and then it's the beach."

Her peck on my lips lasts somewhat longer than I anticipate. I linger on that thought as I linger on my coffee, knowing my Laura. I wave Isabel over and proffer my card, and I get the same story as Bartolo gave me last night.

"Everyone knows you are in the VIP suite. It's all taken care of."

I take the stairs, and when I get to the room, Laura is ready to go. Same pants but now with a loose fitting pale blue blouse in a similar linen material. I slip into my suit, toss my second-to-best shirt on, we grab our things and head to the beach.

The walkway takes us to the beach, where a sign reads 'en topless' with an arrow to the right. I stop to consider, but Laura casually turns to the right. We touch hands and walk, me with my feet completely in the water, Laura just above me on the beach, her toes being lapped by each wave.

"Let's walk to the end of the resort property and look for a place to lay. Just a bit of exploring to start the day."

"Sure."

"I brought some more lotion, but one hour soaking up the sun should be our limit. Walking excluded as long as we have hats and shirts."

Every 20 feet or so there is an umbrella stuck into the sand, with two lounge chairs placed underneath. These vary in color from bold primaries to soft, more subtle shades of blue, red, orange, and yellow. A hundred yards or so down the beach the umbrellas stop, but the chairs continue. We wander for about 10 minutes until we see a sign that signals the end of the Bonita Resort property. There are maybe 20 people on this entire stretch of beach, well scattered out except for one group of eight. We're about in the middle of the age range here, the group of much younger people excepting. About a third of the women are topless.

When we reach the Bonita Resort signpost, Laura reaches out, touches it, turns around, says "let's race" and takes off running. I touch the sign, turn and run, but she's ten or twelve feet ahead of me. We get past two couples to a gap where there are no other people, and she stops.

"How does this look?"

"Great. Should I grab some lounge chairs or just toss our towels on the sand?"

"Lounge chairs."

I walk a few feet to grab the two medium yellow ones closest to us. As I place them next to Laura, I watch her pull off her shirt and pants to reveal a dark, royal blue bikini I've not seen before. Not that there's much to see.

"New bikini?"

"Yes, what do you think?"

"How does one say 'WOW' in Spanish?"

"We should find out."

I draw a circle in the air with my hand, and Laura turns around slowly, one leg bent, as if she's dancing.

"After two kids, do I still have it?"

"Baby, you got it all."

She lays the lounger flat, sits down, turns and lays on her stomach. I stand and watch.

"I saw it at the little shop in the hotel. It looked cute and seemed to fit. We should go in there and get the girls a souvenir. I saw some shirts they may like."

I stand and look.

"Arv, set your phone for 30 minutes. Then it's time to turn over."

I do as requested, and when I look up I see her hands moving away from her back. She's untied the top of the bikini.

"Would you like some lotion on your back?"

"No, we did that in the room. I don't trust your hands. Now, be quiet. I want to listen to the waves."

When my phone alarm goes off, I realize I've been sleeping. I give Laura a soft "hey," then roll over onto my back and pull up the backrest of my lounger to a semi-seating position. I notice Laura is now laying on her back, with her new blue bikini top on, but the straps aren't tied. I look out and watch a few waves come in. When I wake up, I notice Laura has her top off completely, and see it laying in the sand. I move quietly, grab my phone and take a photo. I'm still awake when my alarm goes off. She stands and hands me her bikini top, slips on her shirt and buttons it. I put her top in my pants pocket and we walk into the hotel.

As we are heading for the stairs, a loud voice behind us calls our names.

"Mr. and Ms. Miller!"

We don't recognize the man. He comes up to us smiling.

"I am David's friend Rodrigo, and welcome to the Bonita Resort. I am sorry I was not here last night to welcome you. Is everything to your satisfaction?"

"Everything is spectacular," replies Laura.

"Have you just come from the beach?" We nod.

"Would you like a tour of the hotel? It will take just a few minutes." We nod.

"First, let me apologize that the honeymoon suite was not available. I can move you in tonight if you would prefer it, our guest has had to cancel."

We assure him that we are more than comfortable.

"As you wish. The Bonita has 140 rooms, all on one level except for this building here. The bar and our four suites are on the second level. Have you had a chance to visit the bar?"

We mumble something about Bartolo.

"Ah, yes, he is very good. Will you take a walk with me for a few minutes?"

"Here are three stores, sundries, clothing, and take-away beverages for your room or beach. Anything you want, my treat. David has told me you have two young daughters, correct? Maybe you want to get them a souvenir here to surprise them when you get home."

"Come this way. Past the restaurant is a private dining room. We can easily have up to 40 diners in here, sometimes it is used for wedding celebrations or family reunions and events."

We get to the end of the hallway and walk back towards the lobby.

"Here on our right is the personal quarters of our owner, Phil. He owns many businesses, so he is here only sometimes. He has a room similar to, well, maybe a bit nicer than the honeymoon suite upstairs, and then this private meeting room through this door. Very large and spacious. Sometimes he hosts his business associates here. He had a party that was to use the honeymoon this weekend, but canceled, and they will be here only for a meeting tomorrow. If time permits, I will introduce you."

"Rodrigo," I begin, "this is spectacular, very, very nice of you. But it is too much."

"As you can see, we are not so busy. The true cost to me is what you eat and drink and the souvenirs, all at my cost. It's not so much. But the truth is, you helped David and Alejandro. David and I are very tight, very tight. I have been dating his sister for three years, we will get married one day. That will make David happy, too. You, Mr. Miller, and you, Ms. Miller, David has told me what you have done, taking food to Alejandro for many weeks, keeping everyone safe, and even inviting the two of them into your home and meeting your two daughters. See, he has told me all of this."

"Finally, just last week, Alejandro gets a phone. He says you gave him this phone. It was hard when we did not know where they were or what was going on with them."

"Actually, it was a gift from a friend of ours."

"But it came from your hand. There are 12 people, men and women, and one phone. It is amazing to me. I know many of the people who you hosted, not all of them, but many."

We turn a corner and walk to an outside patio adjoining the owner's meeting room, walk past this into a small outdoor garden area that connects the main building with the next hotel building over. We stop walking while he points out a few flower varieties that have attracted Laura's gaze.

"Have you heard anything of the other four people who were supposed to cross the border?" he asks.

I have to think for a minute.

"No, Alejandro said there were 12 in his group, and financial issues prevented him from moving on past Stillwell. Now that you mention it, I do remember that he said there were to be a total of 16 employees taking the trip, and that one person, maybe an artist, was in charge of that group. I'm sorry, but I don't remember the name he gave me."

"Ah, that would be Consuelo, no doubt. Have you heard anything from her?"

"We are not directly in the loop," clarifies Laura. "We are

way out on the periphery."

"I see. Well, perhaps now that Alejandro has a phone, he can call her."

"I remember when I handed Alejandro and David the phone, they had problems remembering any phone numbers. It was amusing, actually, and quite, quite sad, to watch them recite a name and try to remember numbers. They were alternately frustrated and laughing."

"Oh, you give me a great idea! I know Consuelo, we went to school together. Do you have Alejandro's new phone number?"

We pull out our phones, I read off the number and Rodrigo texts it to Consuelo. Almost instantly he gets a response consisting of a smiling emoji.

"You have done another good thing today, Mr. Miller, and you as well, Ms. Miller. I won't take any more of your time. If I can help in any tiny way, please call me. Do you have plans for today?"

"No."

"If you would like to go to see some sites, there are some fantastic ruins not far, also nearby is a wonderful area for snorkeling. I can arrange this for you if you would like."

"Sure, that would be great."

"Here, step outside." He waves to a car out on the road, lingering just off the driveway to the hotel. He speaks a few words to the driver, and money is exchanged.

We get into a small green car for the short drive to the ruins, then get into a boat and pretend to learn how to snorkel. On the way back, as we snuggle in the back seat, Laura puts her head on my shoulder and whispers.

"I was a bit sorry I did not have time to change into my other bathing suit. Thank goodness you had part of my bikini in your pocket."

"I always try to think ahead."

When we get back, we buy t-shirts and matching sandals for the girls. Again, our room card is refused.

Laura changes into a different outfit for dinner. A blue and grey pattern on linen pants that tie in front paired with a daring, brilliantly white open-front shirt that's cut very, very low and shows off the blue bikini top she wore for part of the day. When we sit down for dinner, Isabel, our server from breakfast, places a Paloma in front of Laura and a Mexican Sunset in front of me.

"Compliments of Bartolo."

We look behind the bar and wave. Bartolo waves back.

"Here are menus for tonight, but Rodrigo has asked me to recommend some things to you. First, a green bean salad sprayed with olive oil, sea salt, pepper and fresh basil. Then, fresh lobster. We can prepare that any way you like, but Rodrigo recommends the Lobster Thermador. This is lobster removed from the shell and prepared with butter, eggs, brandy, cremini mushrooms and six or eight other ingredients that even I do not know, and then placed back into the shell. Very simple to eat and no shells to crack. And for dessert, our classic Creme Brûlée, with caramelized local sugar."

We instantly hand the menus back to Isabel. In five minutes she's back.

"Rodrigo says you should enjoy this with your salad." She puts a martini glass in front of each of us that's the size of Carrol County, Iowa.

Dinner is dazzling. An after-dinner walk on the beach is magical. We sit on our balcony and listen to the gentle power of the waves. A knock on the door, and a waiter we do not recognize delivers two snifters and a small bottle of brandy. Charles, according to his name tag, pours a healthy shot into each glass, places each glass onto a separate wire rack, and lights a tea light under each one.

"About 15 seconds, then enjoy," he says. "Now, hold the bowl of the glass in your hands to keep it warm," he instructs as he hands one to Laura and one to me. "There is more in the bottle, for seconds, and here are matches."

All-in-all, the best day of my life, excluding the days Jan and Jess were born.

28 We have this taken care of

Next morning, we pack most of our things back into our bags, as our bus leaves at 10:30. Miguel has already called the room to remind us. Laura pulls out yet another new outfit (where did she get these? how did they all fit in her roller bag?), today with light tan sandals, light green capris and a relatively modest, short-sleeve, V-neck top in basic white. I've put on my other pair of tan shorts and my light red mixed with dark red, second-best golf shirt.

On our way to the restaurant, we see Rodrigo speaking to a tall, broad-shouldered man. He's wearing a dark suit, no tie, but a dress shirt. Rodrigo motions us over.

"Phil, this is Mr. and Mrs. Miller, Arvin and Laura, the people I was telling you about who helped Alejandro and have been staying with us for just two days. They leave late this morning."

All of us shake hands and exchange pleasantries. Laura comments on the beach, the food and the room. We both thank him profusely. In just a moment, Phil apologizes and walks into his meeting room.

Unlike last night's dinner, we use the menu for breakfast, and both select fish tacos, Laura hot and spicy and me just spicy. It's true, they are not as spicy as the Bloody Maria.

We linger a bit over breakfast, planning a walk on the beach in both directions. We have time for a bit of sun, but decide we got more yesterday than was probably wise. I order coffee and Laura has a second orange juice when we hear what I think are loud fireworks, one, then another in quick succession, and just an instant later, a third.

The sounds seemed to come from the hallway near Phil's meeting room. I turn my head to look that way and see the backs of two men running towards the outdoor garden, a server I don't know standing a few feet from the door with a petrified look on her face, Rodrigo sprinting up the hallway towards the meeting room and just two steps behind him is Laura.

It takes a few seconds for that to sink into my brain. I dumbly look back at the chair opposite me, assure myself that Laura is not sitting in it, turn and look again as Rodrigo and Laura reach the meeting room, and haul my own ass over in that direction.

It only takes a few seconds to get to the doorway of the meeting room, and when I do, I see Phil laying on the floor alongside a long, rectangular wood conference table, Laura kneeling beside Phil and Rodrigo standing nearby, tapping on his cell phone.

"Someone get me gloves from the kitchen and cloth napkins. Lots of them."

It takes me a moment to realize that was Laura's voice. I look up, turn around and sprint to the kitchen. Inside, I mime hands and gloves and a woman picks up a box and starts to pull out a glove. I grab the box from her hands, find the server station, pick up a handful of cloth napkins and sprint back.

I overhear Rodrigo on the phone, but he's speaking very rapidly in Spanish and I can't understand a word. I pull out two gloves and hold them out to Laura, who takes them without looking at me. She takes a gloved handful of napkins and puts them on Phil's chest and pushes down.

There's blood everywhere, leaking from beneath the light blue napkins, down Phil's shirt, pooling on his jacket, puddling on the floor. Laura is sweating as she pushes down, the beads growing on her forehead. I see her look once, twice at Phil's neck and wrist, and guess she'd like a third hand to check for a pulse.

"More napkins."

I race out, back to the server station, grab every napkin there, and get back. Laura nods, and takes a breath.

"Can you put them around? If I let up pressure, he'll die."

I do the best I can, nervous about where . . .

"GLOVES!"

I dig into the box, pull them on as fast as I can. Which is slow, very slow compared with what Laura did.

"Fold them thickly and go around the edges."

I do. Just as I reach for another napkin, there's a commotion behind us. Someone gently takes my shoulder and pulls me back. I see that it's an EMT, gloved, masked and dressed in a paper-like suit. I yield my space; he puts his hand on Phil's neck. I watch Laura's eyes as she shifts her gaze back and forth from her hands, the napkins and Phil's chest to the hand on Phil's neck. The hand moves away, and I see Laura relax the pressure.

The EMT and Laura stand up, and I am surprised to see myself standing too, and to see three other EMT's in the room, which is now filling with police. Rodrigo comes over to Laura and I with towels, and as I wipe my hands, I see the towel that Laura is using grow red as she wipes her hands and forearms.

"Restroom?" I ask.

Rodrigo points to a door at the far end of the room, I go in and am violently ill.

The EMTs bring in sanitizing materials and assist Laura and I to clean up. They give her a few bottles and some materials and talk to her, as I stand nearby, overcome and numb. One policeman, dressed a bit differently than the others, asks me some questions, and the answers I give seem to satisfy him. He seems to be writing down everything in a notebook. He asks where we live, and for a phone number and address.

"Your wife?" he asks and points.

"Yes." He walks over to Laura. Same questions, same answers. I see him compare Laura's answers to mine. Then he asks about what she did, and asks if she is a physician. Again, the answers seem to satisfy him. He has a policeman take a few photos, looks about for shells, then turns to Rodrigo.

"Rodrigo," I hear him say. The rest is in Spanish, and I see him gently lead Rodrigo out the door of the meeting room and towards the main door.

"Arv, let's go get washed up."

"Sure."

As we head upstairs, I notice three or four dark blue vehicles out front, all with flashing red and blue lights. I see an ambulance pull up. Its lights are not flashing.

I'm in the shower and Laura is drying her hair when she hears a knock on the door. The peephole reveals Rodrigo, Laura asks my opinion, and she closes the bathroom door then opens the hotel room door to let Rodrigo in. I call it good, rinse off, dry quickly, pull on my shorts and wrap a towel around my shoulders.

"Mr. Miller, I was just expressing my most sincere regrets to Ms. Miller. This is a horrible, unspeakable thing. But I am so proud of Ms. Miller, she was the first person there, faster than Gabrielle whose only job today was to serve Phil's needs at this meeting. I have never seen anything like this."

"Are we in any trouble?" I ask.

"No, I do not think there is trouble here for anyone. These two men here for the meeting, well, one of them was the man I spoke to you about who had to cancel his overnight stay. He has been here several times before. Phil has businesses with him, at least two other companies. Not this hotel business. And not Phil's transportation business." He smiles thinly at this last comment.

"I am so sorry that your stay with us here has been ruined. I hope you will not carry any mental scars with you. I wish that you will return to join us here at a happier time."

"Please forgive me, but the events today have shaken me. What time was your trip to the airport to be?"

I tell him.

"Maybe it would be best if you go a bit early."

Laura looks at her watch.

"We'd hoped for a stroll on the beach before we left, but I agree," she says. "You probably need to clean this room for your next guest." She returns Rodrigo's thin smile.

"I will get Miguel to bring the bus around, and he will come to help you with your things. If any of your clothes have any stains on them, please throw them away here. Replace them when you get home, and send me the bill."

He and I shake, and he and Laura exchange a brief hug.

"Ms. Miller, you are the hero of the day. So quick, so calm and so skilled."

"I didn't do anything."

"You did everything for Phil. I will not forget your heroic actions."

We finish packing and are walking out the door just as Miguel comes down the hallway. Laura has left her sandals and green capris in the hotel trash can. We walk together down to the elevator, and head out to the waiting van, Laura with her head down except for the briefest glance down the hallway to the meeting room. Her eye lingers for a moment. Then we go through the doorway to the bus.

Laura and I have been married long enough that some portion of our communication is non-verbal. Our chatter with Miguel is muted, consisting of light comments regarding the ocean, traffic and air quality. The discussion between the two of us is tempered until we get into Laura's car at the Minneapolis airport, ready for a two-hour-plus drive home.

29 Unpacking

“I just didn’t want to say anything that could be overheard.”

“I thought so, too."

“It was a professional hit.”

“Clearly. And just as clearly, Rodrigo is right. You are a hero.”

“Bullshit.”

“Trueshit.”

I drive for a couple of miles before I ask her about what she did in the meeting room.

“Arv, I’ve done a handful of shifts in the ER, but never a bullet wound. I’ve been assigned to some major trauma patients, horrible traffic accidents, but by the time I get them, they’ve been pretty well cleaned and stitched. This was . . . gory.”

“God, you handled it well.”

“I don’t know, Arv. He died. Phil, a man we had just met, died. Can I tell you about it? It may help both of us process what happened this morning.”

“If you can speak it, I can listen.”

"I didn't get much of a glimpse of the wound, it was a mess and he'd already lost a ton of blood. That's not accurate. He might have lost a quart by the time I got there. There were two wounds, one I believe directly to the center of his heart, the other a bit above and to his left. The third wound somewhere below and to the right, rib and into the lung territory. He was clearly in shock when I got there, having lost all that blood. Direct pressure is the only way to stop it."

"I didn't think to ask if there was a first aid kit handy, some packing would have been more efficient than the napkins. The direct pressure, no, we study this kind of thing, but reading about it is unlike actually doing it. I wonder what a doctor would have done."

"Probably no more than you did." I take my right hand off the steering wheel and squeeze her left hand.

"I'd ask Dr. Williams, but, and this is what I've been struggling with, do we tell anybody about this? I can come up with as many reasons not to as to."

We're silent for some time, then Laura calls her Mom, tells her when we should be back, and to let the girls stay up if they want to.

We pull into our driveway and are greeted by two grinning, smiling bundles of pure joy. Laura pulls out the sandals and shirt souvenirs, plus a rather gaudy bracelet for her Mom. We grab a bite of cold turkey, a glass of iced tea, and head to bed without coming to a decision. Do we keep it in or let it out?

Sleep comes hard, but it comes. So does waking up at 3:37 am. When I turn over, so does Laura.

"You, too, huh?"

"Yes. Laura, I don't think what happened is going to be a brag story for me, and not even for you, but I do think we should share the story. Your Mom will be proud of you and so will your colleagues. You can learn from this."

"I was coming to the same conclusion. It's not like we did anything wrong. I tried the best I could. Two bullets to the heart and a third nearby isn't likely a survivable event."

"I want to find out what Phil's role was in what Rodrigo called the 'transportation business.' I have to think there's a connection."

"And one that's ended now. Whatever Phil did, he's dead, George's dead, too."

"George isn't dead because of this."

"Neither is Phil. Wait. You don't think Bill's murder had anything to do with the business?"

"No, Carson said he was just a jealous, controlling jerk. Did she tell you that the night before Bill was killed, they'd had an argument?"

"No."

"I forget what she said it was about. I do remember what she told me was the last thing she said to George. She told him 'I'm going out to get a good fuck!' slammed the door and left. Spent the night at a hotel, not with Bill, either. Alone, she told me."

"Jesus, I didn't know that."

Not a sleep-inducing fact, but our mutual exhausted silence

eventually works.

Next morning, as I head out to work, she reminds me, "Classes start Wednesday, and Thursday is a late night too. Are you ready for your last semester of Dinner by Dad?"

"Yes, and no. I'll be interested to hear what Dr. Williams has to say."

"And I want to know what Carol and Doris have to say."

We lock eyes, touch lips, linger there, and go on to our Monday.

I text Lenore, ask her to call. I call her at her suggestion that evening and ask her to look around her sources for news of a murder in Tulum. I spend some time on George's iMac, and list a few Dinner by Dad ideas for discussion with Jan and Jess. I hear back from Lenore later that evening.

"I have news. But first, I have a meeting scheduled tomorrow that I thought you'd like to know about. Tomorrow at 3:30. With Clyde Simpson."

That name takes a while to register. I'm still in Mexico mentally.

Lenore seems to hear my silence. "The state Attorney General."

"Yes, oh, yes." I try to cover. "What's on his agenda?"

"Not his, mine. I requested a meeting, using my now well-honed 'trying to make connections' strategy. I want to find out what he may know about immigrants. Oh, yes, I did get a chance to talk to Lyle Mattern. Just after he lost his job at Watt Metal Forming, he did a couple, actually three, off-the-record-cash-only jobs for George."

"Driving a van."

"Exactly. Briefly, I think he was at the tail end of the pipeline, dropping off one here, two there, and so on."

"That would fit."

"And I didn't see any news from Tulum or from Cancun. Beyond a few deaths that appear to be gang-related. Did you know that some areas of Cancun are not as safe as, say, your front yard?"

"In your professional opinion, does that surprise you?"

"No. I think after I talk to Clyde, we should get the group back together."

"You're on a first name basis?"

"I will be by this time tomorrow."

I roll that around in my mind while I finish up a third spreadsheet, a summary, for Carson. It's getting late, almost 10, the girls are sleeping and Laura is watching what she calls junk TV when my phone rings. It's Calvin Jenkins.

"Mr. Miller, I apologize for calling you so late in the evening. Do you have just a moment or two?"

"Yes, of course. How are you, Calvin?"

"I'm fine. Thank you for asking. I had not meant for this to drag on so long, and for that I apologize. I have reviewed your situation and am ready, with your permission, to close the file. My opinion is that you will not be prosecuted. For one, there is no witness who can specifically place you at Mr. Hanlow's house at a particular date and time. Two, we don't know, and have no way of ever knowing, what Mr. Watt may have done or may not have done with the knowledge he gleaned through your services. Finally, and I think this is a key point as well, is that there is no individual likely to file a civil case, and to the best of my knowledge there is no active criminal investigation into Mr. Hanlow's murder. I can write a formal statement of that if you'd like."

"Actually, yes, I think I would like a short statement in writing. The words you just said would be fine. You know, I'm an accountant and I like to have everything perfected."

"I understand and will mail that to you tomorrow. On the topic of my fee, I owe you somewhat of a refund, as I have spent less time on this matter than I anticipated. With your permission, I'll enclose a check along with my written opinion."

"Thank you, that will be fine." I walk over to where Laura is sitting, wearing a faded blue nightshirt, legs tucked up underneath her. I show her the face of my phone so she knows who is calling, and pantomime a thumbs up.

"If I may ask, Mr. Miller, how are you and your family doing?"

I put my left hand on Laura's head and pretend to comb her hair.

"Just perfect, Calvin. Things have never been better here at home."

The next day, my phone rings as I am driving home. Lenore wants to get everyone together. I ask about her meeting with the AG, but she prefers to tell the story one time. A dozen or so texts later, we agree to meet at Riverside Park on Saturday morning. We'll bring the girls along, and we'll do a group picnic."

30 The interview

The girls are off playing on the small swings and single slide as we unpack baskets of food. Beverages first, all non-alcoholic due to park rules.

I've finally upped my sartorial game, after a quick visit to Kohl's. A light blue linen shirt over a pair of light gray shorts and a new pair of walking sandals, black with orange highlights. Laura has also dressed for the occasion, eschewing her usual sports/fitness wear for a burgundy jumpsuit, fairly low-cut in front with a lace back panel.

Carson pulls up and steps out of her car wearing a dark sage green maxi skirt, that's maxi in the back and knee length in the front. Strappy white sandals and a white crop that leaves a couple inches of her midriff bared.

Lenore, carrying a small white bag, is casually attired in a loose-fitting, striped black, white and grey V-neck top over wine-red capris, starts. "He told me when we scheduled the meeting not to bring my cell phone, or any electronic device into the building. Nothing is allowed. I've been in courtrooms there, I know this, but I let it slide. He did say that some car remotes also set off the alarm."

"I get to the Judicial Center, get through security and into his office. It's my day off, so while I'm casual, I'm clearly not there on a particular story. Not too casual though, a light sweater over my blouse, better slacks, dressy sandals. I remark about the view from his office window, overlooking the park. He says he often goes running down the riverwalk after work. I suggest we walk in the park rather than talk in his office, and he agrees."

"We wander past that new Bubble Tea place on 5th, and I comment on it. He's not interested, but would have an iced tea from Panera. We go in, get in line, and while we wait to place our order I nip out to the restroom. When I come back, I'm wearing this, which Linda has conveniently taped into the inside door of the stall closest to the restroom just seconds after Clyde and I walked in the door."

Everyone's gaze shifts to Linda, who is even more casual. Capris of a jean-like material in a blue jean-like color with a royal blue bikini top, not unlike the one Laura wore in Mexico, peeking out from underneath a crisply ironed collared white shirt, with sleeves rolled up and only the two middle buttons buttoned. Linda reaches into Lenore's white bag and puts something on the picnic table.

"A flash drive."

"Ah, ye of insufficient technology knowledge. This is a USB Voice Recorder. Up to 24 hours of continuous recording. Turns on automatically whenever there is sound, turns off when there's silence. And fits conveniently and discretely."

Lenore pulls the V of her top out and drops the device down her front. She lets go of her shirt, and although I don't stare, I can't see it.

"I positioned it a bit better than this in the Panera restroom."

"We wanted some record of the discussion," adds Linda. "Clyde knows damn well that Lenore knows the policies and procedures of the Judicial Center. He was making a point when he mentioned about leaving her cell in the car."

"So we walk along the couple of blocks to get to the trail in the park. He happens to mention that he likes to have one-on-one discussions on walks in parks. No note taking, no recordings, just thinking time, he said."

"Why did he want a private conversation, if I may ask?" says Carson.

"He's thinking about running for Governor, which means he is, and he essentially offered me a job as his communication director. But that's not why I thought you'd want to hear this," she says as she reaches into the bag and pulls out a laptop.

"But that part is at the end of our discussion. Let me see if I can queue this up to the right place. Remember when I had dinner with Detective Chad Lance? He told me he knew George Watt and Clyde from college days. I asked him if he stayed in touch."

She plays with the PC for a moment, listens, hits a button then another, then cranks up the volume.

"I think Clyde tells a very interesting story, and you can hear it in his own words and his own voice. Here we are."

"I understand you went to school at Iowa with George Watt and Chad Lance. Do the three of you stay in touch?

"You're thorough. Yes, although I was a year or two ahead of them. Can't say we were great friends, might have gone out for a beer once or twice."

"The three of you," Lenore's voice is clearer on the recording.

"No, well, maybe. That's a long time ago, a couple of decades ago or so. It's possible. Why do you ask?"

Clyde's voice is darn clear, too, I marvel as I look at the gizmo sticking out the side of Lenore's laptop. And I smile again as I see myself mentally on a first-name basis with the State AG. Although he doesn't know it.

"Oh, part of it is the 'degrees of separation' concept. Or the stars are in alignment. Did you ever meet Carson, George's wife?"

"Never had that pleasure."

"A friend of mine is helping her wrap up his company. He says it's a bit more complicated than he expected, and has found a few surprises."

"Hmm. What did you want to talk to me about?"

"Well, my General Manager, together with my direct supe, the News Director, have asked all the reporters to develop good relationships with the top people in government, business, non-profits and so on so that when we have a particular story or a question, we can reach out to you."

"You mean so I take your call."

"You're very perceptive. That's it exactly."

"OK, you convinced me. I'll take your next call. And if it's a good call, I'll take your next call."

"Actually, I need your help. You have access to information, sources and databases that I don't. I'm trying to get some information on a murder that took place on Sunday at a resort in Tulum, Mexico."

"Why do you care about that?"

"I'm asking for a friend."

"Are we finished here?"

"A friend who was there when it happened. Who got to Phil before anyone else. My friend who gave him first aid. Who felt his heart stop while both her hands were on it."

"How do you know the deceased man's name?"

"My friend was introduced to him less than an hour before he was killed."

"And your interest is?"

"Personal. A man was brutally murdered by two men, and there's no mention of it in any media I can find. And I looked. The local PD won't return my calls. But also human interest. There was a reason Phil was killed and she wants to know. It seems when you're up to your elbows in another person's blood and you feel their heart stop, you develop a connection. I think she'd like to be able to sleep at night without drugs."

There's an uncomfortably long pause. Lenore puts two hands, palms down, then just one finger up.

"What do you want to know?

"Who killed him and why?"

"What are you going to do with the information?"

"This is of no interest to our viewers. It's for personal use. I want to calm my friend's mind. She needs to know that no one is coming after her or her family."

"Would anyone have a reason to?"

"Go after her? Absolutely not."

"This has to stay private."

"Absolutely will."

"And you'll owe me a favor. Professional."

Lenore makes a hand gesture.

"If it's legal, moral and ethical, yes."

"What was the name of the resort?"

"Bonobo or Bombata or something. I think it was the name of an ocean fish. I'm an Iowa girl, never been to Mexico."

"Close enough. I knew the man to some degree. Phil had a lot of businesses, some of them legal, some of them not so much, some in the middle. This was payback from a business associate."

"Was one of his businesses involved in transporting illegal immigrants into the US?"

"What the hell makes you think that?" This in a sharp, clipped, pointed, wet outburst of words.

"Another friend in Mexico and my friend who is helping Carson."

"Carson?"

"George Watts' widow."

"Of course. How do you make a connection between Phil

and George Watt?"

"Admittedly, I'm putting two and five and twelve together and coming up with 27.036."

"Cute. No, Phil wasn't killed because of the transportation business. It involved another associate in a completely different business."

"How do you know Phil?"

"I met him once on a trip to Mexico."

"Was Chad Lance involved in this? And again, I'm asking personally, not professionally."

"Lenore, do you know Phil's last name?"

"I don't. I don't know if Phil is a real name or a pseudonym. That's how little I know. Maybe that's why I can't find any information in the local media or from the local police force there, although I haven't reached out to the police in Quintana Roo state or to the Mexican National Guard. Yet."

"Lance introduced me to Phil. As just Phil, no last name. He and I went down to the Bonita Resort two or three years ago, a three-day weekend. Did sport fishing. Watched the sunrise. Ate a lot and drank a bit. I try to get him out of his shell every once in a while. He's smarter and more useful than being simply a detective in the Patrol."

"Is he just hanging out, doing the minimum, waiting for retirement in a couple of years?"

"Why do you ask that question?"

"That's the impression I got when I interviewed him about

Bill Hanlow's murder. That was an on-the-record interview."

"Unlike this one."

"Very unlike this one."

"Do you have 15 or 20 minutes?"

"This is my day off. I'm free as a squirrel."

"Hang on, I need to make a phone call."

Lenore pantomimes steps with her fingers. Whispers to us. "He's calling his office, clearing everything for the next hour."

"I like Chad. We're not exactly close, but he's kind of a loner, needs someone to talk to once in a while. I see myself in that role, which is why every year or two we do something together. Guy stuff. Get away, you know."

"I'm not an expert on guy stuff."

"On the Hanlow murder, there's nothing that's worth pursuing. We have solid evidence that points exclusively to George Watt. He's gone, there's no point in pursuing any criminal charges. Civil is of course, beyond my purview, but I can't see anyone besides his widow filing anything. I haven't spoken to Mrs. Hanlow, Chad has, and I think that avenue is closed."

"Phil and Chad had known each other for some time, I have no knowledge of how they may have met. One day the two of them had a meeting over lunch. I walked down the road to another resort, came back and Chad and I went fishing. That's all I know."

"Do you think they had a business together?"

"I have no knowledge of that. You'd need to ask Chad."

"I may. Off the record, of course."

"Of course."

"Do you know anything about a storage unit at SpaceMan #12 over on Hillmont or SpaceMan #4 down on Dundee Road?"

"What are you talking about?"

"Oh, you know, the typical storage units in those places that have popped up all over the last few years. Keep your boat over the winter or Aunt Martha's furniture that you don't want to either keep or sell."

"You'll have to explain that."

"George Watt had four storage units, two here in Des Moines, one in Stillwell, and one in Liberal, Kansas."

"Where in Kansas?"

"Liberal, just across the border from the panhandle of Oklahoma."

"Humph. I'd have to check a map."

"I did it for you."

"What are the contents of these supposed storage units?"

"Two of them were totally empty. The other two had a couple of folded-up boxes."

Lenore points at the laptop, slumps her shoulders and sighs.

"And how did you find these storage units?"

"Oh, not me, my friend who is wrapping up Mr. Watt's businesses. Receipts. Keys. That kind of stuff."

"Another 'friend.'"

"Another friend. Another good friend."

Laura and I both smile.

"You're good, Lenore."

"I work my ass off."

"And all this is for your friend who was with Phil when he died."

"For my friend who was trying to save his life, hands on the gouges that two bullets took out of his heart, unsure where the third wound was, using restaurant napkins to try to stop the bleeding, and feel his heartbeat slowly decrease to nothing. Yeah, that friend."

Lenore makes a circular motion with her hand. Clyde's voice is softer now, but still crystal clear with that same cold steel tone.

"I'm a Democrat in a strongly Republican state. I have aspirations. Do you understand?"

"Completely."

"Phil had a skill. He was a business man. Lots of people want to move from Mexico to the US, but it's hard. If you have no money, or very little, it can cost you your life.

Depending on who you believe, it might be 400 or 500 people a year that wind up dead or missing trying to get here from there. If you have a lot of money, things can go differently. Phil saw an opening in the middle market. The people who did fairly well in Mexico, who had available cash and assets, who had marketable skills in the US and who spoke at least some English. Enough to get along, say, if a customs agent stopped them and asked questions. Smart enough to have a story and to stick to it. Smart enough to help create a story parts of which might actually be true."

"We screened every person. Not me, you understand. I set this up with Phil and Chad while we were at the Bonita. Phil would recruit, screen, screen again, and get them over the border. Chad would handle transportation from just over the border through three stages. Each stage cash only. I know places and people that are looking for smart, skilled workers, managers, artists. Skilled people, you know what I'm saying. Factory supervisors. Web developers."

"I'd identify end points, destinations where they would be accepted, housed, able to find some kind of job right away, able to blend in. The American worker today is lazy and wants too much money. These people work their asses off and are ambitious. Most of all, they are intelligent and discreet."

"Mind you, Lenore, I'm telling you this for you to tell your friend, but also because it's entirely shut down now. No tracing is possible."

Lenore hits a button on her laptop.

"He could have stopped there. He should have stopped there. But some people have big egos."

She hits the button again.

"We agreed on pricing. Phil charged 10k to cross the border. How he got everyone across I don't know, don't want to know and don't care. We charged 2k per leg, three legs. Ron handled the first leg, but he gave all the cash to George. We paid Ron like a driver, I think George drove some or most of the second leg himself and he hired a third driver to take them to their final destinations. Drivers made twelve hundred a trip, so they were happy and quiet. We did 20 to 30 a week for 16 or 17 months."

"I took 20% off the top, Chad 10%. George got what was left."

"We only used white Anglo drivers. Newer vans. Never, never faster than the speed limit. Stopped for restroom breaks only, a few passengers getting out at each stop, then going to another place. About, as I understand, one-third of our customers were female."

"So it was a three-day trip?"

"I don't know the details."

"Did George build a hotel, a dormitory of some kind as a rest stop and charge them on a nightly basis?"

"He may have, but I don't know."

"Are these people successful once they get to those 'final destinations?'"

"I don't know. I'll presume so. I know for sure they are not in Iowa. That was my criteria for finding the landing spaces. I'm a Democrat in a very Republican state. I have aspirations. I take a strong position on illegal immigration.

It's been quite popular. Very popular, actually."

"What do you know about four additional people who left Mexico, got across the border into the US, but haven't been heard from since?"

"I have no idea what you're talking about. Lenore, I am forming a committee to explore a possible candidacy for . . . "

Lenore shuts off the recording and closes her laptop.

"There's more, but it's about his ambition and how he'd like to bring me into the fold. His words, not mine."

"Shit, that's where all that money came from." Carson slowly shakes her head from side to side.

The four of us look at Carson.

"Is that a 'you be quiet, I give you a job' kind of an offer?" asks Laura.

Our eyes shift to Lenore.

"A pretty clear indication. There is no way. But Clyde doesn't know that."

"Laura, you're a hero," says Linda. There's a round of applause, which makes Jan and Jess stop and look over at us. Everyone waves at them, and they go on practicing dribbling.

"So, there's just one issue left that I can see."

Everyone's gaze turns to me. I pause, and realize I'm not nervous around these people, that I'm at last comfortable.

"There are four people lost along that route somewhere.

Alejandro was going to reach out to them, but I haven't heard anything."

"Arv, call him. Now." This from Laura.

I call, leave a voice mail, and get a call back within two minutes.

"Have you heard anything from Consuelo and the others?" I ask without preamble.

"Arvin, it is so nice to hear from you. Yes, we are all doing well here in our new homes. How are you and how are those three beautiful women you are so fortunate to live with?"

I am ashamed. However, this being water under the bridge, I move forward.

"We are all fine here, thank you for asking."

"As for Consuelo's group, they are in Liberal, Kansas. Sometimes they work, doing manual labor or simple restaurant jobs but many days they have no work. It would take any of us four days to drive down, pick them up and come back. It's hard to get away from our work, or to borrow a car. We have two cars now in our group, and ride-share to our jobs and homes."

"Maybe we can pick them up from here.

"That would be the best thing, but they have very little resources left from their initial funds. What with food, paying for the first part of the journey, they cannot pay the sum required."

"Alejandro, when was the last time you talked to Consuelo?"

"Oh, maybe Monday or Tuesday."

"Can I call you back in an hour or so? We're having a group discussion here, maybe we can figure something out."

"I will call Consuelo now. I, all of us, appreciate what you have done for us. You need do no more, Arvin." This with a bit of wistfulness in his voice.

"We'll talk soon."

I explain to the group. There's a complete mishmash of comments.

"I have a van."

"We need a driver."

"It's eleven hours down, eleven hours back and maybe three or four hours to wherever-they-are Wisconsin. That would be at least three, probably four days of heavy driving."

"Having a careful, conservative, white driver seemed important to Clyde. I hate to verbalize, or even think about this, but that makes some sense."

"I can't take that kind of time off work, Laura is starting classes, her Mom is taking a trip."

Silence.

Lenore breaks it.

"I have an idea. Lyle Mattern."

"We just approved his refi," I say. "I believe he has a new job."

I get a couple of stares, but ignore them.

"He starts the week after next, his new employer is shut down this week to re-tool," updates Lenore.

"You suggested I call him Arvin, don't look at me like I ate the last cookie," Lenore laughs.

"Do you think he'd do it?" I ask.

"He's done it before. Used the name Chet. Drove three times after George let him go from Watt Metal Forming. An off-the-books assignment, you see. Cash. He needed it. Poor guy hadn't saved anything, had no safety net when he lost his job."

"We can take up a collection among us," says Laura.

"No. Absolutely not. No collection," states Carson. "I'm paying for Chet to drive them. I probably already have their fare."

"No," says Lenore. "Each leg was paid for separately. The guy on the first southern leg got his, I suspect, for getting them to Liberal. But George wouldn't have seen any money until he picked them up."

"No, please listen to me," Carson says emphatically. "I suddenly have a large amount of cash. I've acquired this under excruciatingly difficult and extremely unusual situations. Gosh only knows what I'm going to do with that cash. But I do know that it was earned and earmarked for the purpose of transporting people from a place they didn't want to be to a place they do want to be. I'm paying for this and I'm not listening to any other options. Lenore, a grand a leg per, correct?"

"Yes. That's what the passengers paid. The drivers got

twelve hundred per leg."

"Four passengers, two legs. But he has to drive to Liberal for pick up and then back here. Lenore, will this guy, I forgot his name."

"Lyle Mattern."

"Will he do it for five grand, cash?"

"I think he'd do it for less, and still kiss you on the mouth."

"Neither of those is happening. I say that without knowing what Lyle Mattern looks like."

"He's married," both Lenore and I say, almost at the same time.

"I'm not doing that stupid shit again. Happy to pay the man, not kissing him."

We all pause, take votes, and, amid a "easy to spend Carson's money for her" comment, agree. I call Alejandro, Lenore calls Lyle and we await callbacks.

"Lenore, I like Lyle, but I can't interact with him on this. And it may be better if Carson isn't involved personally either."

We figure out the logistics of van, keys and cash. Once again, Lenore offers to give up her off day on Monday to manage getting the right things in the right place. We start to break up, promising to text each other when things are complete, when Linda chimes in.

"Veteran's Day is the next official bank holiday, right? And the college shuts down for classes that day, right? Everybody, and I mean Jan and Jess too, are invited to come to our apartment for a sleep over. I never get a chance to cook, and I'm cooking. Bring your appetites. I get thirsty when I cook, which is why it's a sleep over. We have room for everyone, if you don't mind a pull out and the girls can sleep on inflatables."

We agree, back up, and all head back to our cars. On the way through the parking lot, Carson slips up between Laura and I.

"Can you guys scoot by my place on the way home? I want an adult beverage, and don't want to do that alone."

We're sitting at the kitchen island listening to the sounds of the girls laughter coming up the stairwell, laughing out loud at some movie I can't quite recognize. Carson is mixing us small drinks with something dark green, something with two kinds of bitters, rye, cognac, and simple syrup. Laura is cutting the peel off a lemon. We clink glasses, drink, do it again, and then Carson asks us for a moment as she goes upstairs.

She comes back with two, 5 x 7 manilla envelopes, each fat, and a third, bulging, but not nearly as fat. On one is written my name, with Laura's on the other. The third, thinner envelope has no writing.

"I didn't earn this money. And neither did I do what I did for money. This envelope is for Lyle," Carson says as she hands me the thinner one.

"And these are for you. You've supported me, been there for me, without being judgmental, and welcomed me into your lives, and your girls' lives. There's fifteen grand each, a gift from me to you. That's the federal limit on a gift, if it was more, you'd have to pay taxes. Let's not go there."

She picks up her drink.

"To the happiest possible future for all of us, and for all of the passengers."

Then she mixes another drink.

"Oh, I'll rent Lyle a car at the Rent-A-Wreck in whatever-it-is Wisconsin, let me know, will you? He'll need a way to get back here to Stillwater from there. Alejandro should keep the big black van. He needs it if they are car sharing. I'd just sell it for cash anyway. Call it a long-term loan from a friend, or I can sell it to him for $1, as he prefers. Whatever is easy and legal in Wisconsin."

We dive into some finger sandwiches which I help make by keeping my fingers out of the way.

31 Red fabric chairs

We get the girls to bed, and start to go out to the red fabric chairs in the front yard, just as it starts to rain. We go back into the family room, open the curtains and move our chairs to face the window.

"Sleepy time tea or a glass of wine?"

"Tomorrow's Monday, and it's back to normal, school for me, the girls start on Wednesday and you have a couple of errands to run early in the morning. I'll go pour us some wine," says Laura.

We discuss financial planning, my comfort level with my job at the bank, Laura's last two remaining classes, fifth grade, seventh grade, Iowa state political topics. Just before we get to the topic of world peace, Laura stands up.

"I'll be right back."

It isn't long before I see her standing in the bedroom doorway. She's wearing what appears to be a pajama set, separate top and bottom. Neither piece covers very much, and what's covered is hardly hidden. She holds onto the door frame with her left hand and leans a bit to her right, so her entire body is at an angle, filling the rectangular frame of the doorway.

"Arvin, before we both fall asleep, can I have a quick word with you?"

I go in.

About the Author

Red Fabric Chairs is Bruce's first novel. He's also published several poems in two versions of poetry chapbooks published by the South Bend (IN) Museum of Art.

Bruce began his writing career creating and producing radio ads, then expanded into additional media as he moved to and through a couple of advertising agencies, eventually starting his own marketing services firm. He's written for almost every known advertising and public relations medium where a spreadsheet and a handful of bullet points don't tell the story, but words do. To the best of his knowledge, every word he wrote during his advertising career was true.

Which is what inspired him to write fiction.

Made in United States
Troutdale, OR
08/04/2024

21753227R00179